# WHO CARES
# WHO WINS

First published in paperback in 2024 by Sixth Element Publishing

Sixth Element Publishing
Arthur Robinson House
13-14 The Green
Billingham
Stockton on Tees
TS23 1EU
www.6epublishing.net

© 2024 Tim Prescott

ISBN 978-1-914170-56-0

British Library Cataloguing in Publication Data.
A catalogue record for this book is available from the British Library.

Printed in Great Britain.

# WHO CARES WHO WINS

## TIM PRESCOTT

*For my family*

## Acknowledgements

Big thanks to Les Cameron and Meg Ashley for managing to read the first draft and for the feedback.

Thanks for the transformational input and instruction from Gillie Hatton and Graeme Wilkinson at Sixth Element.

# PART ONE

# ELIZABETH BENNETT – OCTOBER 2022

The river ran strong, full of confidence, energised by the overnight rain and freshened by a late October night. Elizabeth walked pretty much every morning. She strode purposefully, her own rhythm invigorated by a dancing river. Sunlight, fresh water and October colours. She listened to the birdsong and she could taste the ocean, her senses sharpened by the fresh morning air and the absence of company. She could feel something. This morning she felt closer to her primitive instincts, a step away from the cultured, twenty-first century woman who had walked the same path yesterday. She was as ready as she could be.

She was tempted to follow the river to the beach but chose instead to climb the path up through the woods. Elizabeth sucked in some big breaths, exhaling each time with a deliberate blow through whistling lips. She celebrated this feeling of readiness, alone with the elements. Elizabeth had her share of human frailty but her body was healthy, and, for a few brief moments, she felt strong.

She was climbing quickly back up towards the town. Then she spotted the cars. Immediately her celebration ended and she was invaded by caution. A quick glance allowed her to scan the scene: two cars, both appeared new and expensive, they were parked in the shade from the trees, early in a morning after a night of heavy rain.

A Range Rover and a BMW. That was unexpected and sufficiently incongruent to shift her caution into mild concern. She could feel an element of fear. Healthy fear, a message from her instincts – something isn't quite right, keep moving, watch with caution and hold your posture.

Her caution may have been healthy, but her attraction to the scene was driven by a competing instinct. She felt a pull that betrayed her aspirational self, that invited her to look into another world. Two male figures stood on the far side of the Range Rover. She felt as if she'd seen this image before.

The smaller of the two men didn't fit with the cars. His clothes,

3

his hair, the hunger in his physique and his skin told a story that shouldn't have included a BMW or a Range Rover. She felt slightly ashamed by her judgment. As she glanced again for three or four seconds from a distance of fifty metres, she guessed that she was walking towards a drugs deal.

Elizabeth had used some recreational drugs during her late teens and early twenties. She didn't count the cocaine that seemed to be disappearing up Rob's nose in ever increasing quantities. Those experiences had given her some insight. She knew what heroin thin looked like and she saw it clearly in his every feature. This boy was heroin thin, and she sensed that this early morning meeting was probably heroin related.

Even from thirty yards away she could see that the other man was taller than his companion, a man with a genetic physical advantage nurtured by obsessive gym work. He wasn't heroin thin, he looked scary in a very different way. Her sense of caution intensified. Again, she spoke silently to herself. Walk quickly, don't make eye contact.

As she drew closer, both men turned their heads and looked straight at her. She met this attention by slowing down. It was an unconscious reaction, their attention somehow adding weight to her stride. Her gaze was drawn to the big man. One half second of eye contact... just enough. Elizabeth felt the tiny hairs on her neck stand to attention as they signalled recognition.

She knew that she was unsettled but her sense of danger had evaporated. Somewhere deep in her gut she knew that this intimidating figure, who appeared to be conducting criminal business, wasn't a threat. She couldn't find a name for him, nor remember where their paths had crossed. But there was no doubt in her mind, she knew him, and she experienced a confusion of powerful emotions. Elizabeth was puzzled. She allowed herself a brief glance back over her shoulder and hurried on towards her home.

•

After an hour of incubation, while in the shower, the memory surfaced. Elizabeth shuddered. It had been twenty years but she had no doubt.

Danny Hutton, still living.

# DANNY HUTTON

Two decades had passed since Danny Hutton's previous encounter with Elizabeth Bennett early in 2002, when he was five years old. By then he'd spent almost a year in the care of the local authority. He was taken into care from a chaotic and abusive family home. His mother, Jeanette Hutton, was herself a victim of sexual, physical and emotional abuse. It kind of ran in the family, had done for several generations. She didn't know how to care for herself, and she didn't know how to care for her unwanted child. Caring wasn't a concept in Jeanette's fucked up world.

Danny's mother actually didn't know how she'd become pregnant. She was seventeen years old, she'd never had a chance, she couldn't see a future, she'd tried and failed at suicide, then she tried tranquillisers. They were fabulous, the most convincing escape she'd ever found. Especially when she washed them down with a litre of cider. Unfortunately, after too many Xanax, some bastard fucked her. Danny was the baby. Stan was the bastard.

Danny's father was a predator and a cunt. He'd suffered his own challenges. Stan and Jeanette had been drawn to one another, finding a thousand ways to re-enact their experiences of abuse, sometimes as victims, sometimes as abusers, sometimes alternating between the two. God only knows who'd done what to Stan... no matter, the net result was a manipulative and quite sadistic man. He favoured abuser roles. Jeanette seemed more comfortable as a victim.

The baby gave Jeanette the currency to secure her own social housing. She felt like a lottery winner. She'd be safe from her abusers, and so would her baby. She had a low IQ, no street craft, and a short lifetime of practice at being trampled on.

Her midwife had ushered plenty of dire prospects into the world, but newly born Danny was the most hopeless of them all. She did her best, alerted the Health Visitor and requested a Social Services assessment.

For almost a year Jeanette was supported and her baby was developing normally. The Health Visitor had to visit at least twice each week and give help that was often beyond the scope of her job description, but she could see how badly Jeanette needed the help. She also enlisted some back up from one of Jeanette's neighbours.

Eventually the Health Visitor discharged Jeanette. She knew that there'd be problems, but she'd given the best help that she could. There were a thousand other new mothers struggling in Teesside in 1999. The midwife's referral to Social Services had asked for a period of monitoring, but contained no substantial evidence of maltreatment. No further action had been taken.

Meanwhile, Stan watched and waited. His interest in Jeanette had lapsed as her pregnancy progressed but he'd re-engaged when he heard that she'd got her own place. With the interfering bleeding hearts fucked off, a thousand lies and false promises, and a couple of dozen Xanax, he moved in.

Stan really was a cunt, he got free housing and regular sex. Jeanette neither consented nor objected. The sad truth was that Jeanette hadn't the resources to manage without help. Stan could cook eggs and toast, he was a better than average shoplifter, and he knew where to score. He was a cunt, but no other cunt was offering help, so he'd have to do. And after all he was Danny's father. Probably.

Over the next three years, Danny adapted as best he could. He was neglected and he witnessed Stan's appalling abusive behaviour towards Jeanette. On a daily basis, Danny watched his two fucked up parents doing their worst, seeing things a child should never see. Over and over again.

He would become distressed but learned that any attempt to interfere, protest, or even to express his emotional reaction, would usually earn him a slap or a kick. So he learned to be still when Stan's mood was black, but there was an element of defiance that never faltered. Danny would watch Stan, fixing an unsettling stare on his father, storing the image, remembering some things that would be best forgotten.

For Jeanette, masturbation was the only way that she could experience sexual pleasure. It was also her most effective method of emotional comfort. During her teenage years, the abuse she suffered in her family home became more frequent, and her only refuge came when she curled into a ball in her bed with her bunched fingers rhythmically grinding around her crotch. Sometimes she made herself sore, sometimes she'd reach orgasm. The key was that she was alone. These moments were a gift from her damaged self to her damaged self.

She thought she'd made her escape when she was given her own house but, as it turned out, Stan had other ideas. She still needed comfort after his frequent brutality, but now she had a young child. She took Danny to her bed and she guided his tiny hands.

Remarkably, some aspects of Danny's development were unimpaired, his language skills were beyond his years... he was a desperately unhappy and disturbed child, with a gift for learning. God only knows where that came from.

His defiant reaction to Stan's abusive behaviour expanded into angry outbursts and around the time of his fourth birthday he started to attack his father. He would charge ferociously, throwing objects and himself with recklessness, he would scratch and bite. There was a primitive, feral power to his anger.

At first Stan tried to laugh it off. He told Jeanette that she'd created a fucking nutcase. But Danny persisted. Stan registered fear and sustained some injuries, and spent more and more time elsewhere.

Jeanette was spending more and more of her time alone with her young son. She struggled, wasn't able to cope, and needed her Xanax and her cider more than ever.

One spring day, a neighbour watched Danny trying to wake his intoxicated mother in the front garden, and called the police. Danny was placed in Malton Court while the domestic circumstances were investigated. He never saw his mother again.

•

As a young child, Danny was a fine-looking boy. His facial features were well proportioned but it was the combination of fear and sadness in his eyes that endeared him. He looked so easy to love.

His social workers found him a couple of foster placements without much difficulty, both during his first year as a looked after child. Both placements broke down within a few weeks. He was too much, too volatile, too strong, too destructive. A rapid series of changes was the last thing that he needed.

Danny Hutton was angry and confused. He spoke to the psychologist. The rage lived on. They talked about it, but the fire in this boy was extraordinary. He was sent to specialist units. Still the rage lived on.

No one wanted to give up on Danny, but no one felt that they could help him. He wasn't just disturbed and bad tempered, he seemed defiant, he wouldn't let anyone get close to him. His caregivers felt defeated by this young and troubled child.

He didn't always sleep well, sometimes he was awoken by bad dreams. He would wake up frightened, drenched in sweat. He was a loner, he could feel the trouble inside of him and he knew it was a problem. In moments of rage he was barely conscious, entirely out of control. He didn't like those times, and as he reorientated afterwards, he could see the damage he'd done and the fear he'd stoked. It was a lot for a young child to think about.

He was receptive to education. Learning at his schools came easily enough, particularly in science and maths. There was a string of incidents that were neatly listed as behavioural disturbances, but, by and large, he was a good student and often genuinely interested to learn.

The years passed, testosterone arrived. Puberty came quite early for Danny, all of his physical changes seeming to be a bit ahead of schedule. It was as if his body had learned from his early experiences of violence and abuse, that he needed to reach a position where he could protect himself. The sooner, the better.

He grew taller and stronger. There was always a bit of a feeling around Danny. What might he do next? Would his destructive anger drive him to do damage so serious that he got locked up? What on earth would he be like as an adult? Those questions formed in the minds of his carers, his teachers, his social workers and his psychologist. And in pretty well everyone else who got half a look at him.

The staff at Malton Court had speculated often about what the hell would happen when Danny hit puberty. They'd joked about it, making back up career plans to give them escape routes when the time came, but none of them expected the reality to be remotely amusing.

He confounded their expectations – he calmed. As a teenager he learned to focus his energy and to understand that sometimes self-control was an option. He could make a choice.

That was a revelation. For the first time in his life he started to question his own impulses and to resist his biology. Danny was experiencing the novelty of choice. He was looking critically at the world for the first time, the gift of adolescence. Danny emerged from the confusion of his childhood with a sense of relief. The power of choice was something new, and that changed his life.

He was more settled, and there were no more excursions into foster care. Danny gradually allowed a few other kids at Malton Court some degree of access. Sean and Beth reached out to him. It would be many years later before Danny realised how courageous and generous they had been with him. Beth was a couple of years older than him and Sean. She seemed to want to be his mum and he definitely didn't want anyone to be his mum. Nevertheless, he liked her. She'd seen the worst of him and he could tell that she liked him. Sean was a weird kid. He should have had the sense to be frightened of Danny but he didn't seem to be frightened of anything. Two courageous children who saw his destructive power and who reached out to him nevertheless, Danny understood that they were good friends.

He was cool with Molly. Sometimes they argued but Danny liked her and she was Beth's best mate. Sally and Lisa were tolerable and sometimes a good laugh. Seth was clumsy, lazy and a bit of a bully. He wasn't a bright boy but he soon learned not to bother Danny or any of his crew.

Gradually, over a period of five years crossing in the corridors and passageways around Malton Court, Danny and Seth figured out how to live as neighbours. Eventually, moving at the pace of elderly sleeping snails, in the dawning of adulthood, they became gym buddies, and then friends. By that time Stevie had turned up, with his fancy clothes and his fancy words. The family was complete.

That was how they all came to think about it. They'd all lost their original families, they were chaos, and they were a family, brothers and sisters. Possibly the most dysfunctional family in the world.

# A DAY AT THE SEASIDE – OCTOBER 2022

The air was a little chilly but there was no wind and the patchy sunlight didn't know whether to signal the end of summer or to say nothing at all.

Sean had arrived first. He was irritated to be meeting at eight o'clock and mystified by the venue. "Jesus, Danny... Saltburn? It's still the middle of the night!" He wasn't an early morning person... his manners would improve once he was fully awake.

Sean had guessed the agenda for their meeting but the location was unexplained.

Danny offered enlightenment. "I live here, Sean."

That was unexpected news. "A retirement home by the seaside? Very nice, Dan."

Danny was always irritated when someone shortened his name, even more so on this occasion because he was uncomfortable about living in Saltburn. More than uncomfortable, he felt out of place, slightly embarrassed, but Beth had delivered an ultimatum. He allowed enough of his irritation to throw Sean a brief warning glance, then he let it go. He was impatient. "Who are they?"

Sean felt a tiny flicker of amusement watching Danny's momentary reaction and then his retreat. He was tempted to ask Danny to spell out his question more fully but he sensed some kind of distraction in his friend's posture. He followed Danny's gaze down a footpath into the woods where a woman was walking towards them. "Local lads, mostly from Stockton. Do you know John Stanton?"

Danny attended sufficiently to have understood that Sean had answered his question but he remained quiet. His attention was drawn to the advancing woman.

"He's a knob," Sean added, even though he'd never met him. He noticed that Danny's attention had not been fully regained. Danny seemed to be watching the approaching woman without looking at her directly. Sean wasn't a man who gave half a look. He raised his head and sent his own inimitable stare straight at the intruder.

She didn't seem to notice Sean's attention. Her eyes met Danny's, then she was gone.

Danny was struggling to refocus. In truth, he expected nothing new from Sean. He had better placed people than Sean to give him information. He wasn't sure why he'd asked him to come over to Saltburn to tell him what he already knew. He'd heard the same name from everyone he'd asked. "Is he running the show?"

Sean had gained an impression about John Stanton. He had heard the chat around town.

"Apparently he's strutting about like he's the big man, loving it. This is second-hand, Danny, I've never met him. But to answer your question…" Sean paused to consider his judgement. "I doubt it. He's from Stockton so he should know all about you. He has a group of guys out on the streets, mostly kids, apparently some claim to be part of a gang. I guess they have some kind of alliance with the Albanians. They've come through too fast, Danny. Suddenly they've got a presence, I can feel a shift in the vibe around town. There's a lot of lines and plenty of chat. I think they've got someone in Malton Court. He's either spent months planning and preparing the ground or he's had help. From what I've heard, he's street level. There's no way he's risen so high on his own. Molly knows him."

Danny turned his head to watch the woman who'd walked past them glance back over her shoulder. Danny had been three months short of his sixth birthday when he'd last spent time with Elizabeth Bennett but he'd recognised her in an instant, just from the sway of her gait. The brief moment of eye contact served only as confirmation.

He didn't bat an eyelid but a shuddering jolt rocked his bones. Where the fuck did she just come from? Who the hell is John Stanton? Selling drugs on my patch and fucking my sister? In my fucking back yard? He hadn't known that Stanton's operation had reached inside Malton Court. Danny told himself he might have left him alone. But not now. He'd seen too many pimps and parasites prey on the vulnerable kids in Malton Court. In truth, Stanton was always going to catch Danny's attention.

As it turned out Sean had given him some new information, he hadn't known about Molly.

"Why didn't you tell me?" Danny was suddenly wound up and frustrated. Sean's message was one he'd already heard whispered but now it was real.

Danny didn't take many drugs, he needed to feel a sense of control. But throughout his lifetime he'd suffered adrenaline surges when he was frightened. He was breathing quickly now and his adrenaline gland was already active. As he'd grown older, he'd become better able to hold himself in check during such moments. He could conceal these changes in mood and biology from most people, but not from Sean.

Sean smiled and kept quiet. He'd seen this a thousand times before… Danny with adrenaline.

Adults and children alike had learned the terror of Danny's adrenaline-driven rage, his terrifying strength. He was beyond restraint, dangerous. Even when he was a young child – especially when he was a young child – everyone, including the staff members at Malton Court, kept well clear when Danny raged. No one would even look at him. Except Sean.

Danny was ticking. "Bastards. I don't really give a shit about the money or whatever the fuck else, Sean, but if Stanton knows the score… and you're telling me he does, yeah?"

"Yeah."

Danny was wound up but he was still able to think. What was John Stanton playing at? Did he really think he could stick two fingers up right in front of Danny's face, with the whole world watching? He was knowingly operating on Danny's turf.

"You're right, Sean, about the Albanians. I met a guy, Erdi, more than a year back. He came to lean on me, gently, too gently. I bought some time. Covid was still around. Me and Beth were buying a house here. It's a long story. Whatever, it doesn't matter now, I guess he's run out of patience. I've no idea why he's got John fucking Stanton up front."

Danny shivered for a second. It was a bit cold but it was tension rather than the weather that chilled and shook his soul.

Sean stayed quiet now, he'd given his brother all he'd got.

Danny took it in. And this understanding that he had to absorb, it was a matter of enormous proportions. That's why he'd bought time from Erdi, he needed time to comprehend that ten years of first building and then prospering would all end. He'd had a pretty steady three years up until his meeting with Erdi. He'd made a lot of money. So too had a handful of his close associates, including Stevie, who for some reason wasn't responding to Danny's messages.

He hadn't done it for the money. It just happened to be the case that the environment in which Danny Hutton felt most able to thrive was a murky and sometimes dangerous world. And that hadn't escaped Danny's intelligent and searching mind. Why should this be his place? On the wrong street at the wrong time of night, a place for the undeserving and for lost souls.

Danny didn't know what to feel now. He didn't know what to expect. Even though he realised that Stanton wasn't the threat, Danny felt a need to maintain his dislike for this man he'd yet to meet. For a moment he allowed reasoned thinking to slip away. His anger – a child – was reacting.

"He's challenging me. Selling gear, Sean, I can take it or leave it. It pays the rent. I'm telling you, Sean, John Stanton's made a wrong move."

*Eee Danny boy, never change.* Sean stayed quiet. He noted the weight in Danny's mood and knew he'd either have to leave, or find a way to restore his newly troubled friend.

# SEAN MURPHY – OUT WALKING

For reasons that eluded Sean, his mother had sometimes felt the need to lock him outside of their family home at night. Four year old Sean walked the streets all night long, out with the cats and the foxes, wondering why there were no other kids around. Maybe that's why he found it so easy to walk into scary darkness. Sean had never lost his innocent, open eyed curiosity.

The first time the police picked him up, he wasn't able to give his address. He didn't know what an address was. He was driven to the police station. In a car, a cop car. They asked where he lived and he pointed and started to describe his house. No one had reported a missing child. A social worker was called but an hour later hadn't arrived.

PC Wilson decided to drive him back to where they'd found him and asked him to show them where he lived. How about that, a policeman who had the courage to think for himself and who also had an imagination. He noted Sean's slow walking pace, the boy's apparent reluctance to return home, and his concern grew.

And as their walk continued alarm bells were ringing in PC Wilson's mind. How come this little lad was out in the middle of the night and why did he seem reluctant to go back to his home? PC Wilson rang the doorbell. No answer. He knocked, still no answer. Then he hammered so hard that neighbours emerged to complain about the noise, changing their minds when they sussed it was police. Eventually Dawn Murphy was awoken and found the energy to open her front door.

PC Wilson was unimpressed, while Dawn Murphy blamed Sean for creeping out behind her back. He took a few notes, swallowed his distaste and went back to the station. The social worker turned up at 8.30am. Five hours after the call. Thank the Lord for joined up inter-agency working.

Over the following weeks and months, PC Wilson kept his eyes open when he did a night shift, cruising through quiet streets, hoping that he wouldn't see Sean. For almost nine weeks his hopes were met.

He was unaware that Sean had seen him a couple of times and managed to hide until his car had passed. Then at 2.30 in the morning PC Wilson turned a corner and saw Sean kick a beer can across the pavement. His heart sank and then sang. The paper work would be tedious, social services would be slow but this time Dawn Murphy's neglect or abuse, whichever it was, would be investigated.

As it turned out, on that particular night, Sean had had a fat lip to carry around the town. Dawn didn't bother to lie this time when she was interviewed by a social worker and by the police. She gave her shoulders a disinterested shrug when she was told Sean would be staying in local authority care for a few days while an assessment was carried out.

The situation had bothered PC Wilson ever since the first time he'd found Sean. While Sean spent a few days in Malton Court, PC Wilson did a bit of community policing. He spent some time with Dawn, talked to the neighbours. Neither Dawn nor her neighbours hid from the truth. Sean's mother was a pisshead, alcohol was her priority. Dawn put him out at night so that the feeling that she had someone to look after went away. If he wasn't there, he didn't need her, so she could go out on the piss with as close to a clean conscience as she would ever get.

Wilson looked inside himself, seeking a sympathetic understanding but he struggled. Dawn told him that when she put Sean out, she really hoped that he wouldn't come back. She didn't wish him dead or even harmed, she just hoped that somehow he'd disappear. PC Wilson felt defeated. He'd gone well beyond the requirements of professional duty, he'd given something of himself. Sean seemed a lovely lad. Alcoholism or motherhood – a tough choice.

For almost fifteen months, social workers did their best to support Dawn's parenting. They worked in good faith although they were always overstretched and often frustrated. Dawn's heart wasn't in it. Desperate alcohol addictions die hard.

Sean didn't talk to anyone about his mum and about his cold lonely nights. Actually he did tell Maisie, his one true love.

But no one else. He didn't understand why but he felt ashamed. Not just ashamed of his mum but also somehow ashamed of himself. Being unacceptable to your mother... not a great feeling.

Sean landed on his feet at Malton Court. Three meals a day, biscuits, safe in bed every night. Those basic needs, food and shelter, hadn't always been met. Sean appreciated the reliability of his care home. He was free from the whims and the cruelties of his alcoholic mother. But he missed her.

He thought about her. She was still in his head. Sean had an impassioned drive to understand why. *Why? Why, mother, didn't you want me?* That question shaped him, it never went away as he tried his best to find answers. Sean looked under stones, walked into darkness, he questioned everything, rejected convention and conventionality with determination and disdain. He was a curious soul and he wanted to know why.

He shared living space for the first time... with six-year-old Danny Hutton, saw him at his worst but they connected. Despite it all.

# ON THE BEACH

Sean was skinny because he'd never learned to make himself a meal and he often forgot to eat. He had a soft mop of mousy hair, balanced by a stubbly beard, a sharp accusing nose and staring brown eyes. All spoiled by a slightly crooked mouth, particularly evident when he smiled or sneered. He had big Irish hands that were almost too much for his long skinny arms. He was a keenly intelligent observer of social injustice, he loved art and music and he had a particular talent for pointing out that the emperor has no clothes.

He brought all of these qualities to his relationship with Danny. There had never been an orderly or predictable pattern of interaction and there was often tension between the two men, but he and Danny were on the same side. For ten years they both grew up as looked after children in the chaos at Malton Court. Workers in the care system came and went. Other residents passed through for periods between a few days and several years but Danny and Sean both kept winding up in Malton Court. They were out finding trouble on the streets when the weather allowed and they played backgammon through the long winter nights. It wasn't a choice or a wish, simply a fact that they passed time together and somehow developed a bond. There were a few happy memories but mostly they'd struggled their way from one heap of shit to another. The key thing was that they'd undertaken their shit-heap struggle together.

Sean was able to look at him when no one else dared. Danny seemed to like that. One way or another, and more than anyone else in Danny's life, Sean had kept him safe. If Sean told Danny to slow down, Danny listened. Sean was the only other man on the planet who was allowed to challenge Danny. Beth challenged him left, right and centre. Obviously.

But even with his courage, his curiosity and their history together, on this cold October morning, on the edge of the woods in Saltburn, he needed to take care that he chose the right words. "Come on, Danny, we'll throw some stones."

Danny was thinking about Erdi and John Stanton. And Elizabeth Bennett. His heart rate was high. He felt sweat laying a coat across his forehead. "No, Sean, I need to…"

Sean felt responsible for Danny's troubled mood, he wanted to get his friend levelled out again. He interrupted Danny's attempt to refuse him. "Come on, Danny man, we'll walk on the beach, we'll throw a few stones. You asked me to come here, for fuck's sake, we'll walk to the beach. I've come to the seaside and I want to make a fucking sandcastle."

This was Sean being the best friend that he could be. He'd seen Danny twitching, struggling for self control and he found the key to a temporary redemption. It was a moment of love. Sean started to walk back down the path towards the river.

Danny sighed and immediately followed.

They walked away from the cars. The morning was coming alive.

It was always beautiful on the beach, light and water, sand and wind. More importantly, there were stones. There were people on the beach, mostly dog walkers. Danny and Sean found their way to the water's edge, waves gently breaking, the salty smell of the sea, the noise of water. They were children and they just wanted to throw stones.

Twenty minutes earlier Danny had been burning with a mixture of confused anger. John Stanton and Elizabeth Bennett had stirred him. Now he was less irritated, and awestruck by Sean's throwing arm. The rest had gone.

It'd always been the same ever since they were kids, Sean had a whiplash arm. An easy rhythmic ripple from his feet, through his hips and shoulders, then his arm unleashed with a snap in his wrist, sending his missiles sailing out to sea twenty metres beyond the distance that Danny's more muscular frame could manage. It was irritating but equally impressive.

The tension in Danny subsided, his shoulders loosening with every throw. For a few minutes, he was free from his many burdens, a rare and precious break from the bounds he could never fully escape. He allowed his worries to slip away in the wind and the salt and the spray. He'd pick them up again later but for now best that children throw their stones. No words were exchanged... the communication was physical, almost balletic. After a while their eyes met and they shared a chuckle. Neither one of them needed to say it but they were remembering the same memories, reasserting their bond.

There was a fight coming, maybe a war. It was important to know who your friends were. Danny suggested coffee and they made their way back to a less inviting set of activities.

"How is Molly?" Danny asked.

Sean paused to consider his reply. "She's okay. You know Molly. She's alive and working. I think she's using, although I'm not sure, maybe she's clean."

Danny was back in control. He noted that Sean's answer to his question had told him absolutely nothing about Molly. "Stanton's a punter?"

"Yeah. I don't know much else, Danny."

"Is he a regular?"

"I think so but I don't know for sure."

"We'll find out. We'll need to get out and watch for a while, catch some new movies, Sean. You up for it?"

It had been a while, more than a year, since Danny and Molly had last met. They'd parted on less than amicable terms. He'd ask Stevie to go and see her. Danny knew he ought to go himself but he knew how easily he got angered by pretty well everything about the way Molly lived her life. Molly knew it too. She'd get nervous in Danny's company and experience shame in his presence. Neither of them wanted or liked their reactions to the other, and so, as close as they were, they tried not to see each other.

The two young men sat like tourists, gazing out to sea while they finished their coffee.

"I'm going back into town, Danny. I'm rehearsing with Maisie this afternoon."

Danny was surprised. "I thought you two were done. Are you back together?" He looked across to note his friend's hesitation.

"We're trying out a few songs, that's all. I'm gone, Danny, catch you later, keep me in touch." Sean was on his way.

# DAN THE MAN

By the time he'd reached sixteen, Danny felt ready for life in the adult world. He was over six feet tall and he was working out in the gym with Seth. He had himself under better control and he felt less inclined to allow others to direct him. Being his own man was a better idea. Adults didn't intimidate him. None of them, not in Malton Court, nor anywhere else.

He lost interest in school. Danny was doing his learning out on the streets. As his school years ended, he was steered into employment. It was a slightly odd experience. Danny had been making his own decisions for the past two years and yet somehow, as his education formally ended, he allowed himself to be nudged towards gainful employment. Somehow he'd suffered a momentary lapse from self determination. His carers were just as surprised as he was when he set out for his first and last day in paid employment.

No one was surprised when he decided against day two. The other kids at Malton Court had bets with each other about how many hours he'd manage without either hitting someone or walking out. But no one could say he didn't give it a damn good try. The next day he started the process of registering self-employed as an antiques dealer, at Max's suggestion. Max described himself as an unorthodox accountant. The unorthodoxy applied to his qualifications and his practice. Danny wondered how many more sixteen-year-old self-employed antiques dealers were out there.

The workers at Malton Court looked at one another with bewilderment and with fear. Danny was sixteen, and on the second day of his working life he declared himself a self-employed antiques dealer. He knew nothing about antiques. He was much easier to look after in those days, no trouble at all and yet somehow more scary than ever.

His indifference with the adults around him had neither malice nor unpleasantness, it was just a bit unsettling. He was already dealing large quantities of weed, and he'd got Max on board. Danny was making his way ably into muddier waters.

For many healthily developing teenagers, hormonal surges fuel uncertainty and clumsy rebellion. Untried feelings of power and sexuality bring confusion and chaos, adolescence can be a troubling transition. Not for Danny... he experienced a new calm confidence, increased clarity and control. These were good years for Danny. He was making his own decisions. He'd found his place and his direction.

The transition through puberty into adolescence and then into the relatively settled young man that he'd now become, was life changing. At first the growing sense of self control felt like a life saved, now it felt like a life to be lived. Danny Hutton was feeling fine.

He accepted his experience quietly, although the profound nature of his development didn't escape his attention. He'd grown up in a world where he had no control and he'd become powerful. He didn't need to shout about it, people could feel it from him and as time went on, he started to feel it within himself.

It was a bit strange for him. For someone who'd suffered such brutality, this progression was impressive. It really was pretty weird. But not unwelcome.

It was a surprise and it came unbidden but it was an undeniable truth, Danny was very exceptionally endowed with power. Paradoxically, at the moment when he appeared to have left the wild child behind, Danny began to apprehend his power and he was more dangerous than ever.

The sixteen-year-old version was over six feet tall, he had a hefty pair of bollocks, purpose and confidence in his stride. Danny seemed to have spent most of his childhood looking at his feet. Well, his chin was repositioned now and he was taking a look around.

Danny spent a lot of time hanging out in Middlesbrough. Staying home and spreading his wings. He got to know his home town. Geographically.

He'd grown up in and around Malton Court, attended the local comprehensive school. He'd always been close to home. He knew his way around the town centre, but the rest of the world was undiscovered. Including the rest of Teesside.

This was Danny at his best, old enough to claim his power and still open to a young man's dreams. He was getting Stevie to drive him places, listening to his stories, truths and lies on their movie nights. His body and his confidence had grown.

His facial features had been endearing when he was a young child, and he still had something in his eyes that invited tenderness, but as he'd grown into his adult form his features seemed to sharpen and his complexion darkened. As a child, Danny's eyes seemed to plead for help, as an adult they gave a different message. He'd become a good-looking young man and there was still visible vulnerability but the innocence had gone. These days Danny looked a bit more edgy.

It wasn't just an important period of personal development, it was also a time when he gained ground with his worldly ambitions.

He formed a new habit. He'd go walking. Mostly by himself but often with Sean, and occasionally with Seth. He'd invited Stevie to walk with him and Stevie had given the invitation careful consideration, thought about how it might be, walking late at night into other parts of town, with Danny don't-fuck-with-me Hutton. A car provided a barrier, shelter and offered rapid withdrawal. Walking and shit, not really Stevie's scene. There were no walking boots in Stevie's locker.

Danny would walk for miles, discovering the length and breadth of his home town. In the darkness, Danny liked the street buzz, he felt alive and in control, he was full of surging testosterone, feeling invincible and sexually repressed. You wouldn't want to get in Danny Hutton's way on a dark night.

Danny was mapping out who was selling, what was selling, who was buying. Watching how it all played out, doing the research. He found his way into the town centre and out to the suburbs. He was interested to look at the more expensive areas of housing. Danny couldn't believe it, no one had told him there were areas like this. Big houses with drives. Some people seemed to be doing okay.

Those slow walks, especially when he went alone, cleared a path for some new learning in Danny Hutton. He saw the world beyond his doorstep, he saw affluence, he saw the variety in the housing and the estates, he saw street sleepers and other people driving flash cars.

Most of the time he tried to be invisible. That wasn't always easy for someone who had grown tall, but he learned to keep walking when heads turned his way. He'd caught a few people's attention back home, especially in the gym, but out on his walks he'd keep his head down, enjoying anonymity.

Once or twice, or thrice, he wandered into a part of town where his foreign body was considered an affront. He was challenged one night by a group of teenagers. They were his age and he was on their turf.

Danny had grown into himself, become self-assured. He felt comfortable with himself out on the streets at night time. The more he walked the streets, the more he felt that it was his town.

There were about ten of them. A few were younger, five or six were Danny's age. The biggest of them asked him what the fuck he thought he was doing on their turf? The question had to be asked, it would have been rude not to, the dozy fucker just about got to the end of his sentence when the seven pound hammer that was Danny's right fist broke his nose and knocked him spark out.

All but one of the others stepped back. The one who'd stood his ground got his bollocks kicked and his bravado shattered. It was a lesson in loyalty. Danny walked through the fragmenting onlookers with disdain, pausing in the midst of them to emphasise his point. That was enough. He started the long stroll home. Danny Hutton's reputation was growing, spreading further afield. And Danny Hutton had learned a bit more about his power.

And over the next two years, his walks continued. He left a couple more calling cards and he asked questions, collecting information, getting ready. It was such an important period in Danny's development, his sense of place and his sense of self clarified. He could see a future, and with each walk and each movie night, he took another step towards his moment.

'Movie nights' was Stevie's phrase, somehow it captured the

sense of entertainment they'd felt during all of the many nights in Stevie's Vauxhall Corsa, watching the streets.

Danny had noted Stevie's arrival at Malton Court – their bedrooms were side by side – but Danny didn't appear to show much interest, he was out and about, walking the streets, making his way. He didn't invest much time getting to know the posh boy. He'd sold him some weed and he'd rescued him from Seth's attempt to bully.

Danny hadn't paid him much attention but he'd been interested by Stevie right from the day he'd arrived at Malton Court. Stevie didn't have a Teesside accent, he spoke confidently. He had a father who had money.

When Stevie turned seventeen, his guilt ridden, absent father paid for driving lessons and an unreliable Vauxhall Corsa. By this time Danny started to find Stevie more interesting than ever. A young man who clearly didn't want to displease him, who owed him a favour, and who had wheels, was exactly the man Danny needed.

The car made a difference and it changed the relationship between the two young men, moved it to a different place. It gave them their cinema seats. They'd been places together, hung out a bit, moodied around, did at least some of the stuff that young folk do. But it takes a long time to build a relationship with Danny Hutton. Stevie could be fun but until the movie nights, Danny and Stevie didn't really get to know each other.

They were parked up, as they had been many other nights, gradually learning more about dealing illegal drugs. They had followed their noses and their instincts, but mostly they'd followed the signposts. Picked up the clues, made the pieces fit together, found the players and identified their roles. Stevie was happy to take direction from Danny and interested to hear about his ambitions.

Seventeen-year-old Stephen Hunter was doing the best he could. The accident which had blown his family apart two years earlier had moved him from a comfortable family life on the North Yorkshire coast to Malton Court. It had been a big change and it had happened overnight. Stevie smoked too much weed and he embraced the crazy kids in his new home. They were all that he had. He tried not to look back and he didn't look too far into the future, Stevie was Mr Mindfulness – living in the moment.

Stevie loved his car, his first set of wheels. He wasn't the first seventeen-year-old to feel the enormous symbolic power that a first car can bring. He treated it like a church and a bedroom on wheels, he had his own private space and he could take it wherever he wanted, or wherever Danny wanted. He got some Bose speakers, kept a supply of weed and condoms and a sleeping bag. All of the things that appeal to seventeen-year-olds happened in Stevie's Vauxhall Corsa. Pretty well every week.

While sitting in the front seats of the car for so many hours, the inevitable occurred… they talked. Stevie did almost all of the talking, Danny was content to listen. Stevie could talk forever and he seemed to have the social skills to feel comfortable talking to anyone and everyone. Especially when he was nervous.

They were a couple of miles from the town centre watching the entrance to a tall apartment block. Stevie spotted a familiar figure.

"Here's Ronnie, back from the pub."

A couple of years earlier, Ronnie had sold weed to the kids

at Malton Court, until Danny had sent him on his way. They weren't quite sure what he was up to now, hence the observation. In Stevie's judgement, based on the desperate punters they'd seen come and go, Ronnie appeared to be dealing small quantities of heroin.

"It takes me back, you know, to when I first got to Malton Court. He was alright, Ronnie, sorted me out with some gear anyway."

Danny sank into his seat. "Ronnie was too interested in teenage kids. I never liked him. But he got me started on the road to ruin in a funny sort of a way… I stole his turf and kicked his arse. How did it start for you, Stevie?"

Stevie knew his role in these movie night conversations. He'd contribute ninety five words out of every hundred spoken. Stevie considered for a few seconds and then responded. "A bit like you, Danny, except I didn't use intimidation and violence, and I paid up front. I bought more than I needed and sold the excess on to kids at school. My folks sent me to a private school near Whitby. It was a boarding school but I was local, I travelled in each day on a bus and I was home at my parent's hotel every night."

Danny offered a second prompt, encouraging Stevie to rattle on. "Did your mum and dad know what you were up to?"

Stevie hardly needed encouragement. "They didn't have a fucking clue, man, they weren't interested, too busy with the hotel. I was doing good business, selling to the boarders. The problem was that I left them to it, you know, I buggered off back home every night. They were in their dormitories, making too much noise. Apparently the air was thick with smoke, even the non-smokers were getting a buzz. Anyway, to cut a long story short, a teacher turned up late one night, smelled the smoke. That was me, bud. The head hauled me into his office the next day. I was busted."

"Police?"

"No, they didn't want a scandal. They called my folks. My dad loved money, Danny. He didn't seem to care about much else. I don't suppose I'll ever forget that day. Well, the bits that I can remember, but the funny thing is, I can only remember half of it." Stevie paused. He was still puzzled by the gaps in his memory. "My mum and dad came over to the school. I had to sit there, the naughty boy, shame-faced while they all talked about me. I got expelled. I started arguing with my dad as soon as we left the school building. He was pissed off, told me I'd wasted his money and my education. I can remember thinking that was typical of dad… the money was his number one concern, my education came second. He didn't give a fuck about me, just the wasted money. It got worse when we were in the car, driving back home, we were both shouting. I can remember that. And it was raining. I can remember the rain. Then nothing. Dad crashed the car. I think I must've got a bang on the head, lost consciousness for a while, I just can't be sure exactly how it happened. Or who was to blame. Me or him. One of us killed my mum."

Stevie sighed. Usually Danny would keep his eyes forwards, staring out of the windscreen while Stevie would talk endlessly, never really sure whether Danny was interested or not. But he felt Danny look across at him. "I was taken to a hospital in Scarborough, stayed overnight. I can't really remember that, but that's what happened. I don't remember the taxi ride over here or any of it, Danny. Suddenly I was in Malton Court and these people who I didn't know seemed worried about me. Yeah, weird couple of days."

They both sat quiet for a while. Stevie's dad suffered major and multiple injuries in the car accident. Stevie had searched inside himself but he couldn't remember the accident. He understood that he may have lost consciousness but there had been no serious head injury. He knew it was possible that he'd blocked the memory. Despite the fate of his parents, Stevie survived with a couple of cuts on the right side of his forehead, a sore elbow and a small bruise somewhere on his left ankle. And that was Stevie… selling recreational drugs to the moneyed middle classes, lacking parental support, and despite close proximity to dangerous events, he had a useful knack of emerging with not much more than a scratch.

He continued his story. "Thank fuck my kid sisters weren't in the car. They were at a different school to me. Mine was all boys. I didn't know any girls till I came to Malton Court and met Sal and Lis. They soon brought me up to speed."

"Yeah, I remember. They thought you were the bees knees, Stevie. It was the way you talked," said Danny.

"Well, it may have had something to do with my charisma and irresistible good looks, Danny!" Until he'd turned fourteen, Stevie was short and his movements appeared poorly co-ordinated, his hair dark and unruly. He'd always liked his clothes but as a child he didn't have the body to wear them. Then he suddenly grew tall, stayed slim and a new fluidity and rhythm infected his movements. He grew his hair and the dark waves reshaped his face, showcasing his dark brown eyes. He grew to become a decent-looking lad.

"It was Sally who got me sorted with a smoke. Probably scored from Ronnie." Stevie had been hesitant as he recalled the car accident, but he was back in more comfortable territory now and in full flow. "Sally and Lisa were brilliant, taught me a few things, Danny. I thought they were my guardian angels. Until Seth threw a hot cup of coffee at me!" Stevie chuckled at this recollection although he'd been less amused at the time. Seth had picked on Stevie because he was the new kid and he hadn't yet made friends with Danny. As it had turned out, it had been Danny who came to his rescue. "I couldn't believe it when you strolled into the kitchen and fucked him off. Seth was twice your size."

Danny asked more questions. "So how was it that you came to Malton Court? What happened to your sisters?

Stevie took in a deep breath. Danny had taken him too close to his past, opened a door that ghosts might walk through. "My mum's sister, Aunt Harriet, took them in. For some reason, she wasn't so keen with me, you know, the dope smoking big brother, the recently expelled nephew who'd caused the accident that killed her sister." Stevie had got his defences back in place. "Fucking aunties, man, no forgiveness. I don't trust any of them."

Danny repeated his first question. "Why Malton Court?"

"Well, there was a room going spare, remember? Next door to you. My dad was in James Cook Hospital. It made sense for me to be in Middlesbrough so that I could visit him, not that I wanted to sit and watch him covered with tubes and bandages. It was the last place I wanted to be. I didn't know where I wanted to be. It didn't matter what I thought anyway, I did what I was told. I had nothing, Danny, no family, no home and no fucking cash. Just you guys."

Stevie really had been lost in the weeks following the fatal car accident. He was expected to be grief stricken but he wasn't, maybe there had been grief in him somewhere but he hadn't been able to find it. His mother's funeral came and went, his sisters were wheeled in and then out again, his father remained in hospital.

He didn't want to go to a new school and his future hung in the balance. His father's recovery took many months and the row that had started in the family car was never fully resolved. "When dad was finally discharged from hospital, I'd already started work."

Stevie still had his job in one of the big warehouses close to the docks.

Ships unloaded their cargo in Teesport where monster warehouses swallowed land, people and produce. It was an easy place to be invisible and to be a legitimate citizen. Stevie kept talking. "Dad found a new house in Whitby, Kitty and Samantha went back to live with him. He asked me but he didn't want me back. I knew that and I didn't want to be anywhere near him. The accident fucked it up for me and dad. It's in the way, we can't get past it. Fuck it."

"Does he blame you?" said Danny.

Stevie was unusually thoughtful. "I don't know, Danny… maybe. He told me it wasn't my fault but I don't know what he really thinks. I don't know exactly what the problem is, we were never close. The thing is, Danny, we killed mum. That's what I did with my dad. We can't sit and watch Eastenders together with that in the background. We can't do it. We both know it. I don't want to breathe the same air that he breathes. I don't want to shit in the same toilet. It's all fucked up."

He paused. Usually he loved these nights, rattling on while Danny mostly listened. Stevie couldn't keep his mouth shut. He told Danny a thousand personal stories. Stevie could see that Danny was happy to listen, interested to hear about his background. Maybe listening was all that Danny could do, he really didn't have the credentials to join into a conversation about middle class family life. Whatever, Stevie havered on, mostly in bright spirits. But this particular conversation had become uncomfortable.

"At least he felt guilty enough to fund my driving lessons, and he bought this car. Fair enough, Danny, you know… *'Sorry, son, for recklessly killing your mum, here's a second hand Vauxhall Corsa.'* Thank you and goodnight. What more can a son hope for?"

In fact, the car was crucial, allowing longer distances as they traced the trade routes that Danny intended to control in the future. The two of them sat in Stevie's Vauxhall Corsa night after night, watching the streets, watching doors opening and closing, figures appearing and disappearing, watching the magic of a dark night, feeling the heat, discovering the secrets and the shame… the backdrop to their friendship and to their working relationship.

It felt peculiar to them both. Stevie had never developed ambitions for a career, and he had no wish to extend his education. But he was seventeen, his family was gone, Stevie needed a future that wasn't inside a warehouse and while he sat in the Corsa with Danny, he found one.

The most surprising thing of all was that Stevie developed a healthy respect for Danny. And he liked him. The miserable control freak, drawn to danger, with all of his destructive power, with the anger and violence inside of him, with his plans to be a drugs dealer, Danny Hutton had found his way into Stevie's affections. Love wasn't blind, it just lacked judgement.

Stevie was good during movie nights. He could talk forever and still watch the scenes unfolding outside in the night. "Hey up, Ronnie's got a visitor."

While a figure waited at the tower block entrance, Ronnie leaned out of his fifth floor window. The door buzzed open and the figure disappeared inside. Probably just a punter. They were waiting to find Ronnie's supplier... they would have to find their target on another night. Good crack though.

•

The movie nights went on for a couple of years and they delivered the goods. Sometimes just Stevie and Danny, on other occasions Sean or Seth would be with them. It was all composed and choreographed by the new in charge and under control Danny Hutton, the coming man. Danny would sit in his room thinking, figuring it out, putting the pieces together, learning the business, finding the players. Then he'd emerge again, round up Sean and Stevie and say, "Come on, guys, we're going to the movies."

And as they learned and planned, their bonds strengthened. At that time, every trail that they followed eventually led to the same man. Nick Singleton was the man. He received imported class A drugs through Teesport and he managed the subsequent distribution. Danny had been watching for nearly two years, and was convinced that Nick was his own man. And indeed he was, right up until the moment that eighteen-year-old Danny Hutton had figured out every detail of his operation, and got his phone number and his home address. Then of course, he was Danny's man.

# MURDER IN THE ORIENT

Danny had followed Nick Singleton over a period of nearly two years, watching and learning. In those early days Danny had needed to take calculated risks… he was on the streets, he handled people and merchandise directly. He knew that he didn't want to offer opportunities to either the local police or to rivals but he also understood that he needed to give clear evidence of his position and of his ruthlessness.

Nick Singleton wasn't frightened but he was listening to the whispers. Nick had had his own journey to travel. He'd watch and wait and if Danny got close, he'd let Ruth do her work.

He heard Danny coming. Two or three people had told him stories about an overconfident teenager who was ruffling some feathers and asking too many questions. Nick wasn't a particularly big man but he had a well developed streak of nastiness and he was well able to administer physical violence. But mostly he left that to Ruth, she enjoyed it. No point spoiling her fun.

There were plenty of frightening rumours about Ruth, including a tale that she'd been a childhood killer and had grown up in some kind of specialised secure detention centre. She had a Scottish accent and she claimed to come from Motherwell. She never said anything more about herself than that and when she did mention her home town, she always showed a sneering amusement, as if Motherwell said it all.

Ruth didn't get sucked into testosterone wars. She wasn't trying to be the alpha male. She liked sharp blades and she got something, some kind of sustenance, from hurting other human beings. Ruth was perfect for Nick. Nick was perfect for Danny.

Danny had been thorough with his research. He had it all worked out. The movie nights hadn't been wasted. He had the complete picture, a panoramic view of Nick's operations. Danny was still only eighteen years old, nevertheless he decided it was time. He was ready.

Nick Singleton would need to be publicly hanged. Danny

would enact his plan swiftly. His message to Nick would be loud and clear and it would be heard all over town.

It was just another movie night, out with Sean and Stevie, when Danny told his companions that he'd be removing Singleton, and that was the word Danny had used… removing. Danny was serious. He knew his own mind but for Stevie and Sean the movie nights were fun. They were having a blast. They were young and foolish enough to be entertained by Danny's rise to power. But neither of them felt ready for Nick Singleton, even less for Razor Ruth.

Danny listened with interest to the rumours about Ruth. He knew that Sean would stand alongside him, even though he wasn't a fighter. Danny appreciated his loyalty and he understood his nerves.

Stevie's position was never in doubt. He was unashamed, almost proud, to be cowardly.

"I'll be washing my hair that night, bud, but you know, I could meet you later for a beer."

Danny knew Stevie's limitations well enough and tended to substitute Seth into the game when a confrontation was anticipated. He smiled to himself while Stevie sought to clarify the parameters of his involvement. Danny wouldn't want Stevie to be a participant in his plan to challenge Nick and Ruth. He knew better than to include Stevie in a street fight, let alone what might occur when he came face to face with Nick Singleton.

"You're the wheels, Stevie. That's all you'll need to do, drive the car. I'll deal with Ruth. With a bit of help from Sean." Danny was planning a dangerous and violent takeover. None of the others would be exposed to such a prospect. It would be Danny's moment.

Stevie wasn't massively attracted to the driving role but he said nothing more.

Sean's interest accelerated. "What does that mean?" He was more than curious.

Danny didn't really answer the question. He had been an inquisitive and a critical observer. He approved of Singleton's management. Nick was a smooth operator and he kept his own hands clean. It wasn't rocket science but a key operating principle nevertheless. Singleton was careful, anything risky or messy was done by someone else. But on this one occasion, for this crucial moment, Danny would have to take a risk and he knew that it may well be a messy encounter.

There was one element of Nick Singleton's behaviour with which Danny was less impressed. In Danny's eyes, Nick Singleton's need to preen his feathers was a weakness. Danny and the others had followed him all over Teesside and sometimes well beyond. Nick appeared to be in full control but he was a little bit too pleased with himself… his personal appearances had become predictable. That gave Danny an opportunity.

Nick liked to spend an hour or two enjoying a drink in a pub. He'd used two or three different venues over the years, but these days The Orient was his preferred option. It was a big pub in the town centre. Nick wasn't overly flash but he liked to be seen. He felt the need to demonstrate his position. Just for a couple of hours, early doors on Friday evenings.

He liked to show Ruth off. By seven o'clock on a Friday, The Orient would be full. A real mix. After work drinkers, early starters, lots of young students, and Nick would be there, with Ruth and a couple of his guys.

Many of the drinkers knew who he was, and they knew to keep a safe distance. There were whispers and there really was a feeling of menace around them. Nick liked that. He could feel the half glances and the nervous tension.

Nick would always park right outside the pub, illegally. A decent quality Jaguar, ninety grand's worth. It was his way of reminding whoever might be taking an interest that he was untouchable, in control and enjoying a fast car. Danny understood the importance of the message. He was less impressed by Nick's mode of delivery. Playing the gangster, dozy bastard.

The day came, Stevie drove, his digestive system squeaking and squirting. He found a space twenty metres from Nick's Jag and stayed in the car.

Danny texted Sean: *Are we set?*

Sean sent a thumbs up in reply.

Sean used The Orient regularly. He'd played a few gigs in the upstairs room. There was no changing room so musicians had to tune up in what was no more than a large cupboard at the front of the first floor where the landlord had his security gear. Twelve cameras covered every square metre downstairs and a computer screen captured each camera's image in a four by three grid. Sean had come into the pub twenty minutes earlier, popped upstairs to the security centre and powered the whole system down.

Danny got out of Stevie's car and walked over to Nick's Jaguar. He booted the wing mirror, more of a horizontal stamp really. The mirror glass shattered, the whole unit was dislodged from the car body, left dangling by a few cables. And, of course, the alarm went off.

Danny moved on swiftly through the door into The Orient. It was an odd, or at least unlikely, set of events. Music was playing but Nick and other drinkers were becoming unsettled, recognising that an alarm was blaring out in the street. Everyone was turning their attention towards the door. Although Danny stood in plain sight, the searching eyes looked past him. He enjoyed a rare moment of invisibility.

He stood still, just a few paces inside the room, breathing fast and scanning table by table. He wore plain clothes – trainers and a black tee-shirt, clean jeans. He was in control. He looked slightly out of place, as if he'd walked into the wrong pub. A young guy looking into the room while everyone else wanted to see what was happening outside.

Danny was a big lad, although not as big as Seth. It was just that Danny had a force within him, some seriously bad energy.

He felt a big surge of adrenaline. He took a few seconds to look around and could sense the growing confusion as he spotted Nick's table. Such moments of dangerous confrontation didn't faze him, he was pumped and he'd learned to trust his instincts. Once in motion, Danny Hutton was unstoppable.

Nick's two meatheads were already marching fast through a parting crowd towards the door. Danny stood aside as they rushed past to investigate the alarm. Danny picked up a wooden stool, walked towards Nick and Ruth and then threw the stool.

He threw it from about twelve feet and with all his force. It hit the top of their table, collecting all four drinks and bounced up into Ruth's face. The edge of the stool seat hit against her forehead and she was knocked out. That was a bonus. Actually, that was the fucking jackpot.

Nick felt several shards of glass cut into his face and neck, nothing too serious but he was dazed and confused. Onlookers were starting to panic, trying to move away, a space opened giving Danny an easy path to Ruth.

Meathead One arrived back inside just in time to catch a glimpse of his boss's bloody face, but he was already too late to help Nick and Ruth. Danny positioned himself next to Ruth on a bench seat. He put his large right hand over Ruth's, which held a Stanley knife. And there they were, the two most dangerous people in town holding hands. And together they slit her throat.

Meathead One made a strategic decision to update his buddy outside with the Jaguar. People were freaking now, screaming and shouting, wanting to get out, frightened to move.

Danny sat across the table from Nick, who was in shock and tentatively attempting to remove fragments of broken glass from his cheeks. They looked into each other's eyes. Nick had blood running down and across his face. He looked like the England flag. He was dazed and beaten, sitting next to his best weapon who was bleeding to death.

Danny was in charge. *This is my town now, Nick.*

Neither man spoke.

Danny got to his feet and walked quickly back out on to the street.

Stevie had kept the car running. He watched Danny emerge back out on to the footpath and moved into action. This really was like the movies. He got the Corsa into gear. He drove the short distance at speed, then braked hard to stop for a few seconds while Danny reclaimed his seat. Stevie accelerated again and they were gone. And so were Stevie's nerves, the unpleasantness was over and Danny was still in one piece. He was a getaway driver, he was having fun.

The Meathead twins watched their departure and found the courage to re-enter The Orient. Sean watched Stevie drive away before he rebooted the security set up back into operation. He went back downstairs and looked around at the chaos, the panic and the damage. Danny with adrenaline. Danny was outside of the car for less than two minutes. Sean decided to leave.

The emergency services did their work. Some witnesses just left the pub, some gave statements. There were accounts which mentioned another person being involved in a fight but no one seemed to be sure exactly how Ruth's fatal cut had happened.

Nick had his cuts tended, a couple of them needing some stitching, but none of his injuries were serious. Ruth died in the pub. The Meathead twins removed Nick, got him into the car and away. The police attended and an ambulance took Ruth away. The Stanley knife was still gripped in her hand.

Danny went back to the gym and spent the evening alone. He was in a reflective mood, thinking about what he'd done. He had a few things to think about.

Danny Hutton, still a teenager, had become a murderer. On a December night, he'd knocked a woman unconscious with a wooden stool, then slit her throat. Ruth was the first and last person that Danny killed. He'd planned it. She was unmanageable, death was the only option. He wasn't proud. But Danny knew then, he had it in him to kill another human being.

He drank whisky while he reflected, a decent Dalwhinnie, heather and honey. He'd looked straight into Nick Singleton's eyes. He knew there was still more work to be done but Danny had asserted his authority, gained position. He examined his actions, his motives and his outcomes. He struggled to judge whether what he'd done was good or bad.

If the whispers around town were half true, then Ruth had a long line of victims. She had in fact killed twice herself. On both occasions the deaths had been accidental when she'd gone a bit too far. Mostly her preference had been to leave hideous scarring… she liked to watch blood running from a fresh wound.

Seth had pointed out one of her victims to Danny a few weeks earlier, a man with two untidy facial scars, one of which covered the full width of his face. He'd heard stories about several others with Ruth's autograph all over their faces. So to speak.

After a couple of hours and a slow glass of whisky, Danny decided he'd done a bad thing. His motives were selfish, the greater good benefits were fortunate but accidental. Despite his negative self-judgement, he slept well enough. Perhaps a bit better than usual. The whisky was a warm friend and, after all, he didn't have to worry about Razor Ruth creeping into his room in the dead of night.

It was the biggest risk that Danny had ever taken. It could have gone wrong in lots of ways. He knew that there was still a possibility that the police would solve the case, but if Sean had cut the cameras, and Sean was good at that kind of stuff, then he'd have to be unlucky.

He needed Ruth dead and he needed Singleton alive. Two days after wreaking havoc in The Orient, Danny took a ride out with Stevie and Seth.

Nick had security cameras at the front and back of his house. Since Danny's untimely intrusion, he had the Meathead twins staying with him in the house day and night. He was, of course, in crisis. He'd talked to as many of his half trusted employees and business associates as he could and it all pointed to a young buck called Danny Hutton who wasn't to be fucked with, apparently. Well, thanks for that guys, timely information.

Nick had nowhere to go. He was in up to his neck. He had shipments in transit, he had buyers waiting. What did Danny Hutton want him to do? The problem was that Nick had faced Danny, and he knew he'd been defeated by Danny's bold and ruthless assault. Now he was waiting for the next move. Nick was struggling.

Meathead One was a vaper, strawberry nicotine. Meathead Two was old fashioned, he smoked cigarettes. Three or four times each day, they stepped out of Nick's house into the garden to get their nicotine fix. It was too easy. Danny presented his argument during their smoke break. Seth emphasised the key points. Stevie waited in the car. Danny showed his hands, that's all.

He gave them a slap, then offered them a job. Nick was relieved. Humiliated but nevertheless, alive and relieved. Danny used him for the next eighteen months and then gave him a generous retirement package. Danny Hutton had made his move and gained unchallenged control of his operations.

Danny had a handful of key contacts, all of which had come through Nick Singleton. Danny became the conductor. Apart from Carl in Rotterdam, everyone was in the north of England. Danny supplied three distributors: Mike Ashton for heroin, Tommy Atherton for amphetamines, cocaine and MDMA, and Saggy for anything unexpected. And he kept things stable, he conducted his business with care and attention.

Danny was the company chairman, Stevie was his CEO. He used Stevie in different roles. Stevie managed the local distribution of cocaine, he supervised the weed farms, and he was good with people. Stevie was always clowning around but he was a shrewd judge of character and he could talk to anyone. Danny understood and appreciated that Stevie stayed calm… he didn't really seem to have an adrenaline gland. And Danny knew that if Stevie questioned him, he'd best listen. Stevie thought in a completely different way to Danny. They had a thousand differences but they filled each other's spaces, covered the cracks. They worked well together.

He made a lot of money from his illegal activities, he'd committed a murder but Danny wasn't a thug. He was a thoughtful operator, a strategist. There was economy in his activities. He did what needed to be done and his timing was precise. He grew to become a very smart businessman and a man of his word. He didn't rip anyone off and he had a carefully judged sense of fair play and business ethics. In Danny's world view, big oil and gas and a thousand other legitimate businesses were the greedy, high carbon cunts who needed policing. Danny was providing services… if nobody got in his way, then nobody got hurt. Unfortunately Nick, Razor Ruth and the Meathead twins had got in Danny's way.

In the years that followed, he maintained his business of hard and soft drugs in and around Teesside. After all of the walks and the movie nights stalking his quarry, he'd taken control. It wasn't about money, he just wanted his own piece of land, a dark place where no one could see him, a place where he could live.

But Danny became increasingly ill at ease with the world he'd won and he experienced a growing dilemma – he didn't want anyone to take it from him but sometimes he wanted it all to be gone.

He'd wrestled with this dilemma for several years without resolution. His prize delivered low satisfaction and high income. Having gained victory over Nick Singleton, Danny was able to focus on other matters. He waited a few months for the headlines to fade away, then he went to find Beth.

# BETH

Beth first met Danny in 2001. She was a few weeks from her seventh birthday when four-year-old Danny first arrived at Malton Court.

She was confused, a young child trying to make sense of a world where tricks of language, alternative truths, seemed to be everywhere. Somewhere around the turn of the century 'looked after children' became the label for children with parents who were either unwilling or unable to raise their kids. So children who were not looked after were called 'looked after children' and those who were looked after were simply children.

Beth was still trying to make sense of her own situation. She could remember what had happened at her mum's house, she knew what her stepfather had done to her. But understanding eluded her.

Surely her mother must have known what had been going on. So maybe it was okay. It hadn't felt okay, it really hadn't. But none of them had spoken about it. Everybody had known but nobody had said anything. She'd become the central character in a sad and unspoken story.

Beth looked to herself for an explanation. She found faults in her own behaviour... had she said a wrong word or worn her socks incorrectly or smiled a crooked smile without realising? She censored her behaviour, trying to understand the faults that brought her stepfather creeping into her room.

No matter how many corrections Beth made to her behaviour, her stepfather's visits continued. She felt like she was nothing, incapable of being a wholesome child, a good daughter. She'd tried to make a difference but she was powerless, crushed and desperately confused.

Beth stopped speaking when she was six years old. No one wanted to hear her story so she became quiet. She'd found her own trick of language, her silence got noisy, her teachers got nosey and the shambles that was her home was suddenly gone. Quietly, she was taken, she was no longer a child, she'd become a looked after child.

She'd arrived at Malton Court a few months ahead of Danny. No one in the care system cared much for Beth. She continued her silence at Malton Court... what was she meant to say? She remembers a woman with prominent teeth, Francis, explaining that her mum had a few things to sort out before Beth could be sent back home.

Beth remembers thinking to herself that even if she'd felt ready to speak, she wouldn't have known what to say. What was a six-year-old victim of persistent sexual abuse supposed to say to the strangers who suddenly surrounded her?

During the first few days, and despite some feelings of relief, she cried a river. Sometimes she was left alone, sometimes a worker offered comfort. She didn't have a clue why her tears kept flowing, quietly. She'd been found and now she was lost. Some of the other looked after children around the Court were unkind in the first few weeks, mocking her silence and her tears. She gave no response. She knew how to speak but by now she had belief in her withdrawal from the world of words, and she felt no need to return.

She waited quietly and her confusion continued. As it turned out, Francis wasn't to be trusted and Beth's temporary removal was extended.

She watched quietly. As the weeks passed, she settled, she paid attention to the world around her, and she experienced a developing urge to reach out to other children. Beth wanted to give something of herself. Unlike her mother, she had a maternal instinct. The everyday order of chaos became a comfort and she did start to reach out (quietly) to some of the other kids.

Beth knew how it felt to be overlooked and unheard when screaming for help. She was quiet but she had courage, she would never look away when she witnessed human distress. This virtue she learned from her mother's neglect, and her stepfather's attention.

Beth had spent fourteen weeks in Malton Court when Danny arrived. She was finding a role in her new home, she was discovering something new in herself, her tears had stopped.

Perhaps there is an aspect of sadness and of something gone wrong when a six-year-old girl develops a compulsion to care, where a burden of responsibility was part of the deal and the opportunity to be a carefree child was not.

Nevertheless, it was the best Beth had ever felt. For the first time that she could remember, she gained a sense of self, a place in her new chaotic family, her existence expanding to include more than a victim. To her surprise, she started to feel more than an occasional urge to speak. Oddly, and even though she'd always known that her mutism was elective, she could never quite find the right moment to break her silence, and she started to worry that she might never regain her voice.

Those first few days of Danny's residency were explosive. He was wild and frightened. Malton Court could be an emotionally charged environment. There always seemed to be someone kicking off. Displays of frustration, disappointment, anger, loss, desperation and impatience were commonplace. But Danny was a bit special.

Beth watched quietly and from distance. The houseparents, the support workers, the visiting professionals, the other kids, every fucker was up a height around Danny. Sometimes he'd rage for what felt like hours, but eventually he'd become exhausted, wasted and lost, shaking, almost unconscious. Beth felt for him.

And so it was on the 12th July 2001 at six in the evening, he was spent, strung out, growling in the corner of a small kitchen, when Beth's hand came lightly to rest on the shoulder of four-year-old Danny Hutton.

"I've left you juice, Danny," she said. Her first words in over nine months.

She left a small beaker of orange juice.

Danny didn't look at her. He kicked the juice across the kitchen floor and disappeared into his room.

•

46

Beth had found her voice but it would be many years later before she escaped her confusion. She'd always felt drawn to Danny, right from the start. She wanted to make him better, whatever that might mean. She didn't know why.

She tolerated her growing pains and watched her body struggle towards adulthood. She knew her developing body offered new possibilities and sensations but she was hesitant and defensive. Suddenly the other kids seemed to be giggling and shrieking, talking about their sexual encounters. Beth felt older and yet at the same time, left behind. She rejected the interest of her peers. If Danny had asked, well… maybe she would have felt differently. He hadn't asked.

Her mother's problems never seemed to resolve. Sometimes she took an interest, sometimes not. Beth learned to live with inconsistency and disappointment. Eventually, after nearly ten years in Malton Court, the world went crazy again… her mother took her home.

Poor Beth had been resourceful and courageous, she'd found her voice and her place. She'd made an admirable adjustment to her life as a looked after child, formed new bonds. Her little group of peers at Malton Court were more than friends, they had become her support system, her family. Then her newly reformed, hero rescuer mother came to reclaim her. Fucking mothers.

Beth and her mother never really connected, it was too late, and although Beth felt some appreciation for her mum's latest try, she was sixteen, she was already more grown up than her mum would ever be. She could find neither the forgiveness for the past, nor investment for the future. She found employment in Debenhams and after less than a year she found her own flat.

Beth had always looked forward to reaching adulthood. The prospect of independence appealed to her, beckoned her with promises and possibilities. She coped, Beth always coped, but she was lonely. She was separated from her friends and her mother. She made occasional visits to Malton Court, keeping in touch with Lisa, Sally and especially Molly. She asked after the boys but they were never around when she visited.

Her friends weren't far behind her, trying to be grown-ups, stumbling out of Malton Court and falling into the bigger world. It was a strange time. For a few years, circumstances had thrown a group of children together. Then came a time when they scattered.

They should have made proper arrangements. Beth had struggled during that period. She'd had her maternal role at Malton Court and she missed that part of herself. She missed seeing the other kids. She and Molly were always close but contact with the other kids became either haphazard or non-existent. She felt adrift, unconnected, almost invisible.

Sean would sometimes turn up to say 'hi' when she was at work. She heard the whispers around town that Danny had earned a reputation but she never saw him. Until he was standing right in front of her across the counter in Debenhams.

They went for coffee during her lunch hour. She was really pleased that he'd turned up again. It had been at least two years since their paths had last crossed. He'd become a man.

He'd seemed to be well on his way to manhood even before she'd left Malton Court. Danny was fourteen then, still wiry in his physique. Beth noticed that he'd got a bit heavier, he was clearly still working out. His face was where he'd changed the most. Changed and aged. His hair and his skin seemed to have darkened and his features had hardened.

But he still smiled a pretty convincing smile and they dropped immediately back into their well established dialogue.

"Well, it's been a while, Danny. Are you okay?" Beth maintained a calm demeanour although she was excited to be in his company again after such a long time.

"Yes, I'm pretty well, Beth. All over the place, as always, but yeah, I'm fine. How are you?"

Beth hesitated, not sure how to answer. She'd survived the early years of her adult life but she'd drifted into a humdrum and oftentimes lonely existence.

"I'm keeping the wolves from the door, busy with work." That was all she could say. She wondered why Danny had suddenly reappeared in her life. "You've grown, Danny, you look well. Has something happened?"

Danny explained himself. "I've got some premises in Darlington, a shop with a flat upstairs. I buy and sell antiques. I want to use the shop, you know, as a retail outlet."

"Oh right, you're doing okay with the antiques business then?" Beth knew well enough how Danny made his living. She raised a sceptical eyebrow and made a less than convincing attempt to repress the grin that was pushing at the corners of her mouth. "Because everybody else in town thinks you're a drug dealer."

Danny glanced around the café. "Yes, thanks for that, Beth, perhaps you could shout a bit louder, there's a couple at the table in the far corner who didn't quite hear. The thing is, Beth, I do want to operate the shop, a proper business, but yes, it would give Max the chance to clean up some money from other sources. I wouldn't put you in any danger, Beth. You know that. And you know about shops. I'll double your wages if you'll give it a shot."

Beth wondered what might be coming. Her relationship with Danny had been straightforward when they were young children. She'd tried to look after him, to find a way to offer comfort to a needy and frightened little boy.

It had got more complicated during puberty. For their own reasons they'd both held back while their friends were discovering and exercising their adult bodies. The truth was that they both had feelings for each other but they'd been paralysed by doubt and fear.

And now he was back offering her a job. He was still only nineteen years old. She'd heard enough through Sean and Molly. She knew that all of the boys were Danny's boys and she knew that Danny helped Molly out with some cash from time to time. She'd been back with her mum while Danny had been learning his trade, and she hadn't looked closely but she knew that Danny's world was dangerous. Danny was dangerous.

Beth had done alright during the previous four years. Her life was dull and dreary but she'd coped with independent living and she was good at her job. After a challenging period in her young life, she'd stayed on a steady path. Beth had grown to become resourceful and self reliant, no wrong turns, no crime, no drugs. No Danny.

There was only ever going to be one answer. Danny's proposal was a crazy invitation to throw away everything she'd worked so hard to build.

"Yes, I'll give it a go, when do we start?"

# DANNY AND BETH: A LOVE STORY

Following Danny's reappearance, Beth's life took a new direction. The safe and repetitive pattern of life that had revolved around a small flat and employment at Debenhams was gone and she set out on a new venture. Her loneliness lifted and she met her new circumstances with enthusiasm.

Over a period of months, Beth got the premises in Darlington into shape. She soon had the shop well stocked, she made sure that the windows invited a closer look and she was making improvements to the living space upstairs.

Danny had to spend time with her at the Darlington premises. There were a thousand things to do, they caught up, and each of them gave their accounts of the years leading up to their reacquaintance. Danny was older, a bit more at ease with himself, he'd grown up. So had Beth, she reflected, looking back through the years. She remembered the pattern of their early interactions at Malton Court. He'd always been passive… she had been the active player. He was filled with tension, and she'd tried to be supportive. They'd come through it all.

Beth started to learn about antiques. Mostly she was learning from her phone but on Sundays she'd cook Danny a meal and then they'd watch the Antiques Roadshow together on the telly. Like a middle aged couple.

Beth had been given limited responsibilities at Debenhams but she had undertaken a variety of tasks and she'd learned about retail. Her decision to work for Danny was a risk, she was breaking new ground. Now she was visiting auction rooms, online markets and recycling centres.

Beth was good at procurement. She seemed able to find what she needed. She made the shop look fabulous and she was great with customers. Danny watched with growing interest. The shop was supposed to be a front for some creative accounting… he'd never imagined a thriving business.

Beth had her own vision. She allowed Max his financial trickery but that apart she was running a successful small business.

She enjoyed her new responsibilities and discovered new talent within herself. She had an appreciation of aesthetics and an instinct for design. She filled her shop with all sorts of interesting antiques and she placed and framed each piece with care. When customers entered, they would often remark immediately on how lovely the shop looked. And it did. Beth, the mother, the pragmatist, the head down and cope girl, had the touch and taste of an artist.

She was a natural grafter and the success of her enterprise grew. She enjoyed it all. She was creating something new. She valued her work but it was still a maternal instinct driving Beth. She'd been confused and uncertain about her emotional investment in Danny when she was a teenager. She was twenty-one years old now and she wasn't confused anymore. She wanted to be with Danny. She wanted children and she wanted Danny to be her children's father. She'd always felt drawn to him but it was only now that the nature of her attraction clarified.

Beth watched Danny. She noted his habits and his moods. He'd given her a ringside seat, regular contact, continuing dialogue. She knew that she needed to proceed cautiously, with patience and diligence. It would be the most important and the most sensitive challenge of her life and yet she always believed that she was the one person on earth who could meet Danny's needs. She was lovingly and meticulously contrived in her seduction.

Beth listened with interest through their catch-up conversations. She guessed that a few of the more gory details had been edited out. He'd talked at length about different brands of whisky. That was unexpected. When they'd been teenagers, Danny had never bothered much with drugs and he'd particularly avoided alcohol. They'd all experimented when they were kids at Malton Court but he'd either been spooked or disappointed. Five years later, still a teenager and he talked about malt whisky like a connoisseur.

Danny had surprised her, she liked that. He told her that he'd rather spit out a mouthful of blended whisky than swallow but he liked a handful of single malts when he was safe in his own home but not when he was working. He gave few details about his business interests but he talked endlessly about the bloody whisky. For some reason the words 'smoke screen' came into Beth's mind.

Of course it suited Beth to stay overnight in the flat above the shop when she would be working in the shop the following morning. Which was most days.

She waited, lovingly and quietly. Danny's appearances were difficult to predict but he still turned up most Sundays, early in the evening. Beth was on the move. She would either find her way to an intimate connection with Danny or she would be refused. She was determined to find out what was possible between them. The prospect scared her but she needed to know.

She knew that he'd accepted her uninvited care in the past and she knew that she was an attractive woman but her apprehension was enormous. She never even knew for sure whether he'd come to the flat. He'd been staying elsewhere since Beth had been at the shop. She assumed he was still using the gym as his living space.

But on impulse after a long Sunday of window dressing, all alone she poured two large glasses of a twenty-year-old Glenlivet and sat in soft light, waiting for Danny.

She waited for more than an hour, feeling nervous. And just as she became so consumed with doubt that she prayed for him to stay away, he walked briskly into the flat. He was surprised by her presence but not disturbed. She gestured to the glass of whisky that was not her own.

He smiled. Beth, he thought, knew him the best.

"Hey, Beth, how are you doing?" Danny looked around for somewhere to hang his jacket, unsuccessfully. He dropped it by a chair, sat down and looked around.

"I'm all over this shop, Danny." Beth smiled as she replied. "It's all coming on, the shop and the flat. I've been sleeping here sometimes, doing some decorating up here in the evenings and it's easy for opening up in the mornings. I hope that's okay? You haven't been using the flat so, you know, I thought I might as well. I had a feeling that you'd come over tonight."

Danny nodded in the direction of the two glasses of whisky. "So I see."

She'd poured generous measures and she allowed almost thirty minutes of small talk to pass before she made her move.

Danny had been tense, polite but nevertheless Beth could feel his tension. Danny didn't like surprises so she spoke in as relaxed a manner as she could.

"Christ, Danny, you've nearly finished your drink. I thought it'd get you relaxed but you still look wound up. Let me give your shoulders a quick massage." As if this was a regular occurrence, no big deal.

She stood and walked across the room and stopped directly behind his chair. It was a big deal. She took the deepest breath in the history of deep breaths and placed a hand upon his shoulder. Not for the first time. But he wasn't a little boy anymore. His shoulders were huge and he felt like granite beneath her small hands.

Then Beth was astonished. She experienced a moment of lust, a really quite raw sense of heat low in her abdomen. Not part of the plan. But no harm. She began to massage Danny's neck and shoulders. He seemed unable to relax. She persisted. What the fuck else could she do now? After a couple of minutes, he arched his back and slid forward in his seat. She heard a sigh and she felt the first signs of softness in the shoulders that were no longer made of stone.

Beth worked her hands instinctively. It was fine, she just needed to figure out how to stop.

"That's starting to feel a bit better. The muscles are softening but I'll keep going for a while." And she did, just for a while. They'd both lost some of their tension and for an immeasurable and inconclusive moment, they seemed to be together, in an antiques business, in a flat above a shop, in a room, in a moment in time, physically, spiritually, in their unspoken dialogue, in their unfolding.

Then she placed each of her hands on the top of his arms. She wanted to squeeze but her hands seemed too small. All she

54

could do was to exert a little extra pressure. She moved her hands back onto his shoulders and for two, maybe three seconds she caressed his almost softened shoulders before she stepped away. "I've made up a bed in the small bedroom. I'm going to get some sleep. Maybe catch you in the morning, Danny."

Danny slept well. Beth laid awake all night, filled with hope.

Danny had allowed her into his personal space, he'd accepted the massage. This was significant, new territory. And just to make sure that her message was clear, she'd given a caress. No words, no space left for a reply. A massage and a caress. Banked and gaining interest.

•

The next morning Beth cooked breakfast and made fresh ground coffee. Danny ate and drank. He had a busy day ahead of him, a few bits and pieces, and his thoughts had been racing but he zoned right in on the bacon and eggs.

If ever there was a moment when a fry up could claim to be a poem, then this was it. The fried eggs were bang on, a hint of brown crisp on the bottom, a couple of bubbles from the spitting hot oil, surrounding a silky wet yolk. Almost pornographic. And Lincolnshire sausage, juicy and slightly charred. The bacon was crispy, and of course there were baked beans, fried mushrooms and plenty of toast. Danny was fully engaged, purring. If there was a God in heaven, and there wasn't, but if there was, every day would begin like this.

He relished every mouthful of this rare treat, a home cooked breakfast.

"You've worked a miracle here, Beth. The flat looks great."

His mood was almost cheerful. Beth didn't want to celebrate too much too early but everything she'd offered had hit the spot. She enjoyed the compliment. "It's a really cool flat, Danny, so's the shop. I really like it here."

"That's good to hear, Beth. You're running the shop, it would make sense for you to live here. The flat's yours if you want it.

I've got a ten year lease." Danny's assessment was objective, nevertheless he felt nervous as he spoke. He hadn't forgotten the massage. He felt as if he should say something about it. He would do just as soon as he'd worked out what he might want to say.

Beth panicked. What exactly was he saying? What was he asking? Shit, one night under the same roof in separate bedrooms and he was gone already! Was she about to evict him?

"I can see it would make sense, maybe, but I thought you were going to live here, Danny."

"No, no, it's fine, Beth. I need to be in town really. Have a chat with Max, he'll sort it." Danny sat forward on his seat, resting his forearms on top of his knees and raised his gaze to look right into her dark eyes.

When Beth had gone to her bed the previous night, she'd felt good. She'd made a bold move and she thought that she'd left Danny an open door. Now he'd decided to walk through it in the wrong direction. Fuck. She could feel his eyes but she didn't want to look at him.

"Great, yeah. I'll call Max then. You're sure about this though, Danny? 'Cos, you know, I'll give up my place in Middlesbrough if you're definite about it."

"One hundred percent, Beth." Danny had in fact offered Beth the flat on impulse. He knew exactly what had happened last night. He'd needed some time to think and yet he wanted to give something to Beth. And it really did make sense. And it felt better to Danny. He'd been taken by surprise, unprepared for Beth's boldness, but at least he'd taken control away from her. Danny didn't wish to be a control freak but so it goes.

He picked up his coat and his car keys. "I need to go."

She just couldn't let him walk out. She needed to speak. "Did you enjoy your massage, Danny?"

He paused on his way to the door and turned his head. "Yeah, it was sweet, Beth." He stopped and turned around fully to face her. "Fucking brilliant to be honest. I don't know how you do it. You're an angel, Beth. You've got the Midas touch with me anyway, you always did have at Malton Court."

And that was it. He broke the spell and looked at his phone. "Gotta go."

He left.

She cooked for him the following Sunday but he texted to say he couldn't get away. Three months later and he still hadn't been over. And then he texted her again. Romantic bastard.

•

Danny had retreated to spend three months wrestling with doubt because he'd understood that a big decision needed to be made. To Beth or not to Beth. Her hand on his shoulder.

Beth had always been able to hold his hand in the darkness. If Danny Hutton was ever going to have a chance in hell at a half decent enduring relationship, it had to be Beth. He knew that well enough.

Sometimes he believed it might be possible, but then his doubt would step forward. Danny Hutton was a man alone, emotionally cold and detached. Danny was tall, he was in good shape, young and strong. He was self assured and vulnerable, both at the same time. He had a moody disposition. He was desperately unsure of himself with sex and with any kind of close, let alone intimate, relationship. Solitude was his best refuge. Women threw themselves at him.

Eleven-year-old Danny had discovered masturbation. He had the body parts and the hormones but he kept his sexual world to himself. Perhaps it was the prospect of reaching his seventeenth birthday as a virgin that eventually convinced him and finally he had consensual sex with another human being. There were no fanfares, no revelations.

Actually it was a huge moment. He'd had plenty of opportunities and let them pass. Not yet ready. And then without a thought, he gave Teresa Howard what for. Teresa and Danny had been at school together, she gave some strong signals and both of them had been surprised when Danny responded. For no particular reason on that particular night, he decided to take his chance. He'd given it full beans. It was okay. It was an orgasm. He'd survived without trauma. He wished Teresa well but it was just a one nighter.

Danny knew after Teresa that it was possible. His interest fluctuated between mild and none at all. Miserable solitude was Danny's default mode of operation, with sex it was pretty well the same, although his inactivity could be misunderstood – Danny had testosterone in buckets but he was caught between drive and desire. He didn't want to look too closely at himself and he didn't wish to examine the history that had confused and damaged him. Avoidance was a more attractive option.

Work had always been the focus, the priority. He was still only nineteen but Danny was a successful businessman. He was a powerful man. This situation with Beth was the first time he'd stopped to think about development in his personal world, about the possibility of a romantic relationship. It was weird. Danny had loved Beth most of his life one way or another. She was the best human being he'd ever known. She cared about Danny. Without reason or judgement. But she really did care about him.

And there was no getting away from it, she had a gorgeous arse on her. And a cute smile. And deep dark eyes. And elegant ankles and a beautiful shape from her neck to her shoulders, and dark straight hair, and humour and compassion and passion and a thousand other things. Fuck. Don't anybody dare call this love. Such appetising prospects were never on the menu for Danny fucked-up-no-love Hutton.

In the end he texted her yet again, asking if he could come and see her next Sunday, maybe watch AR. Better than flowers.

•

Beth was nervous. Danny and Beth in the same building. How big a deal could that be? They grew up together around Malton Court. Beth had risked everything… she'd given her massage, her caress, her message. Danny had been in good spirits. He'd eaten a fine breakfast. Then he'd fucked off for three months. Beth had waited anxiously, quietly, impatiently.

Now he was coming round to watch the Antiques Roadshow. Again. Suddenly. She made no plan this time, the ball was in his court. During the past several weeks, she'd cursed him frequently for his absence, but with all of her anxiety and her moments of irritation, she was excited again now that he was coming.

He arrived late in the afternoon. They exchanged greetings, Beth made a brew and she updated Danny on the shop while she poured the drinks. She was speaking too quickly, driven by her nerves. She should have served whisky. Danny was hard to predict.

He jumped straight in. "I needed to do some thinking, Beth. After you gave me that massage. Not to mention the breakfast."

Beth made a mental note to review her subtlety skills. "Well then, tell me your thoughts."

"You've never done anything like that with me before, Beth. I hadn't expected the message you sent me. Honest, I was surprised. Listen, first I need to tell you, you're the best person I know. And you're fucking gorgeous. Sorry." He wasn't exactly sure why he'd apologised, he seemed to think he'd chosen a clumsy phrase.

He had but Beth appeared to have forgiven him.

He continued. "If I'm about to get a shot with you, Beth, well… you know, if we're, if, you and me, if that's possible? Well, then I'm a lucky man."

Beth was deeply affected. She'd imagined this conversation many times. Rehearsed it phrase by phrase. Invariably their dialogue was quite cold and uncertain. She hadn't imagined a significant increase in body temperature, or the fierce colouring to her neck and face. Beth had held something back for a long time with Danny. She could feel the blood circulating around her ears and her skull. What was this, high blood pressure or love?

Danny continued while Beth tried to listen. "I just wanted to get that out there." Danny looked up with a half smile.

Beth was beaming with a big red faced reply.

"I needed some time to think things through, Beth. I'm sorry but it took me a while. I'm not sure about relationships. I know I'm a pain and I'm miserable. But, yeah, if you're crazy enough, let's give it a go. You'll definitely regret it, Beth, you know what I'm like, I'm hopeless. Even now, I'm still full of doubt, not about you, Beth… I doubt myself."

Beth was feeling great. Her ears were ringing, she felt a bit high. She couldn't really pay proper attention to whatever he was starting to say. When she'd imagined these moments, she wasn't emotional, she was happy but nervous and she imagined a slow and tentative set of steps gradually leading, please God, maybe… eventually… to intimacy. As far as Beth could see, and Beth was a sensitive and insightful woman, Danny had never really done intimacy.

She'd imagined that she'd need to be patient, she never anticipated any fireworks. Now she looked at him across the room and she was full of desire, shocked and excited by her lustful thoughts. This really wasn't Beth at all. Except for today, when it was. Nevertheless she kept her thoughts to herself. For the rest of her life.

She looked again, not taking in what he was saying. She wasn't betraying half of what she was feeling. She concentrated on looking like she was listening. He wasn't half a bonny lad though.

Beth heard enough to realise that Danny was saying stuff about who would live where and really some of it was important. He talked about being a loner, a bit detached, he'd said. And he didn't know whether he could cut it in a relationship.

But Beth was all over it. She interrupted his assertion of doubt. "Danny, I get it, you're not sure, me neither. We'll have to work things out along the way. Great. That's the way with relationships, I guess. I'm not worried, Danny. We'll work it out together." Beth relished the prospect and she believed that they would find their way. Beth could do that kind of stuff. And quite a lot of other stuff. Danny really was a lucky man.

She wanted to put him at ease but still his doubt held position. He had more to say. "I can't have kids, Beth. The thought really scares me. I don't trust myself. I have to tell you that… I don't want to be a father, not ever."

Yeah, thought Beth, we'll see about that. She kept the thought to herself, the second one in five minutes of half listening. Beth didn't worry about what Danny had said. They were both young. Beth wanted children, she would have children. She felt that in her sense of herself as a woman, in her biology. She felt it with certainty. Although Beth knew that children would be a part of her future, she also knew that she wasn't ready yet herself, no point worrying about Danny.

She could hear him, still talking seriously, unable to overcome his doubt, but she felt light and happy. She was smiling but not really listening.

Danny looked at her, puzzled for a second, then he smiled with her. "You're not listening to a bloody word I'm saying, are you?" And they both laughed.

And he crossed the room.

Danny was a masculine man needing to feel in control. He lifted her from her feet and walked through to his recently reworked bedroom. Beth discovered his tenderness and his generosity, and his willingness, momentarily, to relinquish control.

Beth would have children but she and Danny were still young and for once in the love of her life, she was Beth set free. She and Danny had their magical moment and she was unrestrained. She never forgot who she was loving but she gave herself and took him, body and soul.


They each kept a place of their own. Beth kept the flat with the shop and Danny was still living in the building that used to be a gym. Which he now owned.

They were together now.

It was a miracle. That's how it felt to Beth at the beginning. She was a resourceful woman, she was always going to make some kind of a life. Maybe it was a bit more in the balance with Danny and there would always be something dangerous in him. Whatever. They were good. That was the miracle. These young people, victims of abuse, these looked after children, who were both ready to work as hard as was needed, were good together.

They were together now. Until one of them died.

There had been moments of enormous impact in both of their lives... that was how they met, hurricane debris washed up at Malton Court. Mostly their high impact moments had been unchosen and unwelcome, received by powerless children.

As a single event, a choice, a commitment, a change and a dream, this gear shift in their relationship was uncontested. Danny played it down. He got on with his shit as if nothing had changed.

Beth couldn't hide her smile. She was radiant. No exaggeration. She was shining, the first of her dreams had come true, only it was a thousand times better than she'd ever dared to dream. Danny and Beth, they were loving. Danny would be away sometimes for a few days or even weeks. It seemed to work well.

They were together now. Until one of them died. Or until Danny decided to leave.

It was a miracle but they weren't the first couple to discover that honeymoons don't last forever and neither do miracles, especially in the lives of these two looked after children who struggled with trust and intimacy.

After that first few months, Danny and Beth bumped into some unanticipated realities. The most difficult challenge for Danny was closeness. It was as simple as that. Solitude wasn't just good for Danny, it was a survival strategy. He'd loved Beth (in his highly confused way) for many years but from a distance and without romance or sex.

Attending to the maintenance of a close relationship wasn't an easy task. He had no experience to draw on, he'd never had a chance for rehearsals. It wasn't just his lack of direct experience, Danny hadn't even had chance to witness or observe a healthy loving relationship. He was clueless, he was unable.

Nine months after that first night in Darlington, Danny told Beth that he needed more space, he needed to be by himself. He was upset by his failure and he apologised to Beth. Then he ran, despondent and relieved.

•

He'd given his best, he'd paid attention to Beth, watched her movements and her moods. Back at the movies. Watch and learn, that was Danny's method. And he'd made ten thousand observations. Every detail was noted, remembered. The way she dressed, her underwear quickly in place, then her pace dropping as she looked around, considering her choices, before the outer garments were added and the basis of her approach to the day assembled.

He'd watched her as she slept, unconscious and at peace but with moments of interruption – a sudden quick intake of breath, a small groan, a repositioning, a hand escaping her sleep and her dreams to remedy a slipping duvet or a lumpy pillow.

He'd watched her react to music or to her phone, trying to understand this person who he'd known so long without really knowing anything much about her, who seemed to know him better than he knew himself.

But still he felt anxious and uncomfortable, out of place, crowded. Somewhere along the way, Danny had understood that solitude was his best friend. Relaxation would always be a challenge in the company of another person. He should have asked Beth to give him a massage and a glass of whisky, instead he'd fucked off back to the gym and holed up again.

He'd often be gone for a while but this time he'd given an announcement and an apology.

Beth was bereft. She'd allowed herself her moment of unrestrained love, feasting, enjoying the simple pleasure of being a woman in love. Now she chastised herself, she of all people, she who should have known better. She'd won her man with love and guile and now he was gone.

She cried her tears… there were plenty. She wanted to go after him. She knew that would be a mistake but while she'd entertained the idea, she had shaken her head and smiled, realising she didn't know where the gym was. She knew that Danny and Seth had worked out together for years and she knew that Danny had been living there for several years, but in all of those years she'd never seen Danny's home. There were doors in Danny's world which, it seemed, would never be open to her. She'd have to wait.

So she waited. She talked to Molly, who knew nothing. She talked to Sean and Stevie, who said nothing. Fucking Danny Hutton, he had them all where he wanted them, doing as they were told, while Beth took some deep breaths and waited some more.

He reappeared after a couple of months, apologised again and they stumbled their way back to being together. They were together again now. Until the next time.

And so it went on. Danny would get spooked, by sex or some other experience of intimacy, then he'd sink into a quiet mood, out of sorts, like he wanted to be somewhere else. Then he'd go. Just disappear. It drove Beth crazy but she knew she had to find acceptance. Danny was a troubled man and Beth's seemingly unshakable belief in her ability to sooth him became shaken.

Their sex had never been adventurous. At the beginning Danny took control. He could be tender and caring but his experience was limited and his interest uncertain. They both felt a sense of celebration simply because they were together, and to an extent they felt the same way about the sex. They were having sex, that in itself seemed to be a miracle, even though they were both impeded by tension.

Over time they managed to be a bit more relaxed and a bit more communicative, which was better but the pattern was set. They never seemed to make much progress when Beth tried to talk about sex. Danny didn't mean to be difficult, nevertheless it was difficult for him. He was doing his best to deal with it but it was hard. The whole relationship thing was difficult. He wanted so much just to be a normal guy who could do that stuff. His struggle continued.

After a couple of years together, Beth added a second variation to their sex life. Until that time she had been passive, she would leave it with Danny. Beth accepted Danny's advances, she enjoyed the sex, there was no variation and she only rarely experienced orgasm, but she liked the feeling of his powerful uncertain body, the heat in his skin, and she loved the unexpected tenderness of his kisses.

Beth didn't know how or why she decided to try something different, she hadn't planned it. Danny was often wound up, and occasionally Beth could see that he was afflicted by tension. He'd avoid her company, offer nothing, cut himself off from everything. He'd offer no contact in bed.

He would lie on his back, no conversation, no touching. She would lie nervously alongside him, knowing he was troubled, sensing his tension. And she would feel uncomfortable, getting an impression of unmet need, feeling that she should help him feel better. She'd taken risks before, a few deep breaths, then go.

She reached across, her hand moved directly to his cock and she was surprised, he was ready, proud and upstanding, despite the glum face. But even so he gently unclasped her small hand. He didn't speak but his message was clear. But Beth persisted, she regained her hold, this time she raised her head and shoulders, and she pushed down on his chest. He made no further refusal… he allowed her to continue. He was tense and uncommunicative but the sensation in his genitals was exceptionally intense.

Beth worked his erection with a light touch. She noted his groans and she was encouraged. So was Danny. She sat up, moved her left leg across his torso and she was in position. She lowered herself, taking him inside her, intoxicated by her new power. It felt good. When Danny reached orgasm, she witnessed the power of her actions. He was unusually noisy and he was changed. Beth held her position. She had soothed him, it was a generous gift to her troubled man.

Beth never really asked herself why she got herself out of bed each and every morning. There were things to do, she got up and did them. She had talent, she was productive, she was living her life. But why had she left Debenhams to work for Danny? Why had she taken him that beaker of orange juice when they were both small children?

Beth was a woman who looked out at the world, her navel

mostly ignored. The meaning of life would reveal itself in the course of time. Or maybe not. But when she sat astride of her man, heard him cry out, watched his tense body collapse into feathers, she felt herself fulfilled. More in those moments than at any other time. Soothing her troubled man.

After that breakthrough, Beth would repeat her advances when she sensed the need in him.

She practised. Her confidence as initiator grew. She learned how and when to take him. When Danny was the active player, there was more time, there was no rush, desire but not urgency. Beth-led sex was different, it was direct, it happened quickly.

But still their struggles continued. He'd fuck off back to the gym and she'd stay home wondering if he'd ever return. He'd be back when he was ready. Beth learned to be assertive with Danny, and mostly he was compliant. Sometimes she pushed too hard and he'd be gone again or they'd argue and fight.

The Covid lockdowns were unsettling for them both. They did their best to adjust. There wasn't much change to Danny's work pattern although somehow he felt less energised, but Beth's routines were interrupted. Danny did his best, they went out together for exercise, then they went home together to Beth's flat in Darlington. Beth experienced her enforced inactivity as a challenge and Danny was uncomfortable with so much of their time spent together. Just the two of them, watching the rest of the world through closed windows.

Beth couldn't just switch off. She had always known that she liked work. She'd been happy at Debenhams, then the shop at Darlington took things to a different level, a new variety of tasks, the creativity and the commerce. She loved it all. But when the initial lockdown closed the shop, she realised that she needed work. She was no good at spare time. She needed to be busy.

She started to make plans. She had been slowly shifting the Darlington shop away from antiques and was stocking more and more stylish new furniture. Initially she decided to use the time to accelerate and complete that transition.

It certainly wasn't a time to open a new shop, much of the

commercial world was standing still but she and Danny started driving out to Saltburn to get their hour of exercise and a dose of fresh sea air. They'd never bothered with Saltburn before but Beth liked the coast, she enjoyed the small town vibe and she was fascinated to see beyond the urban sprawl. Danny was less impressed. He could walk happily on the beach forever but the town meant nothing to him.

Beth saw the empty shop in the middle of Saltburn's town square and she made some enquiries. She bought the lease, and she had the luxury of several months to shift her energy. She loved the shop in Darlington but it was still part of Danny's world. The Table Leg was Beth's shop, her choice, her own creation. Beth, she just kept on coming.

The vaccines rolled out and the customers rolled in. She and Danny had their struggles. Before they'd got together, she'd always imagined that the beginning would be difficult and that after a while they'd settle. In reality they'd started with surprising ease but they never really settled.

Danny was content for Beth to proceed with the second shop but he played no active part. Unlike the Darlington premises, in which they both had an interest, the Saltburn shop was for Beth. Then Danny started looking at Rightmove, checking out the houses for sale in Saltburn. They felt like burglars, in masks and gloves, wandering around other people's houses. Beth needed neither encouragement nor persuasion. She was taken aback when she realised that Danny was able to pay in excess of half a million pounds for a house beyond her most ambitious dreams, but hey ho, a posh house in Saltburn just up the road from her new scandi shop… yes, please.

She was increasingly confident in her work, happy about the house, but she and Danny continued to struggle. They had started to argue more frequently and he felt desperate for the gym and for solitude, while taking his commitment to the relationship up to a new level. As they proceeded with the house purchase, Danny retreated to the gym. Beth was left to buy it all by herself.

Danny didn't pay much attention but he told Max to follow Beth's instruction. He was mardy as his arse through those weeks. She hardly saw him. Her fantasy of a family home together was fading even before the purchase completed. Then one morning Max phoned and told her the house was hers. That was completely unexpected but it was true, the house belonged solely to Beth.

She was overwhelmed and shocked. She'd assumed that it would be Danny's name on the title deeds. She was reminded of the night of the massage in the flat in Darlington, unable to work out if they were coming together or moving apart. They were all over the place. That's how she felt when the phone call from Max concluded. Was this to be a family home for her and Danny, or was it a generous parting gift.

He'd been at the gym for several weeks. Usually she'd leave him to it, he'd emerge when he was ready but this was different. Beth had more than half a million quid's worth of real estate, bricks and mortar, shelter, a home. She wanted it with all of her heart but she wouldn't live there alone. She phoned him and she told him. This time Beth really told him. She risked everything, became the mother again and little Danny Hutton came running.

The to and fro continued but it was their house. She knew it was hard for Danny and she knew he was doing his best.

He knew that he made it hard for Beth and he wished he could do better.

# PART TWO

# ERDI DJONI

Circumstances outside of his control had directed Erdi's adult life. He fled from Kosovo in 1999 when he was still seventeen years old. He'd lost his family and his homeland. Milosovic's intentions had been clear… the ethnic Albanians who made up more than ninety percent of Kosovo's population were no longer wanted or tolerated. Like many Kosovans over the centuries, Erdi learned to expect hostility and prejudice. He was angry as he travelled through North Macedonia and Greece, and still angry when he arrived in the UK through the United Nations Humanitarian Evacuation Programme a month later.

He tried to become a good British citizen. He lived and worked in Bedford for several years. His physical strength gave him some confidence and made him a target for recruitment into a criminal gang. Erdi gradually side-stepped away from low paid legitimate employment to become increasingly involved with criminal activity carried out by some members of the Albanian community. Better wages.

After years of struggle, he was making a good living through class A drugs, he was prospering. By the time he moved to Stockton in 2019, he'd worked his way up through the ranks of an extensive and exclusively Albanian criminal organisation. Erdi was a big strong man, he was angry and uncompromising, not a man to be messed with. In those respects, Erdi was a bit like Danny Hutton.

Erdi met and married Agnesa in Bedford. She was Albanian and legal. She was a kind-hearted woman and like a million other fools, she fell in love. He managed to wriggle away from Agnesa's questions initially but he knew that he couldn't keep her close without her finding out about his working world. He told her that he was a player in a smuggling operation. She already knew. The Albanians in Bedford were a pretty tight community but she appreciated that Erdi didn't lie to her.

They moved to Teesside, together with their two young sons, and worked out as best they could a plan to keep home and family separate from work. They bought a house in Yarm, a small market town just a few miles from his work base in Stockton, and were a model immigrant family, integrating and anglicising as they developed their life. When Erdi's neighbours watched him pull out of his drive every morning, they had no idea that he was off to supervise the distribution of a shipment of heroin or keep kidnapped sex workers, illegals, in his brothel in Stockton, or to deal with business rivals like Danny Hutton.

Even more bizarre was that Erdi's employees didn't know that when their boss clocked off, he drove back to his wife and two small children in Yarm. Erdi had secrets. He needed to keep his two worlds fully separated.

For Erdi, the opportunity to build a family was a precious freedom, a choice in his own life and a chance to compensate for the brutal losses he'd suffered at the end of the previous century.

Erdi was a refugee who'd made a new life for himself. He enjoyed the power of his position and wealth, he enjoyed success in his black and white businesses. He did his best to sleep at night with the memories and consequences of his suffering. But it was the family – Agnesa, Harry and George – who gave salvation. The children would be good English boys, well educated, encouraged to pursue paths that would make their parents proud. This new Kosovan/Albanian/British alchemy was everything.

Erdi knew that although he was secure in his position in an extensive criminal network, his time wouldn't last forever. He guarded his privacy, nurtured his second life with care and attention. It was beautifully separate from the seedy world over which he presided in Stockton and when the time would inevitably come, he'd take the short drive home and disappear into suburban respectability.

In the meantime, he'd set up several car wash operations that fooled nobody but which nevertheless served their purpose. They washed dirty money and dirty cars. Erdi had acquired several adjoined properties on Fulham Road, close to the centre of Stockton, which served as his headquarters and accommodated a shop and a café. And a brothel. All for the exclusive use of the Albanian community.

While the legal businesses rolled gently along, he oversaw the departure of containers and trailers from Teesport. The smuggling was very professional and incredibly lucrative. There was never an interception. Erdi ran a smooth operation. Initially everything was moved out of area while he sussed out the local operators.

In 2020, during the early months of the Covid pandemic, he received instructions to acquire unused land close to the docks in Teesport and to set up a local distribution network. He also received delivery of three young women to work in the brothel.

# EMINA – A DAY OUT

Emina grew up in a rural environment in the south west of Albania. She was a farm girl. It was a beautiful natural environment, but the life was hard. Her father had a few acres to grow wheat or maize to raise a bit of cash. It was never a fortune but enough in a good year to buy some new clothes for the family or something for the house.

The family kept a few chickens and geese, but the mainstay of their subsistence farming was goats and sheep. They grew vegetables for their own consumption and sometimes fattened up a growing pig. They all had phones, and access to the internet was improving. Some of the farmers had pooled their spare money to buy a few relatively modern items of machinery. Nevertheless, the farming methods and the lifestyle hadn't changed much during the fifty years of her father's life.

Her brother was a big help around the small family farm. He was keen to leave school at the first opportunity and get on with the life that had chosen him. Despite the needs and hopes of her parents, Emina's future was not to be found in the fields and the hills. She did her best, and did okay, but the farm chores never satisfied her. She just wanted to get finished so that she could read her book. It was the only life that she knew and yet somehow she wanted something different. She wanted to know what else might be possible. She loved to dance and excelled at school.

She carried out her early morning farm duties honestly enough but without spirit or interest. She laboured slowly, wanting to be finished but unable to find the energy to work at speed.

Then, as she'd prepare for school, her demeanour would recover. Emina would wash away the smell of goats and sheep, change her clothes and feel re-energised. She could be herself for a few hours. She'd run and skip the two miles to her village school, happy at the prospect of more learning. Her father was proud when Emina's teacher reported a high level of achievement in her school work. Both of her parents knew she would leave the family home one way or another.

The huge majority of young people stayed local and forged their adult life in similar fashion to their parents and grandparents. A few found another path. By the time Emina had reached her fifteenth birthday, she was by far the best English speaker in her village, she was helping the schoolteacher with lessons for younger kids and she dreamed about everything except farming. She wanted to get away, to see more than her small pocket of rural Albania. She wanted to go to the city and watch ballet. She wanted to stand on a beach and listen to waves breaking. She wanted to find love.

After she'd learned everything that her schoolteacher had to give her, she was given two jobs. She continued to do some teaching at the village school and she became an administrator in local government.

It was a small village where Emina and another part-timer were the local government. The teaching was straightforward and sometimes quite rewarding. She liked to see the young kids developing. She had expected the administrative work to be tedious but as it turned out she enjoyed it much more than the teaching. Emina was startlingly efficient. The local council had never before run so smoothly.

Rion passed through for the first time in the summer of 2020. Emina was still only seventeen years old but already two years into her role as administrator and she had become a well known and valued member of the local community. If there was a difficult question to answer or if information was needed, Emina was ready to help.

Rion had asked some questions in the village about electricity supplies as he was looking for a place to start a new business. A neighbouring farmer had directed him to Emina, hoping and expecting that she'd have the required information. Emina remembered him well, Coronavirus cases were few but the requirement for caution and restrictions had greatly reduced the number of visitors from outside of the area. Emina took an interest. His clothes were stylish, he seemed confident, a man of the bigger world. His questions were a bit random and he appeared unconcerned about Covid – he didn't wear a mask and he was travelling freely, but she did her best to be helpful. He went on his way and returned a couple of weeks later, this time with all of his charm.

Over a period of several days he courted Emina. Rion told her about his trips to foreign countries. He'd travelled extensively around southern Europe. That made him the most exciting and interesting man Emina had ever met. They spent a few evenings together. She was seventeen and he wasn't a farm boy. He asked her to spend a day out with him in the hills.

Just for a moment, that's all it was. She was a young woman, charmed by Rion's stories and smiles and for once in her young life she lost her judgement. Just for a moment. And she was there with him, in his car driving out towards the coast. She was excited, exploring new territory, experiencing herself as a grown woman, falling in love in the time of Coronavirus.

The details were difficult to recall, she wasn't sure exactly where they were when Rion pulled over to the side of the road for a break. He gave her some food and they drank beer. It felt like day one of the biggest adventure of her young life. She laid back to feel the sun on her skin. She could feel the alcohol, she was light-headed, happily excited and a bit sleepy.

When she woke up, she was locked in a room with two other young Albanian women and she had a headache. What a moment that was. She slowly regained her senses. She didn't need long to work it out, she'd heard stories from villages close to her own about the disappeared. One young man with his car and his clothes. And his charm and his promises. She'd lost her judgement, just for a moment.

It was a lot to take in. She wasn't enjoying a day out in the hills, she wasn't in love. Not anymore. It seemed almost unbelievable. She fantasised about this mistake being rectified, waiting expectantly for someone to open the door, to apologise.

It couldn't be. But it was.

Her body felt heavy. She could see and hear the two other women but initially, she had no inclination to speak to them.

She just sat quietly, feeling each short breath negotiate with the tense muscles around her ribs.

Over the next couple of hours Emina escaped the residual effects of her picnic lunch. She accepted a bottle of water from her companion prisoners – Debora and Valmira – who had arrived a couple of days earlier.

Debora spoke first. "Drink plenty. We have lots of water," she said. "Not much else, I'm afraid. I'm Debora."

"I'm Emina. Where are we?" She drank big mouthfuls. "What's happening here?"

Their room had no window, an unshaded bulb lit a space of about fifteen square metres. There was a large mattress on the floor and two wooden chairs.

"Valmira and me were kidnapped, kept here. I don't know where we are. We have a bathroom. It's not much but the toilet works. They bring us food and we have water. We sleep together on the mattress."

"Oh my God." Emina looked at Debora, who appeared utterly hopeless. "My God. We are prisoners, three young women. Oh my God."

"We don't know yet what will happen. We don't know." Debora didn't want to accept Emina's assumption.

"Can we escape? Who is here? Can we? We have to try, maybe there's a way. There has to be." Emina looked again at Debora, almost pleading.

"I don't see how, Emina, they have guns. There are always six or seven men. We have nothing, just our clothes and water. I don't know where we are."

Emina tried to believe in miracles. She pleaded to the men who brought food. She was beyond devastation, they were beyond listening.

After two days, the three women were bundled into the back of a van and they travelled all day without a clue where they were going. Emina was terrified but she still held on to some hope, she was determined to escape at the first opportunity.

She wasn't ready to accept the alternative. But there were no escape opportunities. Their journey continued. They were loaded into a container along with thirty-five others, men and women mostly from Albania or Kosovo, but there were a few Syrians and Afghans. They were driven onto a boat and crossed water before resuming road travel. Eventually the container was opened. Bright light and a new country. It was almost exactly a week since she'd set off for her picnic in the countryside. A week's a long time in people trafficking.

Emina met Erdi Djoni the next morning. He was business-like as he greeted his three new slaves.

"I know you've had a long journey. This is England. We're going to drive north. You work for me now, it will be mostly sex work," he said to these three young women who had just had their lives stolen.

None of them spoke in reply. Emina was in some kind of state of shock. She felt paralysed, stunned to such an extent that she couldn't think, let alone speak.

Erdi had a couple of other Albanian guys with him. The six of them drove north for several hours.

The first two weeks of her ordeal broke into a series of memory fragments. She couldn't fully apprehend her own experiences as a linked sequence of connected events. It was as if she just had holiday photos on her phone. Remember the day I was kidnapped, and the time I got locked into the back of a container, or the day I was first raped in a place called Stockton-on-Tees.

The pictures invaded into her mind's eye, uninvited and often, and each time she had to relive her terror. She often felt so tight around her chest that she could hardly breathe. And while she started to live with her loss and her trauma, the men came. Mostly, they were her compatriots.

She became close with Debora and Valmira. They had each other and that was all that they had. For the next several weeks they offered each other comfort when they felt able. During those early weeks, conversation between them was limited, words were insufficient.

They held one another physically, sometimes for several

minutes, swaying or rocking, giving and receiving within the same embrace. And of course they looked into one another's eyes. With understanding and empathy, trying in the midst of their nightmare, to support one another. Somehow they learned and adapted. Emina had a sense of wonder about that, she amazed herself. This country girl with a few vague dreams, loved and valued in her home village, had adapted to her new life as an enslaved sex worker.

# EMINA – A LONG WAY FROM HOME

It was hard to keep track of time and place. There was an atmosphere of deep despondency in the small section of rooms they'd been allocated as their living quarters. They were on the top floor of a three storey building. Every evening they were taken down to the first floor in the same building for work. Sometimes they were given cleaning tasks during the day, in the brothel and in other rooms in the same building. They were never given opportunity to stand outside of the building.

Each of the three young women developed a similar coping strategy. Emina named it 'the zombie strategy'. In their own way they each attempted to withdraw or to be only half present, better still, half dead. When their bodies went to work, they sent their spirits elsewhere, accepting the violence and violation, performing as best they could their new trick of absence.

Emina watched herself and her friends in their withdrawal and became concerned, feeling that she and her spirit spent too much time in separate rooms. It was getting her through but it wasn't living and she resolved to find a better way. That was the beginning, the first sign of a shift in her thinking and her behaviour.

As time moved on, she gradually regained her capacity to think about the future. She forced herself to be awake to her new surroundings, to the men who panted and wheezed and groaned on top of her. For a while she had wished herself dead, then in the midst of her appalling squalor and slavery, she wished to live. Somehow she had to hold on to herself, to be awake, and then to use her best qualities to discover a tiny ray of hope. Or else she'd be lost forever.

Emina was a year older than Debora, twenty-year-old Valmira was the oldest. They were all three fine people. They all had to find a way to survive. There were no rights or wrongs. It just happened that Emina was the first of them to wonder if there might somehow be a way out.

She got organised, she started to gather information and to

form at least the beginnings of a plan. She decided to speak English to everyone except Valmira and Debora. It was a bit left field, it didn't matter to Emina, she'd try to grow in any field. Without rhyme or reason, her language experiment began.

Emina never faltered in her new regime, always Albanian with Debora and Valmira, always English for everyone else. Her friends both noticed her language skills and her changed demeanour. Emina just wanted to do something different, to make those who held her captive and those who held her naked see her differently. To make them look again, to develop an identity as the woman who spoke English.

It was a start and although she felt desperate pain and she had no clear idea about what her next moves might be, she also felt the beginning of spiritual repair.

The rooms above the shops, and in a couple of neighbouring buildings in the same block, provided living space for twenty or more illegal workers and some offices for Erdi and his employees. The woman who speaks English was being discussed through the whole group of buildings. Erdi heard the whisper, Emina was delivered to his office.

Twenty minutes later Emina was escorted away from the offices and back to the small set of third floor rooms that she shared with Valmira and Debora. She didn't really know what kind of an impression she'd made on Erdi. Nevertheless her English speaking had earned something.

The three women had been restricted to just one building, locked in their cramped living space for much of the day and taken to the floor below for their work in the evenings. That had been the limits of their confinement. Until the day when English speaking Emina was asked to explain herself, when she took her first steps out in the open air since the night she'd first arrived in Stockton.

They had walked into a building next door, entered through a heavy wooden door, up a set of stairs and along a narrow corridor before discovering three untidy offices. Her eyes had searched in every direction, everything she'd seen was new information.

When Emina returned from Erdi's office, Valmira was immediately curious and excited. "Well, where have you been?"

Emina took her seat at their kitchen table. She hardly knew where to start. "Not very far, out on to the street and then into another building. Just a few metres along the road. To Erdi's office."

Debora had been very low and quite withdrawn but even she wanted information. "And what happened?"

"Erdi asked me why I've been speaking in English." Emina almost managed to chuckle. "He spoke in Albanian. I answered him in English, of course." Then something unusual happened. She started to laugh. Unconsciously and freely for couple of seconds, then she caught herself, laughing, and her hand reached to her mouth. She wept.

It was a few moments before she regained her composure. "Sorry. He asked me quite a few questions. About how I had learned English, about my job in Albania."

"What did you tell him?" said Valmira.

"I answered his questions. In English. At home I was an administrator and a teacher. I liked doing administration, God knows why, and I was good at it. I told him. I told him that his office looked a mess."

Valmira hadn't seen Emina's English speaking as a thoughtful or strategic action, quite the opposite, she thought that her friend was going bat-shit crazy. Until her excursion. "What was it all about, Emina? I don't understand. You speak English, he asks how you learned. That's it?"

"I don't know, Valmira. Something happened. Because I spoke English. Something happened today. I'll continue to speak English. I need something to happen, anything. I want to get out of here. I want to know who we're dealing with. I just want information. I don't know what it was about, maybe something, maybe nothing. I saw the street, I talked to him. I asked him if I could go back home."

"What did he say?" asked Valmira.

"He didn't give an answer, he looked away, ended the meeting, sent me back here. There's a number 12 on the red door to this building." Emina experienced a rare moment of anger, and for a second she allowed her outrage to overpower her helplessness. She fixed her gaze on her young friend. "There's a world outside. Jesus, Valmira, what's any of this about? You tell me."

•

Emina had been perceptive. Erdi's mood had been amiable enough but the encounter had disturbed him. Erdi had a wall, a barrier to stop him from properly connecting with his power and his inhumanity. Occasionally, the barrier would fail while someone stumbled through. He had that experience as he listened to Emina.

She answered all of his questions boldly in English, she was honest and without malice. Then she asked him politely and with poignant simplicity. "Will I ever be allowed to go back home to my family in Albania?"

She'd cut through. He hadn't seen it coming. He'd paused, momentarily disabled by shame. There was something about Emina that appealed to him. She had disarmed him and she had maintained her English voice but Erdi liked her.

Two days later Emina was again taken to Erdi's office. The same journey with the same escort. Although her first visit had given her her first steps outside in open air since her arrival, the second meeting excited her much more. Two days ago, she'd felt nervous and frightened but not on this occasion… this time she was curious, almost expectant.

Erdi greeted her in a business-like manner. No pleasantries, no invitations to unwanted questions. He spent more than an hour explaining some of the work that was done in the offices. He explained it all in English.

Emina's heart was racing. This was the induction session at the beginning of her new job. For the first ten minutes she listened attentively. Then she asked some questions. Eleven carwashes, the shop, the café, a big group of workers – mostly illegal – and the brothel, of course.

Erdi listened to her with interest. She was asking the right questions. Even in that introductory meeting, Emina had displayed an impressive grasp of the operations he'd outlined to her and she made a couple of suggestions. Erdi had a new secretary. It was good timing. He was extending his operations and he would need to deal with Danny Hutton.

Emina accepted her new job. During the daylight hours she was, in effect, Erdi's personal assistant… in the hours of darkness, she was anybody's and everybody's very personal assistant.

Emina's only aim during this period was to be so good at her new and ever extending duties that Erdi would never want anyone but her to run his offices. She had an avenue of hope, she had some new activity in her life and she had news to take back for Debora and Valmira. Debora was often disinterested, but Valmira wanted every detail.

After a couple of months in her new office job, Emina called her companions together, hoping to gain their support to plan an escape. The three young women were almost nine months into their ordeal, Emina needed to believe that one day it would end. She was nervous about what to say. She wanted to take her friends with her, wherever she might be heading.

"I'm learning more about Erdi," she said. "Maybe it can help us to find a way out of here."

Valmira responded. "How? What have you learned, Emina? What do you do all day?"

"Mostly my work is concerned with the shop and the café. I watch the stock levels, I order food. I record the accounts on a spreadsheet. It's not very interesting. That's all that I've been allowed to do. But I listen, I'm picking up new information every day."

Debora remained quiet, although she was listening.

Valmira was impatient. "So tell us. What have you got, Emina?"

Emina gave information. "The shop, the café and the brothel, they are just for Erdi's workers. He has eleven carwash premises. He has a guy, Zamir, he looks after the admin for the carwashes. I'm not interested in them. Neither is Erdi, except when his

Mercedes needs a rinse. He's buying land at the docks and he's importing drugs. I can hear it all. He talks on the phone, he talks to Luan. He doesn't seem to care that I can hear… what can I do?"

"Who's Luan?" asked Valmira.

"He seems to be Erdi's closest colleague. They are together at some point pretty well every day. He doesn't come to the brothel. He doesn't trust me, he doesn't like me being in the office, I can tell. He won't talk to me in English." Emina paused.

Valmira encouraged her to continue. "What about Erdi?"

"He likes me." Emina surprised herself with this claim, but it was the truth, she'd picked it up even in their first meeting. She was eighteen years old, a sex slave held captive by this man, who was a criminal gang leader. He liked her, that was her advantage and maybe, just maybe, his foolishness. She looked at her two companions.

Debora's interest was growing. "What? You mean he likes you, likes you as a woman?"

Emina felt slightly embarrassed. "Yes, he likes me as a woman. He always speaks to me in English. I work well, I'm polite, I try to please him."

Valmira was unconvinced. "He's never been to the brothel. What are you saying, Emina? Do you have sex with him?"

"No. Sometimes I can sense that he's looking across at me. Sometimes he makes a joke, smiles a little. He likes me, Valmira. Last week he took me out in his car."

Debora had become fully engaged. "Really? Why?"

"I don't know, Debora. There's another guy who comes into the office… Frenk. He doesn't trust me either. He looks after the phones, dozens of them, recharging, switching sim cards. He was ill for a couple of days. Sometimes Erdi uses him as security, watching over me. Maybe that was it, Erdi needed to go out and he didn't want to leave me with Zamir. He showed me some of the land he's going to buy."

Valmira changed the focus. "So you have a computer for the work. And there are lots of phones."

Emina suddenly felt nervous with excitement. This was what she had hoped for. Valmira was getting on board, maybe even Debora. She continued. "There are three computers. One is a laptop, it floats from one person to another, never to me. Erdi has a desktop and so do I. But mine is old, no internet connection. Erdi's computer and the laptop have the internet. It's driving me crazy, Valmira. All the phones, the internet, all close but so far all beyond my reach."

Emina had reached a position where she knew more about Erdi's business than anyone else. She was always efficient and polite, she delivered exactly as she'd first promised, excellent administration and communication.

"I'm trying to think of a way, Valmira. Maybe there'll be a time when I get a chance, you know, to take a phone or to access the internet. I've thought about it. But who do I call? What do I say? I don't know anybody anymore."

Valmira asked, "What about email? Do you have an email account?"

"Yes. I don't know anymore. Probably. But what could I say? It'd be like a message in a bottle, unlikely ever to be read, nowhere to send a reply." Emina had agonised over these frustrations, escaping slavery wasn't easy. "I'm always watching but I have no plan. I need you guys to think with me. We can find a way out of here, we have to."

•

Emina was determined, she was a model worker, she had a mission. And she never spoke a word in her mother tongue. She was incredibly helpful and well mannered in her office work, and at the same time she maintained this expression of defiance.

The tight security around her started to slacken. Perhaps that was a reward for compliance and good work. Maybe it was just laziness. Either way, she no longer suffered the indignity of a minder watching her every move.

Emina was forever watching Frenk, following his routines. Would he notice one missing phone?

She felt bewildered. She was sitting within a few metres of at least half a dozen phones and two internet connected computers. She really was a skilled communicator. She'd got into the nerve centre. She'd come all this way and now she was stuck.

Zamir was in the offices for at least part of every day but he often went out to one of the carwashes. Frenk was often in and out, switching and charging the phones. Fatos, who minded the brothel, came in some days, but not often. Erdi was there more than anyone.

Then on a Tuesday just like any other Tuesday, Erdi stood up from his desk and walked out of the room. Frenk had been and gone, he rarely came in twice on the same day, and Zamir was elsewhere. It was just Emina and Erdi. It had been the same the previous day.

She knew that Zamir's absence was unusual and she recognised her moment of opportunity. Emina didn't hesitate. She was up on her feet and then in Erdi's seat. There was a street map on the screen. She opened a new window, brought up Google and then remembered that she had no plan. She wanted to scream.

She followed her nervous instincts on Google, stumbled through a few links and found a phone number. She reversed her internet steps, closed the window and left Erdi's street map back on to the screen.

She got back to her desk and was immediately filled with doubt. Had she covered her tracks? She felt confused, she couldn't remember, she'd have to go back to check. She took another deep breath, preparing herself but Erdi came back into the office.

Emina sat rigid and still. She could feel her shirt drenched with sweat, sticking to her skin. Her hands were shaking, her heart still exploding. She hoped to God that she'd covered her tracks. She felt like James Bond. It was ninety percent fear with ten percent excitement. Unexpectedly, she had courage. She felt a strong urge to giggle. She'd held herself so tense and tight, she needed a release. But she held it together and gradually calmed herself. She had a phone number. A phone would be good.

Later, during the evening, they were all taken down to work their shift, as they were pretty well every other night.

The sex work was busy at weekends. Erdi paid all of the illegals on his payroll on Fridays and over the course of the following week, the money flowed back to him through the café, the shop and the brothel. The three sex workers dreaded Friday nights. Friday night punters were full of vodka and beer, stinking of sweat and alcohol, sometimes angry or hateful.

Weekdays were much less busy. Each of the women had a core group of regulars, mostly men who lived somewhere in the warren of rooms and passageways on Fulham Road, who took their pleasure without cruelty.

This Tuesday was very quiet. Debora and Valmira both had one visitor each and Emina remained blissfully idle. Valmira's client was in and out in less than fifteen minutes, so to speak. Debora was kept occupied for almost an hour.

Fatos minded the brothel, he took the money and watched over everyone. The bar staff, the women and the punters were all subjects for his unique management style. He was useful muscle for Erdi, in the brothel and elsewhere. He was a nasty bastard. He liked Friday nights in the brothel because the extra numbers and the drinking significantly increased the likelihood of trouble.

If someone made trouble, Fatos would have to eject them, see them down the stairs and out into the street. He never spoke much, he gave no warnings. He delivered his ejections with a well-practiced mix of brutal efficiency, sadism and sheer enjoyment.

For a while he was getting excited, no one kicked off on Tuesdays but this guy had been with Debora for way too long, it looked promising. He was ready to take a stroll down the corridor to see what was going on and who he might throw down the stairs, when Debora and her punter emerged without injury or distress. Fatos was disappointed. It was nine o'clock, the brothel was empty and he was pissed off. He closed up, threw a menacing look at one of the parting bar staff and took the sex workers back upstairs.

Emina made some coffee and sat with her friends at the kitchen table. "Something happened today. I was left alone in the office for a few minutes. I used Erdi's computer and I got on to the internet."

Valmira wanted more. "What happened?"

"I sat down and panicked a bit. My hands were shaking, I was sweating, I could hardly think. I googled Albanian sex slaves. There was a lot of hits. I followed a link, it was a news report, it could have been about us, the story was the same. I followed another link and I finished up reading on a website for the English Collective of Prostitutes. It was interesting, I liked what they were saying." The website gave clear statements campaigning for rights, protection, decriminalisation and self-determination. "For a moment I almost forgot where I was, I got dragged into the surf. I thought about Jane Austen."

Emina looked across at Valmira's facial expression, which demanded explanation. "She was an English writer two hundred years ago. I imagined sex workers dressed like fancy English ladies in bonnets and gloves."

Valmira chuckled. "I don't want a bonnet for my work but a pair of gloves would be good."

"I wrote down a telephone number for them. In London, I think. I don't know what they can do. I had no time, I had to get back to my own desk. I was sweating. I was frightened. Erdi came back in the room seconds later. He'd been to the loo, that was all."

"No, you did good, Emina, you were brave. I couldn't have done that. At least we have a number now." Valmira smiled. "But no phone. What about Frenk's phones?"

"I don't think I can get one. I've watched him, he's careful, he'd know if a phone went missing. Maybe we could steal one from the brothel, Friday nights, when they're all drunk."

Debora had sat quietly, listening but offering no comment. Then she reached into her bag and tossed a phone onto the table. "Make the call," she said, her first contribution to the conversation.

More secrets spilled out of Debora's bag of tricks. Huge news, she had a bar of chocolate! Cadbury's milk chocolate, a full unopened bar. They were excited, with their subterfuge, smuggled milk chocolate, and a phone... a rare moment.

Debora added further news, almost as an afterthought. "I have something else to tell you, I've fallen in love. With Genti, the guy who visited me at the brothel tonight and every other Tuesday for the past several weeks. He gave me the phone and the chocolate. Genti came over four years ago. He's been cleaning cars six days every week ever since." The vacant hopelessness in Debora's eyes had perfectly reflected Genti's own inner world. He'd seen it the first time he bought her in the brothel. For a fiver.

Deborah went on. "We connected, he's gentle, he talks to me. He always brings chocolate. We talk about home, about our families. I know it's crazy, alright. I know. I've struggled, you two know that, you've watched me. I don't know what to say, it's different now. I have Genti."

Emina spoke. "You're full of surprises tonight, Debora. I know how bad it's been for you. But Debora..." She changed her mind, maybe this was Debora's best escape. "It is crazy, I wish you well."

Valmira was less tactful. "He pays for his time with you. He fucks you, then he goes away to live his life." She understood the nature of their relationships with the punters. Some of the men had shown emotional investment, wanting a sense of relationship. Valmira was slightly flattered but mostly amused. Did these fuckers really expect their whores to like them? "This isn't a place for love, Debora."

Debora had no reply. She had her own perspective, she needed her weekly fix, she needed Genti to pay for their twenty minutes of third rate love.

Debora was sexually attractive, more popular with the punters than her colleagues. Some of the men would insist on waiting for her even when she was already occupied and when Valmira and Emina were free. She looked hot, she couldn't do anything else, even when she was clearly miserable. She moved with an easy sway to her hips. If she'd known its effect on the men, she'd have kept still or seated. She had no idea that she was beautiful, or that her natural features and movements set hearts racing. On the rare occasions when she looked at herself in the mirror, she saw herself as fat and ugly.

Genti was kind. He wasn't without self-interest but his kindness affected Debora, reached her at a time when she was almost unreachable. Over a period of many weeks, they extended their dialogue. They talked about everything, including themselves.

About themselves. Debora spoke to Genti about herself. In Genti's company, Debora could have, did have, a sense of self. This fucker, this man who came to fuck her, this dirty little illegal car washer, was restoring Debora's spirit with his kind, kind heart.

A psychiatrist would have diagnosed them both with Stockholm syndrome, or devised a second but closely related diagnostic category, maybe the Stockton syndrome.

As they'd grown closer, Genti had stopped the sex. That had been involuntary, he felt embarrassed. Each Tuesday he'd finish work, eat and then shower. Before he dressed to visit the brothel, he'd stare down at his penis and speak to it, as if it was something separate to him, an independent decision maker who could either make or break his evening appointment.

He'd begin with a few words of encouragement, spoken in friendly tones, he offered incentives. Sometimes he just chatted, small talk, lightening the mood, anything to win favour. He described women who'd used the car wash, hoping to provoke an early show of interest. He told jokes, maybe that was the problem, his penis needed to be humoured. He pleaded. Nothing. Then as he dressed, with his penis out of sight, he'd get annoyed and confrontational, make threats and insults.

His cock had either stopped listening or become wilfully rebellious. Debora didn't think about it, she enjoyed her time with him. She could see how crazy the situation was but she had fallen in love. She thought about him, she reflected on the exchanges from their weekly half hour together. She felt her mood brighten, just a little on Mondays but she'd started to meet each Tuesday with a smile.

That was it. Debora had confounded herself, one part of her stood back, a shocked spectator, watching another part of her, desperately needy and falling towards Genti.

They had nowhere else to go. This was their love affair in full flourish, thirty minutes a week in a brothel in Stockton. Without an erection. Genti worked his shifts, then he was more or less free to live his life. The women were imprisoned, they were either locked inside their set of rooms or watched by security staff while working in the brothel or elsewhere. It was hard to imagine that there could ever be any kind of a life for them.

It was Debora's secret and her salvation. Genti had given her a phone so that they could communicate between his visits to the brothel.

"I know it sounds crazy, Valmira, I can't explain it. Anyway I have a phone, Emina can call the English prostitutes."

# ERDI AND EMINA

Emina's office duties gradually extended. Erdi seemed to trust her. She sensed his interest. He liked her but he was hesitant. She wondered why. He had the power and the opportunity but he seemed restrained. She'd worked well to gain her position and she managed his awkward crush with shyness and smiles.

Her experiences in the brothel had taught her how to please men she despised. She had learned something about the power of her sexuality. She knew she'd won his favour, going out in his car, listening to his boasting. Sometimes, just now and again, she gave him a brief and pretty smile, coy and understated. Just enough to keep him coming.

And he did keep coming, moving slowly, troubled by hesitation but nevertheless, the parameters of their conversations extended. There would be a few occasions each week when the two of them had the office to themselves and these were the moments when Erdi shifted into familiarity.

He'd talk to her about his work and about some of his staff. She recognised that these fragments of private dialogue had meaning for Erdi, she didn't know what he'd do next and she didn't know what she might take from him. She played her role, she indulged him, showing amusement when he attempted humour, listening attentively to his discourse. She'd got herself well positioned and was waiting hopefully with no particular outcome in mind. Eventually her patience brought reward.

He took her out again in the car.

Emina sank into the soft leather passenger seat of his Mercedes and waited. It was just the two of them. There seemed to be no particular purpose to their outing. He showed her the Tees estuary, the docks, the warehouses and the roads, the world that he controlled.

Erdi behaved like a tourist guide, enjoying his knowledge, feeling easy with his power. Emina hadn't been beyond the short stretch of buildings since their first excursion. Her senses were overloaded. She'd never seen a big urban sprawl in her own country. She was riding in a Mercedes with her slave owner who seemed to be attracted to her. She wasn't sure how to feel.

Her curiosity won through and questions sprang from her. Erdi seemed to enjoy her interest, her questions, her innocence, his power.

"What is it like to live here?" she asked.

And he made a speech. Erdi'd had a bad break, his country became a war zone, he lost his family, he stumbled into the UK. He paid his dues, he took the blows.

Yet here he was, all grown up. He'd built a life in this foreign land. Erdi had never stated that he had a family at home but he'd given hints. There had been occasions when he'd left Fulham Road quite late in the afternoon, saying something about being in trouble when he got home late. But Emina had never heard him refer directly to members of his family or to anything concrete about his life away from work. All the same, if there was no one awaiting his homecoming, how could he be in trouble? And if there wasn't anyone waiting for him, why would he resist his attraction to her?

He said that he'd never wanted to leave Kosovo but he was proud of his rise to power in the North East of England. He gestured indeterminately as he spoke boastfully about his new home, in Yarm. Emina gained the impression that she should be impressed. Yarm must be the place to be. It was unlikely to be information of lifesaving proportions but she had something from him, an involuntary gift and for that she felt victorious.

Erdi lived in Yarm, where someone awaited his homecoming.

## DANNY AND ERDI – DANCING LIKE LOVERS

Danny Hutton and Erdi Djoni met on a summer's evening in 2021. Earlier in his life, when Erdi was climbing the ranks back in Bedford, he'd had to deal directly with rivals and to assert his authority from time to time. Since he'd been in Stockton, the man in charge, he'd kept a step back from the front line, kept his hands clean. But he'd done his homework. He'd heard enough about Danny Hutton to arouse his interest and to persuade him that a deputy wouldn't do… he needed to show his face, look his rival in the eyes.

He sent a message through Seth giving the time and place. Seth seemed to know everybody, and if he didn't know them, he knew someone who did. Seth had somehow managed to get himself linked in to every social chain in Teesside.

Erdi sent his message, then waited with certainty for Danny's compliance. They met on a bench close to the library in the centre of Middlesbrough. Danny had arrived early. He actually arrived a full hour ahead of schedule so that he could sit out in the afternoon light, watch the world rushing around him, and to test Erdi's honesty.

The message from Erdi had asked him to come to the meeting alone and in peace. Erdi had sent word that he'd also be alone and attend in the same spirit. Danny was unconvinced, and with an hour to spare, he'd see how well Erdi honoured his promise. He tried to relax but he was watching in all directions.

As it turned out Erdi kept his word, he was alone.

Erdi was interested to meet Danny Hutton. He walked to meet his rival and, although he'd never seen Danny before, he was able to pick him out easily enough. He walked the last twenty metres feeling Danny's watchful eyes.

"You must be Danny Hutton. My name is Erdi Djoni." He gestured, asking permission to sit by his rival, share a seat late on a sunny afternoon.

Erdi's approach was civilised. He took his seat. "It was good of you to make the time to meet with me. I've heard a bit about you, Danny. I believe that we share some business interests. I'm expanding some of my local operations and I thought we should have a chat about it."

Danny was more direct. "I didn't catch your name. What was it again?"

"Erdi Djoni."

"Erdi, thanks. I don't know what you've heard about me, Erdi. I don't know anything about your business interests either. You'd better bring me up to speed. I'm guessing you're from Albania."

Erdi might have objected to Danny's stereotyping but if the glove fits… "No, Danny, I'm a proud Kosovar. At least I used to be. Your guess was close. Albanian is my first language. I came here as a refugee. I'm British now. So I'm told."

Erdi wasn't without appreciation for his new country but he'd never felt welcomed. These are three things that Erdi came to know: no one seems to like ethnic Albanians, Albanians are good at smuggling, Albanians need to stick together. These realisations crystallised as the key to Erdi's understanding of his world and instructed his criminal career.

Perhaps the need to escape Milosevic's crimes against humanity helped motivate Erdi and other Kosovans to develop the smuggling skill set. Once he'd found his way through dangerous territory in the cold and the rain, travelling through the night to cross international borders, the trafficking of people and drugs didn't appear too difficult a prospect. Displaced and angry, Kosovans and Albanians scattered around Europe and sometimes beyond. They were well equipped to evolve international smuggling routes… and for many, there didn't seem to be a great deal of alternative opportunities.

The hungry mouths of the displaced people, unwelcome wherever they went, fuelled urgent and uncompromising innovation. The new generation of Albanian criminal gangs wrote their own rules and rewrote the drug smugglers' handbook. They removed pretty well everyone else in the supply chain, they procured their merchandise in the countries of origin and operated the trafficking from source to final destination.

Erdi had found his way into a powerful and efficient criminal organisation. He was happy that Danny had enquired, he wanted Danny to get a picture. He particularly wanted him to get clear sight of the impressive scale of his operations and of links to a much bigger organisation. Erdi wanted Danny to see clearly that he couldn't compete.

Danny wanted more information. "What brought you here, Erdi, to the UK, to Middlesbrough?"

It was a warm day. Erdi sat back. "That's a big question. Do you really want to know?"

Danny waited.

Erdi looked across at Danny, trying to guess his age. "There was war in my country. My father and my brother were both killed fighting for the Kosovo Liberation Army. I decided to leave. You're much too young to remember, Danny." Erdi paused. This wasn't the conversation he'd anticipated. "It was a terrible time, for me, my people, my country. Everything changed."

It had been a while since Erdi had thought about his family in Kosovo. He'd got himself into the wrong position for a negotiation – he was appreciating his rival's company and he was disarmed by memories of home. He interrupted himself, shifted focus.

He made two demands. First that Danny allowed him to distribute a variety of MDMA products, cocaine, heroin and marijuana all over Teesside, and second that he'd take control of all sex work in Middlesbrough and Stockton. He'd been building a profile of Danny for over a year… he expected a difficult conversation, so he opened by asking for everything.

Danny had sat in silence for a full minute after Erdi finished speaking. Danny wasn't a man who dramatised. He needed the time to think. Eventually he spoke. "You don't want much do you? I get the message, Erdi. You've got the firepower and the connections. I get that. And fair enough, you want my turf. I'm probably not in your league, Erdi. Who knows?"

"I know, Danny."

Danny shrugged. "Maybe you're right. But I've got quite a bit going on, Erdi. I couldn't just walk away, even if I wanted to. And I don't want to. It'd be a shame, Erdi, leaving your home country to escape a war, coming all the way to Middlesbrough to find another. I've been at war all of my life. There's no refuge for the likes of me. We can have a fight if you want one. It could get messy though." Danny paused for a moment. "I'll tell you what, the sex workers outside of Middlesbrough don't interest me, you've got an open door there, be my guest, but not here in Middlesbrough. You leave the women here well alone. Alright?"

Erdi noted the clarity of Danny's response. No malice, no threats. Clarity, eye contact and perhaps a slight smile. Erdi was surprised, caught off guard. He'd approached the meeting expecting first to dislike Danny Hutton, then to bully him into submission. He was having to review the situation. Danny seemed to be thinking intelligently and he clearly wouldn't be bullied.

It was a bit like Trump and Putin, two big boys who, despite their competing interests, kind of liked one another.

"Agreed," Erdi announced. He was happy that Danny had offered a small concession although he was also surprised. He'd heard that Danny had nothing to do with sex workers. It was a start and they were still talking.

The drugs business was a much longer and more complicated negotiation.

Danny told Erdi that he could have Darlington and as many villages as he wanted, and that his operations in these areas would be withdrawn. When Danny's gear reached into these districts, it was down to low level sales people. Danny was an urban Teesside man, he'd never sought to grow further. He intimated that over time, more territory would be conceded, saying he needed to look after the people who were loyal workers… he needed time.

Erdi had made progress and he developed a mood of acceptance. He had no wish for unpleasantness. In some ways Erdi was a confused man. His experiences in Kosovo had given rise to a strong sense of human sympathy and to a cold ruthlessness. For this meeting he'd apply humanity… he kept the cold ruthlessness on hold, as back up.

The negotiation dance was completed. Erdi accepted the scraps he'd been thrown. He'd bide his time. Their meeting ended with spectacular indecision. Neither man had won and neither had lost. They'd met, no blood had been spilled, the future was uncertain.

They sat on the bench outside of the library. It was a decent day, there was a breeze and intermittent sunshine. There were lots of people passing by, the mood was easy, it was a pleasant day to sit out for a while. Their discussion had finished, although Erdi had accepted less than he'd intended, but he got a good feeling from Danny and wished they were on the same side.

He really wanted to stay longer. He would've loved to suggest they got some coffee, and, not for the first time in his life, he realised that some of life's simple pleasures are not always available to criminal gang leaders.

"Well, I must go." Erdi stood up as he spoke.

Danny also got to his feet.

They turned to face each other and they both noticed that Danny was significantly younger. They were the same height, both big men, but Erdi had put on a few pounds during the past several years. He was the heavier man but Danny was in better shape. They were getting along perfectly well, nevertheless, neither of them could avoid such observations.

Erdi gave a smile as he reached out to shake Danny's hand. "Good to meet you, Danny. Goodbye." It was quite a formal farewell.

They both started to walk away. In the same direction. They'd managed their meeting without difficulty, handled themselves and each other with calm and dignity. They walked on side by side, both suddenly desperate for the other to be gone.

Danny spoke, rescuing them both. "I'm parked just across the road."

"So am I." Erdi was grateful. He asked Danny how he rated the Range Rover and they walked on, talking about cars. They were parked together. A few of the local folk hadn't failed to notice a hundred and fifty grand's worth of wheels parked on an unlikely street and were hanging around to see who the owners might be. Danny was recognised, but not Erdi.

They said goodbye for a second time and got into their cars. Danny waited and allowed Erdi to drive away. They'd gone their separate ways.

Both men felt relieved.

Danny allowed mixed feelings to confuse him. The drugs markets had given him control of his own life. It had always been a strategy for managing his life. The money was a bonus, the drugs were irrelevant. During his late teenage years, it had been a compelling drive. There had never been a long term plan, no exit strategy. But as he sat in his Range Rover watching Erdi drive away, he felt temped to concede.

None of it was fun, it had become a burden. He felt like he was carrying a sack of shit and that he was tied into a tight corner of his own making. He surprised himself and wondered, after the meeting with Erdi, if maybe he could get himself free.

•

Erdi watched patiently over the next fifteen months. The Covid pandemic brought more lockdowns, the normal patterns of life were disrupted. Everything seemed to slow down. Erdi started to think that Danny had changed his mind, broken their agreement. He wasn't going to ask Danny twice, he'd been generous asking the first time. He decided to step up the pace. He needed to make a move but he didn't want to be seen. He needed a disguise. Thank goodness for John Stanton.

# JOHN STANTON

Billy Stanton and his wife Ellie had three children. John, the eldest, was born in 1989. Billy was like his dad, handy with his fists, misogynistic and a bully. John was expected to follow the family line.

Ellie cared for infant John diligently, and she loved her young son but she knew that in the end John would become his father's child. For generations the Stantons were identified with masculinity and violence. John would be educated into the family tradition. He would either be a hard man or nobody at all. It was a strange thing for a young and inexperienced mother, to care for her baby while expecting to dislike him as he grew older.

Ellie's expectation became reality… she knew her husband all too well. Billy was teaching John how to throw punches before the child could talk. John was never going to become a doctor or a lawyer. He survived his father's learning agenda and the physical abuse that was normal life in the Stanton family. He learned from experience and his father added focused instruction to ensure that no detail from his demonstrations was missed. John learned to fight and he understood his place in the world. He'd never seen life beyond his close surroundings. Survival had always revolved around petty crime, drug use and violence. John accepted his fate.

In the world that John grew up in, these qualities were valued, and so was being male. John Stanton was a hard man, the product of his upbringing and environment. Just like everyone else.

John never married. He lived in the same council house for all of his life. Ellie had managed to escape with help from her eldest daughter. When John got sick of the sight of his father sitting on a grubby sofa watching old westerns on the telly, he gave him notice to leave. That left John and his youngest sister, June.

June was bullied and criticised throughout her upbringing, suffering bouts of depression. She always felt anxious. Somehow she had been left behind, kept on in the house with John as the domestic help, cleaning and cooking for the big brother who treated her badly. She had no confidence and no friends. Just John.

John Stanton was involved in everything that went down in Stockton. Drugs and stolen goods were common currency. He held position but had no ambition. John met Erdi Djoni in a pub, The White Lion, early in the evening towards the end of August 2022.

When John entered a pub he'd scan the faces around the room, watch eyes fall to the floor all around him. It was a buzz. He'd earned his notoriety and occasionally, just for a moment or two, he'd enjoy it. But on this occasion when he entered The White Lion, Erdi Djoni kept his head held high. He met John's gaze and grinned a hard man's grin.

John was aware that there were several houses on his estate that had Albanian residents and he'd heard that they were a tight knit group. From what John had heard, they were growing a lot of weed. There would be three or four houses, always in the less fashionable parts of Stockton, set up as cannabis farms.

He'd made a show of his indifference when he'd been told that they weren't to be messed with but this was his first direct encounter. He'd seen them around in little groups but they usually kept to themselves. So he was surprised by the lone figure. He returned the grin and issued a greeting. "You've got some balls."

Erdi gestured an invitation for John to sit with him.

John took a seat.

"I'm Erdi. I was hoping we might have a chat, John. Can I buy you a drink?"

Erdi seduced John with the ease of a man accustomed to getting his way. He told him that he'd made importation arrangements for some class A drugs and he needed John's help to set up a local network of sales outlets. He told John that he'd earn good money and enjoy the protection of Edri's compatriots.

John was blown away. This was an opportunity. He thought he'd won the lottery. When he'd started the day, no such prospect existed. He hadn't seen this one coming. His reputation must've spread further than he'd realised.

Poor John… he never asked himself why on earth Erdi Djoni had chosen to offer him this gift.

# ROB AND ELIZABETH

Elizabeth emerged from her shower, still wondering how on earth Danny Hutton had reappeared in her life. She was curious but really she wanted to focus her thoughts on more immediate concerns. She had enough to worry about already… she'd married the wrong man.

•

Rob grew up in Surrey as an only child, receiving mixed messages from his dedicated mother and his disciplinarian father. This was the mixture of familial dynamics that shaped his development… his mother gave the best of herself and his father criticised.

Both Rob and his mother were subjects for his father's critical voice. He ought to have sided with his mother, their shared positions suggesting a natural alliance. But instead, he identified with his father. The one who had the authority and control, the man in charge. The one who could be a bit of an arsehole. And on that basis, Rob shut himself off from the warmth his mother offered and learned to live in his father's cold house.

Rob made models. The model kits were provided by his father. Apart from discipline and criticism, they were his only gifts to a son who didn't really interest him much. Rob might have won approval if he'd been good at sports but he had neither interest nor inclination. High achievement at school might have won more recognition. Rob had managed at school but he was unexceptional. His father had no doubt that Rob could and should have done better. It didn't really matter how well Rob might do, his dad was only ever going to criticise.

The models gave Rob one delicate strand of connection with his dad. He had a steady hand and he seemed to understand how things fitted together. His father would never say that he'd done well or offer any direct praise. But he'd look at each newly completed piece and he'd find something positive to say, about the model rather than about Rob.

For example, he might point to the design qualities of an aeroplane wing. In those occasional moments when his father took an interest, Rob felt himself rewarded… he appreciated the value of cold contact. And that was enough for Rob. It had to be, there was nothing more.

Rob's mum had no interest in models and yet she would give him praise. She could see how perfectly he built them. His mother's comments were about Rob, they were complimentary and warm. Nevertheless, Rob knew that his mother held no enthusiasm for his hobby and he found himself not only unconvinced by her praise, but also resentful. He decided that her comments were dutiful. She couldn't give genuine investment and Rob felt she was letting him down.

He got through childhood. He wasn't a popular boy but he kept his head down and survived amongst his peers. He took A-levels in maths and chemistry and went on to university in Sunderland. He needed to feel distance from his parents.

And so it went on with Rob. He added a mediocre degree to his mediocre A-levels and gained employment in local government where he worked for the next nine years. Rob had good practical skills and he was an organised worker. If his people skills had been better, he'd have progressed to a senior position but each time he applied for a promotion, he got knocked back. He seemed to have found his level.

He met Mark in September 2016 when they worked together at the council offices in Middlesbrough. Rob had never found it easy to make friends but he and Mark got along. Mark also liked models. It was actually Mark's suggestion that they design their own model kits and Mark's idea to create a series of iconic model buildings from cities across the globe. Really, when it started it was a bit of a nerdy thing, they were passing their time with a hobby. They worked long and hard and it became something real. They built prototypes, improved them and they could see they had something a bit different.

Rob saw an opportunity. He formed a company and arranged manufacturing. Before the end of 2018 they were selling on

Amazon and a couple of specialist digital platforms. For a year or so the orders were patchy although the trend was promising.

Then Covid hit. It was exactly what they needed; everyone forced to stay home, while Mark and Rob marketed their home entertainment projects. Perfect. Rob sent bad energy to the vaccine developers and prayed for the next big variant. He wanted the pandemic to last forever. He did the maths, each Covid related fatality seemed to deliver two sales. Pile 'em high, bury them deep.

They both left their day jobs and Mark watched with interest. He hadn't expected this level of success. The sales suddenly increased and he couldn't understand how he'd allowed Rob to take sole ownership of the company. And sometimes it occurred to him that he hadn't made such an allowance. Nevertheless, he was a salaried employee and Rob was the boss.

Rob loved it. Until now, mediocrity had been the best he could achieve in the less than glamorous world of local government. Nothing exciting ever happened to Rob... he stayed at home by himself and made models. Once or twice a week he went out for a cold fuck with a local sex worker. That was it. Well, it was different now. He was an entrepreneur, a success. Thank the Lord for Coronavirus. Thank you, China.

When they'd first become friends, Mark had taken Rob out in the town and had introduced him to Stevie. Mark had always been partial to a toot, but not Rob. Rob had always disapproved of illegal drugs (just like his father), dangerous poison for fools, dreamers and lawbreakers. Rob had always supported the war on drugs but he wanted to see more powerful weapons. He advocated for much stronger punishments, including labour camps and military service. A few years in the army was exactly the right remedy for these losers.

With his own business and the money flowing steadily into his bank account, Rob reviewed his position. He felt like a rockstar now, and cocaine came with the territory. Rob made the necessary adjustment to his thinking. It was a good drug for Rob, his confidence, which had already grown with the company success, got a further boost up each nostril pretty well every night.

During this rock 'n' roll period, Mark secured a large mortgage to buy a house in Saltburn and he met Elizabeth. She was a few years older than Rob and she was the same height as him. But those minor irritations aside, she was cool, she had a cool job, she looked good and people seemed to like her. Rob had a vacancy for a rock chick and Elizabeth fulfilled the essential criteria. She was the only applicant.

Rob was having his fifteen minutes, he wanted to make it count. He courted Elizabeth with all his charm and some of his new money. With the right chemical support, it was almost fun. He had to use persuasion and he had to persist. He gave plenty of both and he won the fair maiden's hand in marriage.

Rob enjoyed it all. He won praise and the money flowed. If he and Mark had been experienced in business, they would have been busy creating a second series of models... they would have formed a post-pandemic sales strategy. But Rob was way too busy being a rock star and Mark was quietly planning a return to local government.

Mark was so seriously pissed off that he decided to stay for a while. He didn't like Rob anymore, and he wanted to watch him fall. He became mildly sycophantic in his behaviour, smiling at everything Rob was missing. He accepted the dinner invitations and continued to draw his inadequate salary while he waited for the company to fail.

Rob wasn't as absent as Mark had thought. He could see that the flow of orders had dried up and he watched his bank balance decline and then his overdraft grow. Rob simply didn't know what to do. Mark was the only person who might have some ideas but he'd ripped his only friend off. Rob was on his own, fantasising about divorce and bankruptcy.

•

Elizabeth was in a reflective mood… maybe it had something to do with Danny Hutton.

She'd recognised some of Rob's imperfections, including his rather controlling manner, quite early in their two year old relationship. In truth, Elizabeth was never fully convinced by Rob. She was already into her forties when they'd first met. The clock was ticking. Rob was succeeding in his business. He was clearly making an effort and he seemed very keen. It was just that occasionally he could be a bit critical and he seemed to be taking an awful lot of cocaine. She consoled herself with the 'nobody's perfect' argument, crossed her fingers and said the biggest 'yes' of her life. Rob's new and uncertain wife moved into his heavily mortgaged house.

It only took a few weeks of sharing Rob's house as husband and wife for Elizabeth to recognise that things had changed. Rob had been attentive, even considerate during their courtship but once he'd secured his prize, the effort level dropped. As the months passed, more changes occurred.

Incrementally, she felt herself being manoeuvred into a position of subservience. She simply hadn't accepted that such a thing could happen to her. She considered herself to be a strong and independent woman.

Nevertheless, Rob's demands increased. He started to give her instructions about how to perform tasks around the house. Rob expected Elizabeth to learn his routines and to maintain the same order in the house. He liked his shirts to be hung in a wardrobe in a particular colour sequence and with the second to top button fastened. These fussy particularities applied everywhere. Every item had its place. That's the way Rob liked it, everything neatly in place, including Elizabeth.

That had been the trigger for their first major fight, a misplaced shirt. It seemed ridiculous to Elizabeth… she could still remember every word of that frightening encounter.

"Jesus Christ, Elizabeth, it's fucking chaos in this house. Nothing is ever where it's supposed to be, not a single bloody thing," Rob had said.

Elizabeth had already learned to stay calm when Rob showed irritation. She'd steadied herself. "What are you looking for?"

"My blue shirt. Has it disappeared or is it just that my wife has misplaced it? I wonder which is it?"

She'd tried to stay calm. "I'm sure it's in the wardrobe, Rob, let me look." Elizabeth was trapped, he'd got her on the defensive but still she'd managed to walk across their bedroom, desperately hoping for resolution. She found Rob's shirt, the colour easily spotted.

Rob had snatched it from her. "How difficult is it to hang a shirt in its proper place and fasten a button? Is it too much to ask? Have I married a cretin?"

He'd been too close, too angry. She'd seen him show flashes of irritation but that was the first time that Rob got properly angry. In truth he got angry and downright nasty. He'd leaned over her until his face was just a few inches from her own and shouted at her. She'd felt specks of saliva hit her mouth and cheeks. Her husband for less than a year… he'd looked hateful.

The memory had stayed in her thoughts, replaying for the next several days. There were moments when she wondered how on Earth it could have happened. She examined the detail of what each of them had said, trying to identify what had triggered such an angry display. She could find no explanation. Maybe he had problems with the business. Whatever. It had blown over. She would've liked an apology. Never mind.

They were still newly married. Lots of couples have teething problems, house rules have to be negotiated. They'd work things out and settle down. She believed that she and her husband would make it work. However, Elizabeth kept noticing how precisely she was conforming to Rob's instructions, including the hanging and ordering of his fucking shirts.

As it turned out, the direction of travel didn't change. Rob's angry outbursts and his cutting criticism became more frequent. He didn't want grown up discussions about how they lived, he just wanted Elizabeth to fit in with his life, to be his wife. He really seemed shocked by Elizabeth's objections. She'd married him after all, hardly rocket science?

There was coercion and there was cruelty but to a passing observer they looked like success, good citizens, their lives fulfilled. Rob thought it was all fine, he just wished that Elizabeth would try harder and moan less often.

His criticisms and his instructions all became more frequent and more brutally expressed. Elizabeth started to see her relationship as a mistake. She felt trapped. He'd moved her into his house in an afternoon, and she wondered how easy it would be to leave. She suspected that Rob might be a difficult man to get away from. Elizabeth was perplexed… surely she was as free as a bird. Where had this prison come from?

The pattern of their interaction was set. Quite rigidly set. She learned how best to keep things on an even keel. It wasn't fun for either of them. Rob didn't seem to mind. She was doing what he expected of her. They were settling unhappily into their slow death together.

Elizabeth had always done what was expected of her. She worked hard at school, she went to university. Her only rebellion was to study social science. She trained as a social worker and then she got a job. She gave it a good go but she wasn't suited to the work. She drifted in and out of a few different jobs over the next several years.

Rob was her third big relationship. She was a forty-four-year-old self employed interior designer. Rob had liked that, he thought it was a cool job. Rob wanted his wife to be cool.

The work was cool. It took her twenty years but Elizabeth had found her talent. She could look at an empty room or a room filled with mediocrity, and in minutes, sometimes in seconds, she could form a vision, apprehend the mood. Those moments of imaginative transformation thrilled her every time, magical moments.

Elizabeth had made a fair number of wrong turns. Interior design wasn't one of them. She loved it and she was good at it.

Rob's tendency to criticise was injurious, he made her feel small. While she was trying to find a way out from her marriage, she needed her work. She was always busy, she was winning friends, she was treated respectfully and she was valued. The satisfaction from her work sustained her. She was deeply troubled and often hurt by her husband but if she continued to work well, she would find her way forward.

Her mind offered solutions, fantasies really, violent fantasies in which she turned the tables on Rob. She knew that she had to find a way to leave him, and one day she would, but in the meantime the fantasies kept coming. Sometimes she used a knife, sometimes a hammer. Once, in a dream, she shot him with a Colt 45. She wouldn't know a Colt 45 from any other handgun but that's what it was. She blew his brains out. She felt both relief and pleasure as she watched the blood drain out from a messy wound.

Earlier in the day there had been a disturbing encounter, a brush with the past, a glimpse into another world, a primitive world (probably) where things might be out of control, where the violence of her fantasies might be made real.

Danny Hutton didn't belong in the same world as Elizabeth. It's the same in towns and cities all over the country – dump estates side by side with more fashionable and affluent residential areas. Parallel worlds, each with their own values and subcultures. Somehow, despite geographical proximity, they remain entirely separate. Well, usually. It had just been a passing moment when their worlds had overlapped – enough for Danny to get into her head. Surely he couldn't properly find his way into her world.

Elizabeth was nobody special. She had enjoyed the benefits of a middle class upbringing, her father emotionally cold and her mother lukewarm on a good day. Nevertheless she'd spent her childhood in an environment that provided stability, her parents' best approximation of love and education. There had been no significant trauma, she had been protected from danger. She never felt huge warmth for her mother or a strong connection with her father but she'd always felt safe and she was grateful for that.

The primitive impulses of her internal world were in contrast to the calm and civility of the world she chose to live in. The sudden reappearance of Danny Hutton had disturbed her and yet she wanted to see him again. She wanted to know how Danny Hutton was and how the hell had he found his way back into her world. Danny Hutton didn't belong in Saltburn. The last time she'd met him, poor Danny didn't belong anywhere.

Elizabeth and Rob were hosting a small dinner party. It was just Becky and Mark. Elizabeth got along okay with Becky but they were Rob's guests. He employed Mark and much of their conversation would be work related. Rob expected Elizabeth to be the attentive hostess, to serve food and wine.

The boys had disappeared into the lounge. Becky stayed in the kitchen, chatting while Elizabeth completed the final preparations for a foody dinner party – avocado, crushed pistachios, shit like that. In the kitchen, Elizabeth tried to focus on the food. She was aware that Rob's business was struggling and was glad to give him some time alone with Mark. Nevertheless, it was her early morning walk that occupied her mind.

"I saw a man called Danny Hutton today."

Rebecca sipped her wine. "Do I know him, Liz?"

Elizabeth shook her head. "Probably not, Becky. I haven't seen him for twenty years. I was a social worker, one of my many failed careers! I placed him with a foster family in Stockton. He was four or five years old then. He was a lovely looking lad, handsome and tall for his age but Christ, he was full of trouble, poor little bugger."

Becky made a noise – an expression of maternal sympathy.

Elizabeth continued. "No, seriously, Becks. I'd never encountered such a troubled child. He was taken into care from very violent and disturbed parents. God only knows what they'd done to him. He was filled with rage and he was incredibly strong for such a young child. Honestly, his rage and strength were incredible. He was unmanageable. It sounds terrible… I mean, he was lovely but when he lost it, he was really destructive."

Rebecca felt her interest growing. "Fuck. What happened to him?"

"I don't know. You know, Becks, sometimes you can look for five minutes at a young child and you feel that you can guess their future. I sort of had that feeling with Danny Hutton. It felt that there was no way to save him. Five years old and already too far gone. I could only imagine, well, dread really, the damage he might create as he grew older. I was working with looked after children and he was on my caseload. I was young, quite inexperienced. To be honest. Becks. I didn't even feel comfortable with children. I didn't know how to talk to them. I was way out of my depth. But I think he was at least able to see that I was trying to help him. I hope so."

"What did you do with him?"

"I failed him, Becky. I tried but I couldn't help him. I walked. Left my job. The first time that I met him, he rested his head against the top of my left hip and I watched in disbelief as his small hand slid between my legs. He seemed to expect that his sexual advance would be welcomed. I've never forgotten, I was so shocked. But I really felt for him. He was needy, sometimes he held my hand. I can remember like it was yesterday, Becks. I found him two foster placements. They both broke down after a few weeks. The foster parents cared for him, tried to, even with their many bruises... they'd also seen his vulnerability and neediness. They were disappointed by their failure but they couldn't cope with him. I felt the same way. I really wanted to find a family who could make him better. He was the most damaged and dangerous little boy I'd ever met."

Becky could see that Elizabeth was affected. "I'm sure you did your best, Liz."

Elizabeth wasn't so sure. "He seemed to be beyond the reach of help and I could only imagine his future as more violence and more failures. I felt a connection with him but I couldn't save him. I was criticised for the early breakdown of the foster placements and my confidence as a social worker collapsed. A couple of months later I changed jobs. I never went back to social work. I didn't ever want to feel the way I'd felt as I failed to find a way to help Danny Hutton."

Rebecca had entered the kitchen light at heart and in five minutes her mood had changed. Nevertheless, she was compelled by her friend's story. "Christ, Liz, I mean, fuck. Where did you see him?"

"He was in the town. At the top of a path by the woods. I'm sure he didn't recognise me and at the time, although I knew that I knew him, I couldn't remember where I knew him from." Elizabeth carefully crushed the last of the pistachios. "I was showering after I got home before I realised who I'd seen. It was twenty years ago, Becks."

Becky was intrigued by Elizabeth's tale. "What was he doing?"

"I could be wrong, Becky, but I immediately assumed that a drugs deal was being conducted. The cars didn't fit with their clothes. He was with another man. I felt a bit unsafe and I just wanted to get past them. For a brief moment our eyes met. I felt a strong attraction and a sense of foreboding both at the same time. It was weird. I had a lot of different feelings. That was it."

"Wow, how exciting." Rebecca's enjoyment of the drama was growing.

"A bit scary actually, Becks, but yeah maybe there are some new drugs in town." Elizabeth looked around to find her glass of wine. She rewarded her successful search with a medicative gulp, then led Becky through to the lounge to join the boys.

"Oh well, every cloud has a silver lining," said Rebecca, following her host.

The evening passed in relatively smooth fashion. Rob's charm, abundant early in the evening, reduced as his alcohol and cocaine intake progressed. Once his slightly acidic criticisms of Elizabeth upgraded to poorly disguised insults, the guests issued thanks and departed.

Elizabeth was tired. Rob was never pleasant. If an evening at home together passed without open hostility or belittling criticism, she felt she'd had a result. Rob's maltreatment was still progressing. Initially it was always verbal abuse, more recently he'd used his hands. She couldn't understand what it was all about, this display of sophistication. The food, the wine, the clothes, such fine clothes in which her unhappy marriage was dressed.

# PART THREE

# MAISIE

Maisie waited outside of Sean's terraced house, cold but not downhearted. She'd known Sean for a few years and punctuality had never been his strongest suit. It'd been a few months since they'd last played together. She had no great expectations. It never went very far. They were practising three songs for an open mic night. She sat on the garden bench in front of his bay window and shook her head as she looked at the mess that had once been a small garden.

Maisie lived a busy life, she didn't mind that too much, but a few minutes alone with her thoughts, shivering in Sean's overgrown garden, was a welcome and peaceful break. Such was her life. She'd fled her family home soon after her sixteenth birthday and nearly fifteen years later she felt like she was still running, trying to protect the distance she'd gained.

Sean arrived, twenty minutes late but sober.

"I was just about to give up on you," she said.

"I'm sorry, Maisie. I had to go over to Saltburn." Sean took a seat beside her on the bench.

"I'll forgive you. I was enjoying a bit of peace, Sean." She looked at him with a smile and a shiver. "Not the cold though. What were you doing in Saltburn?"

"Nothing much. Throwing stones mostly, drinking coffee. How are you, Maisie?"

"I'm alright, Sean. Overworked, underpaid, smiling when I can. I was thinking, looking back… I should know better." She took his hand, surprising them both.

Maisie and Sean had some magic between them. They had their ups and downs but the chemistry that had first attracted them to each other and that still united them in music had meaning for them both. But Sean had let her down too many times. She'd given up on any hopes that he'd become the sober and reliable man with whom a proper grown up relationship could be possible.

She had tried, but in the end she'd sent him away. It broke Maisie's heart but she'd arrived at the same conclusion as everyone else who knew Sean… he was an interesting man, sometimes compelling, but he was a drug best taken in small doses. *Come and see me tomorrow, when you're sober. Or maybe next week.* It had been a painful disappointment, but Maisie was tough, and she needed to sing.

"Tell me what you were thinking." Sean sat back, failing to notice Maisie's shivers.

"Christmas 2002, as it happens."

Sean chuckled. "I was five," he said.

Maisie smiled again. "I was ten. I sang in the school concert. We all had to audition. Most of the kids were stopped after a few bars but I sang the whole song. All I Want For Christmas. I couldn't understand why Miss Jones let me carry on right through the song. I didn't know until then that I could sing. I didn't even realise that I knew the lyrics, it just came out of me. All the other kids were staring at me when I finished, then they clapped. I blew them away, if you'll forgive my modesty. Ten years old."

For the three weeks that followed her audition, Maisie became Miss Jones's darling girl. She did one song by herself and then a duet with Sue Bellamy, who was almost posh. Despite her shabby clothes and her family's reputation, Maisie gained favour. She was teacher's pet and she had a new best friend. She was excused from lessons to practice her songs. She was going to make the school concert a success. What a good girl. Maisie had the voice of an angel. Perfect for Christmas. All Miss Jones wanted for Christmas was Maisie. Just for Christmas, just like a dog.

"My dad wouldn't let mum come and hear me sing. Bastard. So I was the star of the show but my mum wasn't there. We had a crap Christmas, dad was drunk, no presents and no fucking turkey, the same every year. I just wanted the holidays to end so that I could go back to school." Maisie sighed. She tried to avoid talking about her family and mostly she didn't look back. She brought it to an end. "It's all a long time ago…"

Miss Jones had blanked her after the holidays, so did Sue Bellamy. She was Maisie again, an unwanted Christmas dog.

"Can we go in? I'm freezing."

"Yeah, in a minute."

"Sean, I can't sit here all day, I have things to do, work, that kind of stuff. I came to rehearse, not to sit here in the cold." She looked again at the overgrown weeds and empty crisp packets. "Why don't you look after your garden? It's a mess."

"It's called re-wilding. We're sitting in the middle of a complex eco-system. But you blew them away, Maisie, you haven't forgotten that. And at least you carried on singing afterwards."

Maisie corrected him. "No, I didn't. I didn't really sing again till after I'd left home. I joined a choir... they were in vogue. It was a brilliant sound. Honestly, Sean, what a revelation, every Thursday evening, the sound of thirty voices working together, the best moment of my week. I was only sixteen and working all the hours I could at the pizza house. I can't remember how it ended. I joined a rock band after that. Completely different. The choir was more fun." Maisie had found other opportunities to exercise her vocal chords. She could release her voice sweet and pure and she could harden the edges. She had impressive control, although she never really thought about her delivery, she just sang.

Maisie was twenty-four when Sean fell in love with her. He was still just nineteen. To be fair, Sean fell in love just about every time he went out of the house. Nevertheless, Maisie knew that they had something special. She loved to sing for him. He'd give her his lyrics and play the guitar.

Sean wrote songs without a melody. He started writing song lyrics as a child. He had been good at English for ten months, Year 8 at school. Mrs Jenson told the other kids what to write but allowed Sean to write whatever he wanted. He thrived. He was given permission to be himself, freedom to roam. He mostly wrote prose to begin with, descriptions of nature, sometimes personal diary pieces, he was wide open. Then he started to write song lyrics but he couldn't sing and he couldn't play an instrument so he moved to poems.

Sean was eighteen when he taught himself to play guitar. Right from the start, he'd written lyrics and created guitar accompaniments but that was as far as he could take it. Until he met Maisie. She was able to find a melody and a way to make the words fit with the music. In a way that sounded exactly the way that Sean couldn't quite hear in his imagination. That's a tough task but Maisie could do it. She always picked up the emotional tone from Sean's writing. She held the key to all of his melodies. Surely that was the person to fall in love with.

The magic worked for them both. He gave such rich and raw materials. He gave her his music and his trust. Maisie understood sadness and disappointment... she knew about anger and disillusionment.

They were bonded by their art but Maisie had just about managed to withdraw from the emotional entanglement that had tied her to Sean too closely during the first two years of their relationship. These days it was music and friendship. She knew she shouldn't have held his hand, feeding him another shot of false hope. Too late, Maisie was fiercely independent, a strong woman, a fighter. But once in a while she wanted someone to put an arm around her shoulder, someone to lean on. There was no one else, there was only Sean.

He'd put her through some turmoil, messed her around, and sometimes she took a little more from him than she should. Fuck it, surely to God he owed her a few minutes here and there. And sometimes she let her longing and her neediness run free, held him tight, tore at his skin, took his love and his loving. Then she'd pull back and he'd be hurt. She didn't know what else she could do. She needed him but he was impossible.

As if by magic, he reclaimed his held hand and wrapped his arm around her. Maisie nestled her head against his shoulder. He seemed to be able to sense her needs sometimes. She'd stopped shivering, she felt warm.

"Let's go inside. You can play me some music, Sean. I want to sing."

# STEVIE – COMING IN FROM THE COLD

Stevie got a cold. It was October… why not? For a week he sneezed and coughed. He recovered and emerged back into the world. He'd noticed one or two rogue deals taking place before his cold had hit. A week later, it was clear to see that there was a new player in town. Almost too clear. He saw a couple of mopeds slowly approaching a café. The lead bike pulled over and the two young guys on board watched the second bike trundle on for another twenty metres to the waiting punters. The wraps and the cash were quickly exchanged and the mopeds disappeared.

There were drugs in circulation that had nothing to do with either Stevie or Danny. It wasn't unusual. Middlesbrough was a port, an obvious target for smugglers. Inevitably there would be opportunities for entrepreneurial criminals and risk takers.

Stevie understood that better than most. It was the professional domain in which he'd forged a career. He felt secure in his own share of the market and he didn't really mind when new players emerged, so long as they kept clear of Danny's trade. Nevertheless, he liked to think that he had his finger on the pulse. There were risks as well as rewards in the drugs business sector, opportunities and threats, and these fuckers on the mopeds were new boys. He bought fresh milk and cigarettes, then headed home, time for breakfast and a phone call to Danny.

He arrived back at his flat in town and made the call. "Yo, Danny."

Danny had been waiting to hear from him. "What's happening, Stevie?"

Stevie was ready for the question. "Mopeds and dirty wraps… thought you'd want to know."

"Yeah, so I've heard. I spoke to Sean yesterday. Where've you been?" Danny asked.

"I've been ill. I haven't been out for over a week, until today. It's a bit weird, Danny. The guys I saw this morning didn't seem to give a toss. Do you know who they are?" Stevie's curiosity was growing.

"Yeah, I think so, but I want to take a look myself. We'll need to catch up, Stevie, I've got a feeling that this might be serious. We might need to put in a few movie nights," said Danny.

Stevie smiled. He remembered those days, too right he remembered them, special days. "Just like the old days, Danny. Sounds like fun."

"I'm not sure about that." Danny wasn't able to echo his brother's sentiment. John Stanton, Erdi, Elizabeth Bennett… it really was starting to feel serious. "We need a meeting, Stevie, all of us. There's trouble coming. When did you last speak to Seth?

"Weeks ago, I can't remember. What's happening, Danny?"

"Can we meet at your place, tomorrow night, eight thirty? I'll tell Sean. Can you give Seth a shout?" Danny was seriously uneasy but he was ready. Ready to fight, ready to walk away.

Stevie was more cheerful. "Yeah yeah, I'll call Seth. We can meet at my house." He'd bought a house out in the suburbs three years earlier. Mostly it had stood empty while Stevie continued to live in his rented flat close to the town centre. It had been Max's idea. Stevie had proceeded without much interest but the value was increasing and it provided a garage for his Corsa. "Brilliant… movie nights and a board meeting. I'll see you tomorrow."

# THE BOARD MEETING

Sean and Danny arrived in good time and good spirits. The agenda was depressing, but the prospect of a couple of hours together was welcome. Seth had been invited but he couldn't attend, he had Covid.

Stevie had no doubt that he was the coolest guy in town. He didn't spend much time in his semi-detached house in the suburbs. He didn't like it, he thought it was a property more suited to his parents... well, to his dad. It was an investment and an embarrassment but at least it provided a space for board meetings. He'd furnished the house badly... it felt more like a two star hotel than a home.

Danny and Sean settled into his panda skin sofa, cracked open their beers and got ready to rip the piss out of their host.

Stevie was in his element. Stevie Jobs, Chief Executive Officer, called the meeting to order. He'd hoped they would all sit around his dining table, taking notes on their phones, forming plans, but Danny and Sean weren't co-operating.

He grabbed himself a beer and found a seat, returning from the corporate world and resuming a more natural role, as petulant Stevie. "I can't believe this lot... they're everywhere, seriously, flying about on bikes and mopeds. They have no right. They haven't earned the right. They're kids, Danny, just young kids."

Danny smiled at Stevie's objection. "So were we, Stevie."

"We had a car, Danny. We kept a low profile. We were young, I'll grant you that, but we weren't kids. What exactly do we know about these scummy fuckers?" Stevie hadn't caught up yet. He'd lost a week with his ill health, he had no information and he hadn't really stopped to think what it would all mean. Stevie often needed to speak his thoughts in order to see them. "What's going on?"

Sean responded first. He had none of Stevie's anxiety. He had neither financial nor emotional investment in the business. Nevertheless, Sean was always ready to help Danny out. They both knew that. Danny employed him and paid him a wage, gave him additional cash. Danny had bought the Beamer and he paid Sean's rent by standing order. Nevertheless, Sean considered himself to be a sponsored artist… he didn't actually work for Danny. And as such, he felt that he owed Danny nothing but his friendship.

Sean offered his information. "I've heard from at least three different people that a guy called John Stanton is the man with the beans. From what I hear, he's nothing special. He's from Stockton. What else do you need to know? It's all happened in a couple of weeks. That's too fast. There must be someone else working with him. Danny?"

Danny's lightness of heart was gone. He wasn't fully himself, he was hesitant. "Yeah, I can't be sure yet but I think the Albanians are involved. That's bad news. Terminal, probably." He paused.

And it was noted by both Sean and Stevie… his words of warning, his hesitation, a hint of resignation even. They heard Danny speaking and they looked across the room at each other, both feeling the same way… disappointed, a bit shocked. If Danny believed, they all believed, but the atmosphere in the room had changed, belief seemed to be in short supply.

Now they all felt the gravity of these fragments of a new story, of their emerging understanding of what was taking place, and what it would mean. The mood was sombre.

Danny wasn't ready to say much, he had a lot on his mind. Including Elizabeth Bennett and the prospect of early retirement. He sat up. "Let's cruise for a few days, see what we find, see if we can find Stanton. I want a good look. I'll have to speak to Erdi again. If I can find him."

In the past, board meetings had always been fun, a group of young lads making plans, plenty of piss taking. Then they'd leave with smiles and heightened spirits. Not tonight. Ten minutes of discussion to identify a serious threat. That was pretty well it. It was like bad sex… it didn't last very long and nobody enjoyed themselves.

# TOGETHER AGAIN

Danny and Beth had owned the house at Saltburn for over eighteen months. Beth had become accustomed to his patchy presence in the house. She knew that he was trying his best.

It had been almost five months since they'd last had sex. She and Danny had drifted aimlessly in their struggle with intimacy and they hadn't managed to find a way back. She could see that he was tense and downhearted when he arrived back from his meeting with Sean and Stevie. She sensed his mood and gave him plenty of space.

Beth felt sorry for him but sometimes she could have laughed. She looked at him, a big powerful man and a frightened child. He was trying so hard to be with her. For years he'd always gone back to the gym when he was troubled but occasionally he stayed in Saltburn. She knew that was against his instincts. He was trying to demonstrate commitment, to show his progress. He was hopeless, he looked lost.

He poured and drank a glass of whisky, then she watched as he disappeared up to bed.

She desperately wanted to follow, to be there for him. But she knew her man. She waited, knowing he wouldn't sleep. She kept him waiting for another twenty minutes, then she climbed into the bed beside him. She knew what was needed.

He was very tense, surprised by the directness of her advance after a such a long period of abstinence. His first and habitual response to her searching hand was refusal but his erection was clearly interested. Beth continued. She stroked him, feather light, almost tickling. It drove him crazy, then she gave him a squeeze as she gained ascendency. She sat astride him, sensing his need and noting her own accelerating involvement. She rubbed herself against his erection. Her intention had been to give but now she was taking, panting, and then he was inside her. It was electric. They were together now.

He cried out so desperately that she worried he was hurt. The tension exploded out of him. Beth dismounted. She felt elated and he allowed her to rest her head on his shoulder, a rare treat.

She'd always found the courage to reach out to him and she did then. "You were wound up when you came back home tonight. What's wrong? I'd like to know."

She felt his chest rise from a deep breath. "Nothing serious."

"I'm not stupid. You had Sean over to Saltburn, early in the morning. You've had tonight's meeting, and you looked bloody awful when you came back. I want to know what's happening."

"There's someone else muscling in on my turf, that's all. It's happened before. I'll have to sort it. No big deal, it'll be fine. I could do without it, that's all it is. I could do without the whole show, to be honest, Beth."

Beth remained quiet.

Danny spoke again. "I've made a lot of money. Maybe I should cut and run. I feel like I've had enough. I don't know."

Beth was surprised. Danny rarely discussed his work. "If you want out, do it. We don't need it, you don't want it. It's a no brainer. Get out, Danny."

"Maybe you're right. It's not an easy thing to do though, walking away."

Beth tried again. "Why not? Just walk. It's easy, walk away." She waited for his response but he remained silent, the pillow talk window had closed.

# A FAMILY REUNION

Back in the day, when they'd still been teenagers, they had enjoyed the movie nights. There had been a feeling of excitement, the confidence of youth. It had been genuinely entertaining, they'd watched some great movies.

Danny hadn't expected that he'd have this task to perform again ten years later. Nevertheless, over a period of five consecutive days, Danny, Stevie and Sean combined in pairs to drive around different parts of Middlesbrough and Stockton. Seth should have been with them but he was still recovering from Covid. Eternally.

They went into the town centres and out on to the estates. They could see the street selling all over town but nothing more. It wasn't fun anymore and they weren't really movie nights. They were watching it all unfold in broad daylight. Stevie's initial observation had been insightful – these kids just didn't seem to give a toss.

Sean was particularly bothered by how many young kids were involved. Ten and twelve-year-old couriers pedalling their bikes and peddling their wraps. There were lots of teenagers on mopeds who made no effort to look anything other than law breakers. They rode red lights and footpaths, proudly and foolishly defiant.

Danny was more concerned about the numbers. They were everywhere, all nobodies but plenty of them, easy to find, easy to watch. He quickly started to lose interest. He needed to get a close look at what John fucking Stanton was all about and he needed to think about Erdi. These kids on bikes were a distraction, a waste of time.

Danny was uncomfortable. His sense of control felt compromised, someone else was calling the shots, goading him. And Elizabeth. Somehow Danny was mixing her in… she seemed to be part of the puzzle. She'd appeared at the same moment, suddenly visible. John Stanton remained hidden and so did Erdi, but they all seemed to be sending unwelcome questions. As yet, Danny had no answers.

It was the fifth fruitless day. Danny had almost decided to give up. They'd learned as much as the streets could teach them. He and Sean had been cruising, then they parked up close to a small group of shops. It seemed quiet, then a bit of fun started outside a post office. It was early in the afternoon, the best part of a November day, and there were a few people coming and going. It was always a place to hang out if you had something to sell. Some people were still picking up their benefits in cash and would take the opportunity to score as soon as they emerged, freshly endowed with the king's shilling.

A middle aged couple, a man who was tall and skinny, probably in his forties, and a woman who looked a bit younger, were having some kind of a disagreement. Something in the scene caught Danny's attention. The movements, the sounds. His guts were churning, he started to sweat. He was remembering fragments of what he'd spent most of his life trying to forget. Danny was watching intently, almost entranced. He'd stared at this man before, defiant and afraid. A long time ago. He remembered the voice.

They were shouting at each other and the tall guy was starting to push the woman around. It was unpleasant, a bit of a mess on the footpath but no one was getting murdered.

Sean had seen them. He was much less interested. Sean saw a pair of losers, losing again but Danny's fascination held. Then he opened the car door, got out on to the pavement and threw up on the footpath by the side of the car. Sean was taken by surprise. There'd been no warning, Danny had been fine, now he was sick.

Sean jumped out and rushed to check what was wrong. Danny didn't say anything, he wiped his face with his hand and spat out the acid still left in his mouth. He heard Sean ask if he was okay. He wasn't. He didn't answer, he walked quickly across the road, passing the front of the post office as he approached the altercation.

The argument was turning nasty. The man was the aggressor. He shoved the woman hard against a brick wall and she cried out in pain, holding on tightly to her bag nevertheless. Her face contorted with fear as she anticipated her fate. She never even saw Danny.

Danny with adrenaline. He almost seemed to glide, his movement graceful and swift. His right hand grabbed the back of the man's jacket and Danny steered him around the side of the post office, away from the eyes of a small but gathering audience.

Danny held his grip, keeping the man's back in front of him as he moved him into position. Then he released his hold, turned his hand ninety degrees so that his fingers pointed to the darkening sky. He moved his hand up to cup the back of the man's head, and smashed his face hard into the brick wall.

The sound was somewhere between a thud and a crack. It was an unusual sound, bricks and mortar meeting human flesh and bones. Twenty years of waiting, better late than never. The blood and pulp that had once been Stan's face slid down the wall while Danny strolled calmly and briskly back to the car, still full of grace.

There would be no reprisal, no reporting. The protocol for cinema trips included the preservation of anonymity. But this unplanned announcement that Danny Hutton was alive and well would do no harm in the current circumstances. Danny was recognised by most of the lowlife in Middlesbrough. There was a possibility that someone would have recognised him. Not a problem, the proud population was neither a friend to the police nor a supporter of law and order. And of course, no one crossed Danny Hutton.

Sean had started to follow Danny but it was all done and dusted before he'd had time to catch up. They got back into the car together and Sean drove back towards the town centre.

"That was interesting. Was it just a way to break the boredom or did reason have a part to play?" It was a bit frivolous, quite inappropriate and very Sean.

Danny didn't answer and he offered no explanation as Sean drove back into the town. Danny was shaken, unable to speak about what had just happened. It felt like a dream. Sean knew his friend well enough, he'd ask him again on another day. Danny jumped out of Sean's car and then straight into the Range Rover. He was gone. Sean watched him drive away, concerned and curious.

Danny decided not to drive back to Saltburn. He drove out onto the moors, found himself a quiet lane and parked up. He needed some time, trying to understand what had happened. For the first time in more than ten years, Danny hadn't been in control. He'd felt a compulsion. He was sickened and confused, barely conscious. He felt like a lonely child, about four years old.

He had time to think about it now. Danny had spent many hours out on the moors. He was from an urban environment but he liked areas of coastline and he liked the North Yorkshire Moors, stark and beautiful. When the noise inside his head grew to be too much, he felt the need for moorland, stillness or at least slowness. And the quiet.

Although it didn't take much more than thirty minutes to drive from Middlesbrough, he'd never visited the moors until his twenty-first year. He'd been with Beth for his first visit. She wanted to see a sculpture, a seated man. Beth had enjoyed the day out, but Danny was completely blown away. Such magnificent landscape.

And he liked the sculpture, a bearded man sitting with a bag or a briefcase resting on his lap, gazing out across the hills and the dales. He returned to look again a few times more before the sculpture was relocated in the summer of 2019. Danny was guided by this piece of art… he saw a man with his work rested upon his knee while gazing miles across the land, gaining perspective. He did the same. He could bring his work here, think about it for a while with a sense of the greater world around him. In town he was a big man, out on the moors, in the greatness and the beauty, he felt wonderfully small.

It was three in the afternoon but already the light was in transition. It was still too early for twilight but the light hovered somewhere in between daylight and darkness. It was a magical light, a photographer's dream. There was a red kite drifting without effort, in full command of the clear sky, surveying the land. And Danny watched, he could have watched forever but the kite circled higher and found an escape from his vision.

Danny was ready now. He knew in his bones, in his soul, in his suffering, that he'd connected with something or rather someone from his early life. Danny had never asked about his parents or his past. Maybe he'd picked it up from one of his many social workers but he seemed to know better than to ask. He had been told almost nothing about his mum. Apparently she had a lot of problems. That had been enough. *Don't go there, Danny, let sleeping ghosts die.*

There wasn't a father's name on his birth certificate so he'd never know for sure but he was guessing now that the man he'd attacked had to be from the part of his life that he couldn't or wouldn't remember. During the few seconds that he'd held the man's jacket, he'd picked out the smell of stale alcohol and sweat. It all fitted: the sound of his voice, the movements, the stink of him. It was him alright, whoever the fuck he was.

He could still sense it in his nostrils. Beth was a few miles down the road, in the house that she insisted he share but Danny felt like he had nowhere to go. He'd have to sit and suffer the stench that might be his father until it found its way out of his nostrils again. The magical light slipped away and darkness took its turn. He started the car. Beth had held him close and warm after the board meeting but he couldn't face her now, he needed solitude. Fucking fathers.

# RETREAT AND REVIEW

After the unexpected disturbance by the post office, Danny retreated to the gym. He felt tired. He didn't really understand why. Usually Danny was a bit over-energised, feeling that he needed to be active. He lifted some weights... he gazed out from his windows. He was waiting for inspiration or clarity and there was no sign of either. Everything felt heavy, except the weights. He was packing in plenty of reps.

Elizabeth's sudden appearance, then the pond life surfacing at the post office. Danny had struggled for twenty years to escape his past. Suddenly the things that he'd been running away from for all these years were right alongside him.

It all felt burdensome. He needed to send word to Erdi suggesting a meeting, but he'd have to wait for Seth's recovery. He wasn't too concerned, he knew that it wasn't a good sign, but as things stood, Danny still hadn't decided exactly what he wanted to say. He decided against any further days just cruising, it was a waste of time.

He needed some time to get himself focused again after his day out with Sean, redecorating the post office wall. He hadn't been back to Saltburn since it had happened. These were the times when Danny lost belief in his relationship with Beth. He couldn't be with her when his internal world overwhelmed him. He couldn't be with anyone.

After three days, tormented by his own company, he arranged to meet Stevie and Seth to sort out a more focused agenda to help locate John Stanton. He'd given Stevie a time thirty minutes before Seth was scheduled to join them. He wanted a few minutes to talk with Stevie alone, share some thoughts. He'd excluded Sean altogether. He didn't want to hear Sean's questions about his recent violence because he had no clear answers.

They'd had a pretty good look around during the previous week, watching someone else's drugs circulating freely. Young kids with nothing much to lose. But nothing more than that. John Stanton remained unseen.

Danny drove out by the football stadium to meet Stevie who was waiting in the Corsa.

And there they were again, it was the same car but they were ten years older.

Stevie was in the driver's seat, Danny alongside him in the front passenger seat. "Hey, Stevie. How are you doing?"

Danny hadn't told Stevie about the post office incident. He felt no shame, no sense of regret, he just felt unsure about it all. What could he tell his friend? That he'd decided to smash a man's face into a wall because of his voice and his smell? He hadn't told him about Elizabeth either. Nor had he mentioned his temptation to walk away. They had a few things to discuss.

"Yeah, good. Where have you been, Danny? I thought we were getting busy. What's the score?"

"We've sat and watched, Stevie, but we've got nowhere. We'll have to think again. I've asked Seth to come, we'll get him caught up and I'll ask him to get word to Erdi, arrange a meet." Danny was frustrated by their wasted time. "Have you talked to Molly?"

"No, me and Sean are going to see her tomorrow night. What are you thinking, Danny?"

Danny had a thousand thoughts, his head felt crowded. He needed to share at least a few of them with his friend. "We've seen it coming, Stevie. I'm not sure about Stanton, I've never met the guy and I still want to get a closer look at him. But no, this is it, mate… this is the Albanians."

Stevie answered quickly. "What does that mean? This is it? I don't understand, Danny."

Ten years earlier, Danny had enjoyed many hours alongside Stevie in the Corsa. Back then, he'd felt comfortable and confident on the streets, he had a clear vision. It felt different now and in some ways it was different. All these young kids, Erdi and John Stanton… but Danny himself had changed. Twenty-five-year-old Danny looked out through the car windows with more critical eyes. He experienced a sense of distaste as he witnessed from close quarters the mess that street dealing of crack cocaine and heroin can make.

"I don't know. We'll have to find John Stanton, follow him for a couple of days. I'll try international diplomacy."

"I'm not sure that I'm following your train of thought, Danny. Great yeah, we'll find Stanton, you'll talk to the Albanians. Then what? What's the end game? I don't like these twats scooting around like they fucking own the place. I don't need this. I'm cool thanks. I mean we've done this bit, Danny. I didn't give a fuck when we were kids, it was necessary, an investment. We had to do the leg work, we were building the business. I'm twenty-six, Danny. I've got a strong customer base, I'm a low risk operator. Seriously, man, I don't need these dickheads fucking it up."

Danny could relate to his brother's irritation. He was having similar thoughts. "We're not interested in these guys, we just need to get as much of the story as we can. They're foot soldiers, they don't matter. If there's a war, they'll be front row cannon fodder, never issued a uniform, sitting ducks with second rate weapons. They'll help us find the generals. Maybe. And yes, I agree, they're an irritating bunch of fucks. But right now, on this particular mission, they're all we've got."

Of course Stevie knew the score, although Danny's comments had further heightened his concern. "When you say 'if there's a war', help me out here, Danny, what do you mean by that? Who exactly is John fucking Stanton?"

Stevie's whining discomfort wasn't helping Danny's mood. "That's the point, Stevie. I want to know more about John Stanton."

Stevie asked the million dollar question. "Then what?"

Danny decided to voice his indecision. "Listen, Stevie, we've had a good run. But I need to tell you, this is serious. This guy, Erdi, he's a part of something, a big organised network. That's what he told me. Too much for you and me. So you know, Stevie, it's serious."

"Yeah, I hear you. Fuck. Fuck it, Danny, I hear what you're saying, it's serious, we've had a good run, I'm listening, but I don't have a clue where we're heading. What's the end game?" Stevie paused for a second but he had more to say. "You never told me about Erdi. I didn't know we were under threat from an Albanian criminal organisation. I watch the fucking news, Danny. Jesus."

Danny noted Stevie's displeasure. At least Stevie had got the message. He softened the blow. "I'm not panicking, Stevie. Erdi didn't make threats, but fair enough, I should have told you. Seth will be here in a minute, we'll work something out. I just thought I'd better give you the heads up. I'll let you know if things are going to kick off."

Danny understood Stevie's nerves. They were brothers, no question about it. Danny would kill for him. They both knew that. Stevie definitely wouldn't kill for Danny. They both knew that as well.

Stevie exhaled slowly, took a fresh look around the street and spotted a figure of interest emerging from another car across the road. "Seth's here, better late than never."

Seth crossed the street, opened the back passenger door and took his seat. "How you doing, guys?"

Danny gave Seth his customary greeting. "Good to see you, Seth. We're all over the place."

"I should hope so," said Seth. "This brings back memories, us three in the old Corsa. What's happening?"

Stevie and Seth had never really got on particularly well, but they accepted each other because that's what Danny wanted.

"We're all over the place, man," Stevie took his turn. "You alright for coffee, Seth?"

Seth absorbed Stevie's indignity without distress, he had heard the question a thousand times before, pretty well every time he and Stevie met. He'd learned to let it pass.

Stevie loved it every time.

Danny was impatient. "Seth, you remember in the summer last year, you gave me a message to meet Erdi Djoni outside of the library? I need to meet him again. Do you know where to find him?"

"No," said Seth, "but I can find Davey Cooper. It was him who gave the message to me last year. Davey's solid, he'll pass it on."

"Speak to him today, Seth." Danny remained focused on the

task. "There's a guy from Stockton called John Stanton. Do you know him?"

This was Seth's first involvement. He'd spent the previous several days coughing and sneezing. His test kits had all been negative but he was convinced he'd had Covid. He'd recognised the symptoms from a previous episode, which had also produced negative test results.

"I've seen him around a bit over the years. He's a knobhead, fancies himself, loves a mirror. But fair do's, he's a big lad and he's handy. I saw him in action a couple of years ago, he likes an audience. He drinks in The White Lion in Stockton. He's not in your league, Danny, not on any level. Sean used to know his sister – Maisie."

Danny was agitated and relieved. He converted both emotions to anger and there was a snap in his voice as he brought their boys brigade meeting to a conclusion. He turned first to Seth. "Jesus, Seth, if you'd told me that yesterday, we wouldn't be here now. Sean still sees Maisie, they've been rehearsing some songs."

"I thought she'd dumped him years ago," replied Seth, who was forever underestimated. He was valuable muscle but he was often excluded from the more cerebral parts of the business. While the others had been cruising the streets for several wasted days asking their questions, Seth had been at home coughing and sneezing and in possession of all the answers.

Stevie was encouraged. "Nice one, Seth. That's progress. I won't need to bother with Molly."

Danny turned to Stevie. "No, go and see her, find out what you can. Bring Sean up to speed, maybe he can have a quiet word with Maisie, but we don't want to send any early warnings. Talk to Molly. The both of you can go to Stockton tomorrow. I want to know where he lives, where he hangs out and what he eats for breakfast." Danny was annoyed that he hadn't asked Seth earlier, but delighted to be given his first proper look at John Stanton.

During the moments when Danny recognised the wisdom and benefits of early retirement, he felt lethargic. When he recognised an enemy, someone to fight, he seemed to perk up. He knew it was all wrong.

# SETH

Seth and Stevie went to Stockton together the day after they'd met with Danny out by the football stadium. They figured that John Stanton either lived close to The White Lion or he had reasons to visit, it was the obvious starting point. Stevie waited in his car and Seth for once turned up at the agreed time, free from Covid symptoms.

Stevie started the script. "Fancy a coffee, Seth?"

Seth manufactured a face to signal a bad mood. "Yeah, I want Costa, so find a drive thru and get me some caffeine." Seth spat his words out with as much menace as he could muster, he wasn't an actor but he could see that Stevie was surprised. He'd planned this the previous evening: he planned to show offence, mention Danny's absence and then watch Stevie start to panic.

As it turned out, he thought his joke was so funny that he couldn't keep his face straight to complete the script and a loud outburst of full laughter brought a premature end to his less than impressive acting scene. Then he gulped a breath of air and laughed on and on. Stevie was laughing with him now, somehow reacting to Seth's pathetic joke as if it had been the funniest moment in world history.

They had the giggles. It went on until it became painful. Even then they were still having mini eruptions and they were both nervous as they realised how easy it would be to start again. Eventually they managed to stop, they were settling. Then they made the mistake of looking at each other and off they went again.

Stevie and Seth never hung out. They had nothing much to say to one another, they'd learned to get on well enough but their conversation had never extended beyond an exchange of information. There was no ill feeling, they were just different.

They'd never done this before, not as grown men, just the two of them in a small space for what might be several hours. They were both tense. Until the giggles, a new shared experience. Neither of them knew what to say. Stevie started the car and drove to a Costa, bought the coffees and some flapjack and drove on to Stockton, parking thirty metres from the entrance to The White Lion. Stevie unhooked his seatbelt, his shoulders hung loose. The tension gone, he fancied a chat with Seth. For once in his life.

"How are you, Seth?"

"All over the shop, man. I'm good enough, Stevie. I'm breathing."

"Yeah, good man, breathe on."

Stevie hesitated.

Seth spoke again. "What's the score, Stevie? All of this with Stanton... what's the story?"

"John fucking Stanton is running some gear, irritatingly good quality coke, more than decent heroin. It's all happened pretty quick. Too quick, Danny thinks. And Sean says that the Albanians are involved." Stevie interrupted himself. Seth's attempt at humour still occupied his mind. "Fuck, listen, Seth, what you did today, you know with the coffee routine, it was funny, man. Seriously, Seth, I liked that."

Stevie surprised himself with this comment. Seth's moment of humour had really taken him by surprise and he realised that Seth must have thought about it beforehand, planned it out so that they might get on better. He didn't know that Seth had that in him. He got back on track. "But yeah, you notice that Danny isn't here today, he's got some shit with Beth and the shop. Anyway, we're designated to watch the hot lead and Danny can't be arsed to turn out. He wants the detail on Stanton but he's interested elsewhere. I think Danny's gonna walk away, leave Stanton and the Albanians an open door. They're too big, Seth, too many. And Danny knows it. Oddly enough, I suspect that Stanton hasn't worked it out yet... it's the Albanians who are in charge here, Seth. John fucking Stanton's the sucker who's being used to draw the heat. I mean, from what Sean tells me, Stanton's a dickhead but for Danny, he's irrelevant. We'll find out where he lives, check for family and whether he still drinks in the Lion. Then we'll fuck off."

Seth appreciated Stevie's candid reply and gave himself some time to let the information sink in. "I hear you, Stevie. Fuck, man, if you want the truth, I hope he does walk away. But I've known Danny for a long time, Stevie. I've never seen him walk away from anybody. That's worth remembering. Stanton's handy, I mean, maybe I could take him, I'm not sure. I don't know what tools he carries or who's with him." Seth paused for a sip from his coffee. He stared out into the street, his thoughts drifting, remembering all the way back through the years that he'd known Danny, and he'd spoken truthfully, Danny had always stood his ground.

Seth continued. "I was twelve when I first met Danny. My mother died. She had diabetes, died from a heart attack. She wasn't even forty. She found life hard going, ate too many fucking cakes, fed me too many cakes but she did her best. She was a bit of a tragedy really but at least I got twelve years with her and you know, she didn't abuse me or anything like that."

Stevie was astonished. This was Seth, this was personal disclosure. He didn't have a reply. Seth was way off script. "Yeah…" He hesitated, trying to find a word in response. He couldn't think, but words came. "I made it to sixteen before my old lady died. I was even luckier than you, Seth."

Seth went on. "I was a fat kid, not huge but enough to get picked on. I didn't know what to do, I tried to be invisible but I was too fucking big. It was a teacher, Mrs McCarthy, who saw me getting pushed around at school. She took me aside one day and asked why a big lad like me didn't hit the other kids back. So I plucked up my courage and I whacked this kid. Dave Thorpe. I'd got myself so psyched up for it, I lashed out with all my strength and caught him smack in his teeth. Anyway, to cut the story short, that was that, I was the unpopular fat kid who could knock Dave Thorpe's teeth out. It was about the only thing I learned at school, Stevie, but hey ho, I've earned a living from it ever since. More use than a GCSE in Geography. God bless Mrs McCarthy, my kind of teacher."

Stevie could still feel an impact from Seth's unexpected

conversation. The giggling had relaxed them both. He didn't feel the need to say anything. What the fuck.

Seth went on. "After mum died, I went to Malton Court. Danny and Sean were already there. I was quiet enough to start with but after a few weeks I thumped a kid called Tony Hirons. Rattled his fucking brains, I can't remember why. I couldn't believe it when Danny came to see me in my room. He was only nine, big for his age but so was I and I was twelve. He just walked straight in and kicked me in the bollocks, told me that was for Tony and walked out again. It had been five years then since Mrs McCarthy had put me straight and for five years no one laid a finger on me. I couldn't believe it. I was nearly a foot taller than Danny, twice his size. Anyway I was more careful after that, I knew I had to be, I still pushed people around but only kids who didn't hang out with Danny. That's why I had a go at you, Stevie. Everyone thought you were a flash bastard. I thought I had a clear path. I couldn't believe it when Danny came in and took your side."

Stevie smiled. "Yeah, that was poor judgement, Seth."

Seth accepted the insult. "When you moved in, it was hormone city... a few of them were finding out what to do with their tits and bollocks, messing around, just having a laugh, you know. I was a bit older, Danny wasn't interested so we started going to the gym, left the rest of you to get on with it. I thought you guys were still kids, I thought me and Danny were the big boys. We'd stopped being kids."

Stevie reflected. "I can remember, Seth."

"I'll tell you what, Stevie, Danny can pump iron. We were in the gym nearly every day, young lads among grown men, plenty of mean fuckers. No one spoke much to us, a few guys stared at us, you know, intimidating stuff. I was shitting myself but Danny kept dragging me back. He didn't bat an eyelid, Stevie. I remember thinking that he can't just kick these guys in the bollocks like he'd done to me. But then I watched him lifting the weights, looking straight back at these guys and I wasn't so sure."

Stevie listened, then he smiled. "He'd have kicked any fucker's bollocks, Seth."

"Yeah, he probably would have. Anyway, there was never any bother, Stevie, but he was cocksure of himself. I knew then that I'd stick with Danny, whatever he wanted to do, I'd be with him. You never saw Danny when he was a kid. I missed most of it. He was calming down by the time I went into care. That's what Sally and Lisa told me, apparently he was completely out of control when he was really young. I don't know what happened to him, Stevie, but I'll tell you what, somewhere along the line somebody made Danny Hutton angry and they made a fucking good job of it. He's carrying some high energy."

Stevie chuckled. "Can't argue with that."

Seth continued. "So no, he won't walk away, Stevie. When Danny shifts into gear, he's fast and powerful. That's when me and Danny started to get on, back in the gym. If you didn't know Danny, you'd never believe this shit. He was still only fourteen or fifteen, he never said anything in the gym. I kept my head down but Danny had his chin up and he looked at everyone, he was straight back at them, eye to eye, and fuck he could pump iron."

Stevie smiled. "But that's how he was with everybody. Our friend was a remarkable teenager. Danny was going places, no one could've stopped him."

Seth nodded in agreement. "The guys in the gym watched us bulk up. I lost the last of my excess weight. I was well ripped then, Stevie. I was full grown, a couple of stones heavier than Danny but he could still lift more than me. We were both in good shape. After six months at the gym, the locals were giving us a cheery greeting, showing their respect. I was seventeen, Danny was fifteen, two fresh faced lads in a backstreet gym, rubbing shoulders with the local hard men."

Stevie remembered. Danny and Seth had suddenly become close, changing from boys into men.

For Seth, the memories flowed fast and strong. "Danny still didn't talk to anyone but it started to feel like it was our gym. You couldn't make it up. I'd always felt, you know, like I didn't fit in. I knew how to bully but I was a scared fat kid under the surface. At least I had been until then. I was looking at myself in the mirror and it didn't look like me. I was lifting my head at the gym and scary guys were either looking elsewhere or giving me a friendly smile. I was somebody. Because of Danny, I was somebody."

Stevie was enjoying listening to Seth. He'd never heard him talk so much. Or so well. He felt disappointed in himself. He'd written Seth off years ago as a brainless meathead. In Stevie's view, Seth was a thicko, a man with big biceps and a small brain. Stevie was slightly amazed every time that Seth managed to form a full sentence. He'd never known about Seth's journey into the care system.

It was interesting now with Seth in full flow, effortlessly reeling off several long paragraphs, that his subject was Danny. Stevie was a bright man, he understood things. Although he took pleasure in the listening, he quietly and gently chastised himself. Seth was a better man than he'd realised and as he listened to him now, he recognised the strength of feeling that Seth had for Danny. He'd never seen that before. He felt foolish and he felt regret about his dismissive assessment of the big guy sitting in his car.

"I can remember that, Seth. I didn't know where the gym was but we all saw you two getting into shape. I was shagging Lisa but suddenly she had the hots for you. Suddenly you had big fucking guns on you, you looked like you were made of rock. Seriously, you guys were both ripped. I remember telling myself never to fall out of favour with Danny 'cos I thought you'd kill me with your bare hands."

Seth chuckled. "I didn't know Lisa fancied me, nobody said anything. Shit, I missed my chance there. Anyway, Danny started to take me places. He'd tell me he was going out and ask if I wanted to come with him. He had it all worked out, Stevie. Well, not all of it but he was building his reputation. He was sending a message out into the streets. We cracked a few heads... the message needed to be clear. Sean was there mostly, then you started driving and the core team was in place."

Stevie was positively beaming now. He felt good, he liked to remember those days. A bunch of young guns out and about. He hadn't known that, like himself, Seth had a dead mother and an absent father. Danny was so focused back then, fearless, bold and ballsy. Filled with certainty, eyes on the prize. "I loved that time, Seth. I took more drugs than you and Danny, so did Sean, so did just about everybody, come to think of it. But it was you guys that gave me the most smiles. We were a team. No, that's not the right word. We were family, man."

Seth nodded in agreement. "It seems like a lifetime away now though. Fuck it, Stevie, we're older now. I didn't give a shit whether I lived or died in those days. Tell me this... if Danny doesn't walk away, and he won't, what do we do? I mean there were some dangerous fuckers around ten years ago but no guns and no Albanians. I had muscle, you had brains, Danny had it all and Sean made us laugh, built the spliffs. No one could match us. We started the wars and we won them. We won't win this one, Stevie." Then Seth dropped the bombshell. "I've got Jen and the bairn to think about."

That jolted Stevie. "Who the fucking hell's Jen?"

"My missus. She works at Sainsbury's Local, she's a supervisor and she's only twenty four."

"You fucking what? What are telling me here, Seth? You've never mentioned anyone called Jen. I've never seen her. Are you for real?" Stevie was reaching new levels of astonishment.

"I didn't know what you'd all think. I thought you'd think I was a daft cunt."

"Seth, man, you are a daft cunt, you don't need Jen to make that claim. I have to ask Seth, did I just hear you say 'the bairn'?"

"I've got a baby boy... Daniel. He's thirteen months, trotting about now. I never knew my dad, Stevie. I want to be there with Daniel all the way through."

"Jesus Christ. Jesus fuck the Pope! Christ! So how much does Jen know, Seth? Like, for example, does she know what you're doing today?"

"Not exactly. She knows that I do work for Danny."

"Does Danny know about Jen and Daniel. Is he the fucking Godfather? Excuse the pun."

"He doesn't know. I've kept quiet about it. You must be some

144

kind of psychologist, Stevie. I can't believe I've told you about them. I've told Jen a few bits and pieces. She's not happy about it. She wants me to get a job in one of the big warehouses. Don't get me wrong, it's been a blast and shit, but yeah, walking away would suit me fine."

Stevie was in a state he'd never experienced before. Clearly Seth's story was truthful and yet his first emotion was disbelief. In the space of fifty minutes, Seth had morphed into a completely different person to the one he'd ripped the piss out of the previous evening and indeed for the previous ten years.

New Seth had a different role in the coffee sketch. He was a stream of personal disclosures, he was a husband and a father and he was contemplating a career change – hitman to shelf stacker. Pretty fucking weird. Nevertheless, he liked it, he liked new Seth and he wanted to meet the baby. "Hey, can I be Daniel's uncle? No cancel that question, I'm your brother, Seth… I *am* Daniel's uncle. I can't wait to meet him, man."

Seth wasn't entirely sure that thirteen-month-old Daniel was ready to meet his Uncle Stevie, or what Jen would have to say. He'd let the cat out of the bag now, he'd have to rely on Stevie keeping his mouth shut. "Listen, Stevie, keep that to yourself, will you."

It wasn't meant to be a question. "Absolutely, Seth, your secret's safe with me, my friend."


They were ready for a long day but they got lucky. Less than an hour had passed when Seth saw Stanton and another guy walking towards The White Lion. Seth recognised both men.

"Here we go, Stevie, target identified, walking towards the pub on the opposite side of the road. John Stanton and Finn Duncan. Irish lad, hard as nails."

John Stanton and Finn Duncan were in The White Lion for less than an hour. Stevie followed Stanton as he walked back to his house. All done in a day. Home address, drinking hole and Finn Duncan. More than enough.

# LOOKING FOR LOVE

Sean was a law unto himself. He didn't like unanswered questions and Danny's altercation had left him puzzled. He wondered why Danny hadn't given him an explanation. He'd heard Danny bring an end to this new group of movie nights, but he wanted to understand what had happened. He'd returned twice to the post office and spent a couple of hours watching and waiting. So far he'd learned nothing new but he was determined to continue.

Stevie provided an update as they made their way to find Molly. "We've located Stanton. Me and Seth found him at The White Lion in Stockton."

Sean expected more. "And?"

"He was with another guy, Finn Duncan. Seth knows him. I don't know, Sean, that's all. We can watch him now, see where he leads us, I guess. We'll see what Molly knows." Stevie wanted to give Sean a message of confidence but it wasn't easy, Danny's hesitation was bothering him.

Sean noted with interest that Stevie appeared to know nothing about the altercation out by the post office. He said nothing more.

They weren't an impressive team, Stevie and Sean, shuffling awkwardly on a street corner on the wrong side of the station, at a well established pick up point where men came to find their prostitutes. They looked like naughty school children. The Albanian criminal gang better beware.

This wasn't a place to pause unless you were either working or kerb crawling. Stevie was embarrassed, trying to find the facial expression that communicated disinterest in prostitutes, trying to blend into the background, trying to be invisible. Pam had based her business there for five years, almost as long as Molly.

They'd been in position for less than five minutes when she approached.

"Do you boys need some help?" Pam raised her thin black eyebrows. She scratched the top of her leg, teasing her almost non-existent skirt up and down, kindly offering a clue about the kind of help she might give. Just a few pounds, twenty quid's worth of heaven, say your prayers, sing your hymn.

She was a mate of Molly's. Sean had met her before. He'd half expected to be approached by a kerb crawling, skin crawling, sex seeker. He was delighted to have been identified as a punter. Perks of the job. "Hello, Pam. We're hoping to catch Molly."

Pam remembered him now. "Dirty bastards, two at a time, Molly won't do it." She chuckled, glad of the company. "Just move along the road a bit, you'll spook the customers. I need to earn some cash. Molly'll be back in a bit. He'll drop her across the road."

They complied. And Pam's information was good. Before long, a car pulled to a halt across the road. It was a dark blue Audi with a personalised number plate.

Stevie recognised the plate, the car and the driver. He turned his back... he didn't want Rob to see him. "Well, well. Rob Thomas out for a bit of extras."

Molly was in a bad mood.

Sean told her that they needed to talk to her but she sent them away, she was working. He could see that she didn't like her friends watching her at her place of work. In her work clothes. Sean knew better than to argue with Molly. She was furious. He really wanted to get some information but Molly was clear in her message. He ushered Stevie away, accepting her instruction to visit her flat the next morning.

Both men were glad to be walking away.

Sean was curious. "Who's Rob Thomas?"

"I sell him his gear. He's made some serious money selling model kits. He only got married a few months back. He's a knob, he likes his coke." Stevie hadn't enjoyed their outing and Molly wouldn't spare them five minutes. Not the best use of Stevie's time. But Rob Thomas... that was an interesting little bonus. Never any harm in knowing a newly married man's dirty secret.

Stevie was keen to be somewhere else, anywhere else. "We can meet in the morning and go to Molly's."

"You'll have to go on your own, Stevie. I'll be asleep." Sean wasn't an early riser but he had no intention of sleeping late. He'd be back out to the post office, trying to work out who or what had angered Danny.

Then Stevie remembered. "I hear you and Maisie are back together?"

Sean sighed mournfully. "I wish. I see her sometimes, she still sings with me. We're playing at an open mic night tomorrow."

It really wasn't a matter for amusement, but Stevie was amused nevertheless. "Oh right, very nice. What's her surname, Sean?"

"Stant… you are fucking kidding me." Sean felt embarrassed. He hadn't made the connection.

Stevie chuckled. "You've been sleeping with the fucking enemy, Sean. Although fair do's, not as often as you'd have liked."

# LUAN

Luan was Erdi's most trusted and senior colleague, his number two. Erdi had started the hares running, it was Luan's job to follow their track. He'd been keeping an eye on John Stanton and he'd caught sight of Danny and the boys out cruising. A message had come through – Danny Hutton had requested a meeting with Erdi. It was all unfolding according to plan. John Stanton was drawing the heat. Danny was reacting. With a bit of luck, one of them would kill the other.

Then Luan heard about Danny beating up someone who was unconnected to both Erdi and Stanton. That made no sense. Luan decided to investigate. He'd spent some time parked close to the post office, an hour or so when he'd had spare time. He'd drawn a blank from the first two visits but his third effort was more fruitful.

Luan was good at his job. He'd taken the time to identify some of Danny Hutton's people. He recognised Sean's car first, a white BMW. His heart rate quickened but he drove slowly, right alongside. There was just Sean in the car, asleep.

Luan smiled. He decided to exploit this fortuitous encounter. He parked his grey Lexus in front of Sean's Beamer and stepped out into a crisp cold morning. He opened Sean's car door and punched him. Just a sharp straight jab, then he watched Sean's rude awakening.

It took a while for Sean to orientate but he got there, and through his pain and his shock, he looked his attacker in the eye. "Why did you hit me?"

Luan's explanation was brief. "I'm John Stanton." He jumped back into his car and disappeared.

# MOLLY LOPEZ

Molly Lopez knew very little about her parents. Her father's identity had never been revealed. She never got to learn about her Spanish family, she had her mother's surname, the only clue to her roots. Southern Europe had given her beautiful skin but for Molly the Spanish heritage made her even more different, when all she wanted was to be the same as everyone else. She was born to a fourteen-year-old mother and 'given up for adoption'.

A married couple without any children of their own completed the stressful period where their suitability had been assessed and they had waited patiently for a fresh new baby from an anonymous womb.

But just a few days before Molly was to be handed over to her new parents, they changed their minds. The adoption never happened. Molly was still less than three months old and already she'd managed to lose two mothers. Careless.

Molly had two foster placements early in her childhood. She was with the second foster family for nearly three years. Her luck seemed to have changed. But it hadn't. Her foster mum died, it brought the placement to a sad end, it broke her heart and it broke Molly, who was already broken.

A few weeks short of her fifth birthday, bedraggled and thrice rejected, Molly arrived again at Malton Court.

She was an active child, she did what she could, she got on with her life… she had no other option. Five years old and she'd figured out that nobody wanted her. She was a child who was unloved, and despite her resolve and her energy, her sadness had the better of her. She felt worthless. She thought she was good for nothing.

Until Beth turned up she'd never made a friend. She got a different social worker every few months and one of them instructed against further foster placements. The social worker moved on, the entry in Molly's case record remained. She became a permanent resident at Malton Court. It was like an airport, kids landing and taking off in all directions, and amongst all the chaos and changes, Molly stayed put. And she was more all over the place than any of them.

She was a fiercely loyal friend and somewhere in her heart she kept a few splinters of gold. Molly's heart had a few other splinters to be fair. She could flare up over something or nothing, but she would soon cool down again. She hated school and she hated kids who had parents. Fair enough. Her moods defined her, she was Molly, she was moody. Molly'd had a crappy childhood.

Puberty was terrifying. A bunch of new hormones, hairs growing, her body changing shape, menstruation and mood changes. It was everything she'd ever dreamed about. In her worst nightmares.

Unloved and unlovable, Molly became promiscuous during her early teens. She didn't like the sex but she liked someone wanting her. She liked seeing boys who were pleased because they'd fucked her. She liked her fleeting moments of weak power. Then she'd got her habit, completing a perfect set of credentials for survival sex work. Every heroin cloud has a silver lining.

Beth never gave up on Molly. It was just as well because Molly was lost for a while. She'd had her stomach pumped a couple of times when she was fifteen. She had still been in care back then and the safety nets caught her. It was more dangerous after she moved into her own bedsit and was injecting heroin. Beth had found her once when Molly had overdosed. Beth called the ambulance and later pointed out to her friend that she was lucky to be alive. Molly was unconvinced, she was a survivor. Whether she liked it or not.

For three or four years, Molly's life was particularly difficult. She was often very depressed, filled with self loathing, shooting too much smack, eating either crap food or no food. She was thin, her skin was grey. She was in her early twenties and she was dying.

It was during those years that Danny stepped away from her. He was with Beth by this time but he always kept space in his heart for Molly. During Molly's lost years, Danny would get upset seeing her in a grubby flat… dirty needles, dirty floors. He got angry with her. It didn't matter how loudly he shouted, Molly wasn't listening. So he'd stepped away.

Many human beings find themselves reaching a crossroads, facing a tough track. Life had dealt Molly a bad hand. She grew up as a miserable and unwanted looked after child to become a sex worker with low self-esteem. She suffered episodes of depression and she had a heroin habit. Her home was a hovel and she had no experience of personal power. Somehow, from these circumstances, Molly found resources within herself and started to claw her way back.

That's as good as human achievement gets.

She still chased the dragon from time to time, especially when setbacks occurred but she stopped injecting. She wondered whether taking care of herself might be a better idea, and she hoped that one day she and Danny could be friends again.

# MOLLY IN THE MORNING

Molly preferred Sean. She was comfortable enough with Stevie and she liked him well enough, but she was much more comfortable with Sean. Molly had ups and downs and she knew she wasn't always good company but with Sean it made no difference. When she got very low and she was miserable company, Sean actually visited more often. He washed a few pots, turned the radio on. He accepted her even with the bad choices she made and in all of her moods. Stevie was a bit more judgmental, although not as bad as Danny.

Stevie had phoned early in the morning to say he wanted to come and have a chat. After she'd sent them on their way the previous evening, he thought best to give her forewarning. Molly had still been in bed. She'd had a couple of hours now to get herself together and she was curious.

"So what's new, Molly?" Stevie made his way into Molly's tiny flat, noting that it looked unusually clean and tidy.

"Apps and shit. It's been a while, Stevie. How are you doing?"

"Yeah, yeah, all over the place." Stevie was the least enthusiastic user of their traditional greeting.

Molly was impatient. "Well, Beth called and said that trouble's brewing and now you're paying a visit. So I assume it's true?"

"Not if I can help it, Mol, but yeah, you must've seen these fuckers shooting about on mopeds. Pain in my arse. Kids and halfwits. Apparently one of your punters is involved so we need to gather a bit of intel. It's a guy called John Stanton, he lives in Stockton." Stevie left it there, just waiting for Molly to respond.

"Yeah, I know him. He's been coming to me for two or three years. He's a creature of habit, or he always used to be. I didn't know he was coming all the way from Stockton. He was always a Thursday man, quite early in the evening, always sober, a bit rough. He pulls my head back with a handful of hair, he doesn't do eye contact but he does look at me. He's been coming on different days but still early in the evening. He probably goes for a few pints after. And yeah, he's full of himself. I don't like him. If Danny wants to waste him, that's fine with me."

Stevie was watching her. She looked alright, better than he'd expected. He looked around again. It had been about a year since Stevie had last visited Molly. She'd been a mess and so had the flat. Molly had used heroin since she was fifteen, but her habit didn't take hold until she'd moved from Malton Court into her flat when she turned eighteen. It had been a challenging time for her, trying to live independently for the first time. Molly had struggled.

She went on struggling for the next several years.

But today the flat was tidy and Molly had some colour. She looked better than Stevie had seen her for years, so much so that he diverted the conversation. "You're looking well, Mol." He saw her eyes roll so he tried again. "I mean it, you look good."

"Fuck off, Stevie." Molly had always been unable to accept compliments. Just about any form of positive regard sneers at her and then runs away.

"No, seriously, Mol. I haven't seen you looking so well for ages."

Molly tried a bit harder this time. "Fuck off, Stevie." No need to rewrite the speech but the extra volume did the trick.

Stevie tried a different tack. "Have you got the kettle on or what, dozy fucking cow."

"That's better. Grab a seat. I'll make us a brew." She was more comfortable with the insult, back in familiar territory. She made the tea and sat with him. "How are you, Stevie?"

"I really am all over the shop, Mol. I'm nervous. This has all happened fast and I don't know where it'll take us. I mean, you know what Danny's like." Stevie wrapped his hands around his hot mug of tea.

"Yeah, he's a grumpy, controlling and bad tempered psychopath," Molly interjected unhelpfully.

"And not always easy to read," Stevie added. He was indeed disturbed by whoever his rival might be, but he was also concerned about what Danny would do. So far Danny was calm, organising the movie nights, getting the lie of the land, learning about who he would have to argue with. Nevertheless, Stevie didn't know what to expect, Danny had talked about giving way, which was unlike him.

"Stevie, why do you wait for Danny to make the decisions? Why don't you decide for yourself?" Molly loved all of her brothers, Danny more than anyone but she didn't have him up on a pedestal. Stevie could take Danny's road to hell if he wanted to, she'd find her own way.

The question surprised Stevie. He had no answer. He abandoned the diversion and refocused. "Stanton's having fun, playing the big man. We need to pin him down, you know, see where he fits in. Anything you can tell us. It's not really about Stanton, Molly. I mean, he's heavily involved and I suspect he might get a fucking when the fun really starts, but there's a big group of Albanians behind him."

"Oh right. Interesting."

Molly's interruption was unexpected.

Stevie was curious. "Why?"

Molly paused. She had her reasons to keep her information to herself. She didn't answer his question. Instead she shifted the focus back on to Stevie. "So what's going to happen?"

"Fuck knows, I've stopped myself from thinking about it, Mol. It's depressing me."

That struck a nerve and Molly snapped at him. Her angry eyes found him across the kitchen table. Stevie winced even before she spat her words out.

"You're worried, Stephen. You should be. But you're not depressed."

"Alright, alright, Jesus fuck, what's wrong with you? You asked me a question, I was good enough to answer. Excuse me, Mol."

"Sorry, I didn't mean to snap." She softened again. Molly blew hot and cold, she always had done. "It's just that I do get depressed, Stevie, and I know what it feels like. When I'm low, I don't pop round to a mate for a moan and a cuppa. I sit here and cry… that's depression, Stevie. I can hardly fucking move, can't get up off my chair. I hear you, Stevie, there's something happening.

Everyone's talking about it, and if the Albanians are involved, you should be seriously worried and very careful. So should Danny. They're ruthless bastards. Just don't call it depression."

Stevie was a bit shocked by what Molly had said. He'd never taken that much notice of Molly. She was always a bit of a miserable bitch. Molly's disclosure was bringing him right down, but he decided it was best not to mention that to Molly just now. Instead he tried to lighten the mood. "Life's tough, Mol, but we've all got to rise above it. No fucking good moaning, is it?"

Molly snapped again. "You don't have a fucking clue, Stephen."

Stevie decided not to argue, not when she was calling him Stephen. And Molly had a point, he was clueless. "A perfectly well reasoned argument, Mol. I stand corrected. Who exactly are the ruthless bastards you referred to?"

"Never mind that." She paused to take a breath and she almost decided to answer his question. But Molly was being real, real with Stevie. She'd talked to Beth and to Sean about her struggles with anxiety and depression, but she'd never imagined a sympathetic response from Stevie.

She still felt the same way, wishing she'd never mentioned it but she had and she held her line. "I've suffered with depression since I was a kid. I didn't have a clue myself back then. I thought I was shit, I still do sometimes. It's hard, Stevie. I feel paralysed, the world turns to crap. I hate myself and I can't lift a finger to change anything. I take anti-depressants, I take anything I can get hold of when I'm really bad. Especially if there's a chance it might kill me. Seriously, Stevie, that's how it feels, kill or cure equally welcome, both better options than staying depressed."

Stevie realised that his attempt to shift the conversation had failed. Suddenly everyone was going off script. Seth and Danny yesterday, now Molly was at it. "For fuck's sake." He couldn't think of anything else to say.

Molly hadn't finished. "When nobody's ever wanted you, except to fuck you, you wonder what must be wrong with yourself. You're worth fifteen quid with your knickers off in the back of a car... apart from that you're worthless."

She couldn't quite manage the first person with that little vignette. She was just about looking at him, finding just enough courage to seek eye contact. She'd said some things that she hadn't expected to say, and she needed to make sure he'd heard. She wasn't crying but tears were running fast down her cheeks. Her eyes were fixed on his, waiting.

Stevie really didn't have a clue. He didn't know what it was like to be Molly, he didn't know about depression and he had no idea about how to handle this fucking conversation. His usually reliable stock of witty one liners offered nothing. He had to look up. He was fearful as he raised his gaze and suddenly affected when eventually their eyes met. "Fuck, Mol, I didn't know. I didn't know."

"Well, you know now." Molly was sobbing now, quietly and steadily. Stevie had heard her, so now she could cry.

Stevie was a long way outside of his comfort zone. He was intensely uncomfortable, watching a young woman crying and talking about her mental health. Stevie always had a line, he could talk for Britain and right now, with his need for something to say so strong, he choked on his silence. Molly had told him she gets down sometimes, that was all. He felt destroyed, impotent.

"I don't know what to say, Mol." He pulled three papers off his Rizla pack, slowly, still with his eyes connected to Molly, and his spirit. He built a joint, not too much weed but enough. Enough to help them both. They took their smoke, felt the medicine, thanked God for THC.

Stevie was drifting, stoned. He lost sight of John Stanton… he wanted to give something to Molly. "Listen, Molly, do you need some coke? I mean on the house, babe, as much as you like."

Stevie's ridiculous attempt to offer help was so wide of the mark, so utterly ridiculous and so Stevie, that Molly was amused. Which was a bit annoying. She'd made a bloody good job of being heartbroken and affronted, she didn't want to blow it with an eruption of laughter. But she was stoned as well and she and Stevie had always resolved their unfinishable conversations with humour, sharing laughter. "Okay, I'll take a kilo."

Stevie was a bit shell shocked and he needed a second or two before he caught up with Molly and joined her infectious laughter. Relief. He was grateful. He knew that Molly had trusted him. They were laughing now but their conversation had been deadly serious. He wouldn't forget. All the same, he was happy that they'd found an escape. Stevie was hearing some unexpected stories and he was just about coping. So he rode this fucking nutcase wave of new communications, this fashion for reaching out, risk taking, this new art of conversation.

Their laughter started to ease. Stevie felt okay in a weird sort of a way. He hadn't gained anything new on John fucking Stanton, Molly had made him feel intensely uncomfortable with all that personal disclosure and mental health shit, but nevertheless he felt strangely okay. "I've got your back, Mol. Anytime, day or night."

He listened to himself. Sounding strange, like someone else. This wasn't Stevie, he didn't really do empathy and emotional support. Fucking weird. Fucking sisters.

They were both relaxed now. Stevie had visited for a purpose, it was work. In her own inimitable way, Molly had moved them to a more personal agenda.

She released a long sigh. She'd escaped the tears and laughter. "I bet you weren't expecting all that, Stephen."

"No."

"I'm doing okay at the minute, Stevie. I'm not depressed. I do have a history of drug addiction so an unlimited supply of coke is the last thing you should offer me. Silly sod. I'm trying to clean my act up. I haven't injected for months. I'll never put another needle in my arm as long as I live. But I know you meant well." Unlike Stevie, Molly hadn't lost sight of why he'd come. "How serious is this trouble?"

"It's serious, Mol."

Molly asked again. "What kind of serious? Will you lose a few quid or will somebody get killed?"

"Yeah, good question." Stevie thought for a few seconds. "It'll be more than a few quid and I don't know, but probably."

Stevie's reply reflected Molly's own judgement. "I need to speak to Danny."

This was an unexpected development. "Yeah?" he asked.

Molly stayed quiet.

"Why?"

"If Danny gets himself killed, I want to know that I warned him. Tell him I need to see him. Either today or tomorrow."

The glow from their earlier conversation faded and Stevie felt like a messenger boy. "What is it, Molly? Just tell me."

"I know a bit about some Albanians. I can't keep it to myself after what you've just told me but I need to talk to Danny." Molly could see that Stevie wasn't happy. Men and their fucking egos. "You bring him, I'll talk to both of you."

That helped, Stevie was almost restored. "Okay. Will you be in later?"

"I need to work for a couple of hours, I need food for tomorrow. So either come between five and seven or leave it till the morning." Then she thought for a moment. "I don't think you should wait till the morning."

# HELPLINE

Emina's first phone call had been brief and for Molly it had felt dreamlike. Molly had first contacted the English Collective of Prostitutes a year earlier and during the past few months she'd held several meetings with other sex workers, mostly in Middlesbrough but also from other towns and cities in the North East of England.

The sex workers wanted to be able to work safely, on their own terms. They also wanted the police and the rest of the world to stop treating them like criminals. It was an agenda that matched Molly's concerns very well. It had helped Molly. She was more able to think about how she worked. It had helped her to take a few steps towards self-respect. These links to other sex workers gave impetus to a process of change. Molly carried some deep wounds. Recovery is relative but she was relatively well.

Then, from out of nowhere, Emina had called. Molly had immediately picked up the foreign accent and that had focused her attention. She'd raised her left hand to cover her left ear to shut out any competing sounds. She'd listened to an unknown and foreign voice speaking an extraordinary message. It had felt quite unreal.

Molly noted the slow and deliberate enunciation, as if her caller was reading her words (she was). Each word seemed to have been chosen with care. But even still Molly could feel her caller's urgency. This is what Emina had written and what Molly heard:

*Molly, you don't know me. The English Collective of Prostitutes gave me your number. Please listen to me. My name is Emina. I'm in Stockton, Fulham Road. There's a café and a shop and a red door with a number 12. I am one of three Albanian women, kidnapped and held captive. We are sex slaves. We have a phone but I don't know if we'll manage to keep it or get a charger. You cannot call me, or the police, that would be dangerous for us. We need to get away from here, we need help, please will you help us?*

Molly had been shocked. She'd asked how she could help and Emina had said that she didn't know how. There was a few seconds of silence, then Molly had said, "Yes, I'll help." She heard Emina say, "Thank you, Molly," like a child instructed by parents to always be polite. Then Emina had ended the call.

Over the next several weeks, more calls came from Emina, always quite late on Tuesday evenings. The calls were brief to begin with but as time passed Molly and Emina gradually developed a sense of relationship. They exchanged information and Molly built a picture of her new telephone friend.

Emina described the pattern of her day to day life. She talked about Debora and Valmira. And she talked about Erdi, the Godfather. Sometimes the two women explored ideas for escape but neither of them had much to offer.

As Molly learned more from Emina, her desire to help grew, but so did her feeling of impotence. Each time Emina talked about Erdi, managing shipments of cocaine, running his little empire, Molly was reminded of Danny.

It was a testing set of considerations for Molly. She was hearing Emina's desperate story within Erdi's dark and dangerous world. Emina was fiercely critical of everything Erdi was involved in, including illegal drugs. Molly was a long term user. Danny was the only person who might be able to offer an avenue of hope and he was an English version of Erdi.

Molly talked to Emina about it all, the morals and the practicalities. It was a challenge for both of them. Molly felt herself to be less than perfectly equipped to set sex slaves free but she wanted to try. She went over to Stockton. She wandered up and down Fulham Road a couple of times and saw the buildings. She knew that part of Stockton well enough. That was weird, standing in the road, watching a few people wandering in and out of the shop or the café and wondering if she and Emina were just a few metres apart.

They were from different worlds and they were in different worlds but during their series of telephone calls, they built a bridge, where they stood together, looking both ways, with an ocean of deep water beneath them.

# WAITING FOR MOLLY

A process was unfolding. It had started, there could be no turning back. The wheels were in motion. Something was going to happen. That was how Stevie suddenly felt after receiving Molly's information. The period for preliminaries was all done. He felt that he was approaching an ending.

He'd intended to meet Danny after talking to Molly to pass on information and to report back from his trip to Stockton the previous day. Molly's unexpected urgency had affected him. He'd been unprepared for Molly's mental health shit and he certainly hadn't anticipated the Albanian connection. Stevie was spooked.

He was back at his flat waiting for Danny to arrive. He was in an unusually reflective mood. His conversation with Danny out by the football stadium had been brief and, in Stevie's mind, unfinished. But there had been enough said for Stevie to understand that his friend was considering the unthinkable. Danny seemed ready to abandon their territory and allow their business to be taken over by an aggressive rival. The whole show would be over.

That wasn't a prospect that appealed to Stevie. He didn't want to find himself in the middle of a turf war. He didn't want get himself killed but he didn't want his way of life to end either.

Stevie enjoyed being the slightly edgy drugs dealer. It had become a part of his identity. He knew his product well, he knew his customers. He understood his business model – decent drugs for decent people at a decent price. Even in the early days selling skunk at Brent Hall, he'd noted the effect that his position as dealer produced in others. Stevie realised that buying illegal drugs is different to buying a bar of chocolate. For most buyers there is probably only one retail outlet. It's not a good idea to upset your supplier, so the customers treat the dealer well, smiles and gratitude, even though there may be less appreciative sentiments below the surface.

Stevie liked that. He found there was something special about the transaction, the etiquette of the exchange, those moments when he still held the gear while the punter had to wait until he was ready. Those were the moments when he felt the power of his position, the magic of a street deal.

The money was fun and there was plenty of it, but there was more to it than the money. The business was his connection to Danny, and Danny was the most important person in Stevie's life. The two of them had chosen a controversial path… maybe they'd taken a wrong turn. None of that mattered, they'd travelled together, grown up together. That's what counted.

He'd been a misguided, middle class kid, expelled from school for selling weed to his mates. Now his family was gone and he was under threat from an international criminal gang.

And what the fuck was happening? Danny conceding, Seth father to a son, Molly this morning, John Stanton, the Albanians. It all seemed to be happening way too fast.

He wondered what else was still to come from Molly. He hadn't had time to think. He needed a proper conversation with Danny. His doorbell rang, he checked on his phone… Danny was standing on his doorstep. He was early.

They still had a couple of hours before Molly could see them. Stevie took the opportunity to ask a few questions. "Come in, Danny. Have a seat."

Danny sat. "How are you, Stevie?"

"All over the place, mate. Believe me. Me and Seth found John Stanton. He still drinks in The White Lion and I followed him home. So, you know, that's done. Molly had nothing new on Stanton but she claims to know something about the Albanians. Your guess is as good as mine, Danny."

"Yeah, well, we'll find out soon enough. At least we're making some progress now."

Stevie was unconvinced. "Progress towards what?" His anxiety was getting the better of him. He pressed on. "I mean, where are we heading here, Danny? We work together, I'd like to know. What you said the other day, it sounded as if you were ready to give Erdi whoever the fuck his name is a clear path. I'm in this with you. We need to work out what we're trying to do. Me and Seth found John Stanton for you. Now what?"

Danny took his time. "The truth is that I don't know. I don't have the answers. We can keep an eye on Stanton now, I guess that's something, but it'll be Erdi calling the shots. I don't like what he's doing but we've never had a situation like this before. They're bigger than us, Stevie, that's a fact. What do you suggest? Do you want to go to war?"

Stevie had no suggestion. The prospect of war terrified him. He remained silent.

Danny continued. "I first thought about winding down just over a year ago, after I'd had the meeting with Erdi. I don't want to do this forever. I have to get out at some point, you too, Stevie. Maybe this is the right time."

Stevie was listening. He'd listened to Seth the previous day when Seth had pointed out that Danny doesn't walk away from anything. "Do you mean out completely? I mean, can't we make an agreement? We could map out the territory, give him a big piece. We don't have to get in each other's way."

"That's what we did when we met last time. No, Erdi's sending a different message in a different way. He could have come to see me again but he chose the John fucking Stanton route instead." Danny looked a bit lost. "It could get a bit tasty, Stevie, you'll need to keep your eyes open. Seth will get a message through, then I can have a chat with Erdi. I'll do what I can but right now I don't have a clue what's coming. So look out for yourself. You, Sean, Seth, we'll all be of interest."

Stevie was unsettled. "You look out for me, man, that's how it works. I make people laugh, sort out their coke, I don't do looking out." His comment was just panic. He had his knowledge and skills... looking out for himself wasn't amongst them. The seriousness of it all was even more apparent to him now. Hostile attention from violent criminals wasn't an attractive prospect for Stevie. He'd lay down his arms and run for his life if anyone aged ten or over became threatening.

But quite where he'd run to and what he'd do next was starting to worry him. "I'll watch out but is it all over for us? What am I going to do? Sit in my front room playing on the Xbox?

Not really. What about you? Small town shopkeeper? I don't think so, Danny."

"No, probably not." Danny was irritated. "I'm just telling you, Stevie, it's serious, potentially very dangerous. You need to know that. If you come across a miracle shop in the meantime, pop in and buy us a couple."

Stevie backed off. Danny didn't have the answers. "Listen, Danny, don't leave me out in the cold. Talk to me, man, keep talking to me. We'll go and see what Molly knows. We'll work it out." He looked across at his friend, his brother and protector, full of fear and confusion.

# FRIENDS AGAIN

Their last meeting had ended abruptly. Danny had stormed out of Molly's flat. Her determination to treat herself like shit exasperated him. Survival sex work to support heroin addiction isn't a lot of fun, and it's not an easy watch for friends and family. It's a destructive cycle, often desperate. Molly didn't like doing it and Danny wouldn't watch. Couldn't watch.

So they were both nervous. Even though months had passed, Danny would offer neither apology nor olive branch. He followed Stevie into the flat and they all sat around Molly's kitchen table. Danny's chair was wobbly. He suspected that Molly had arranged that deliberately. She had. That's how childish their conflict was, it had always been the same. But she was glad to see him.

"We'll have a row in a few minutes, Danny, but I need to talk to you first." And she smiled back at him when his miserable, mardy-arsed face produced a grin. Ice broken. "Stevie was telling me that some Albanians are involved in all this new gear."

Danny nodded. "Yeah, that's right."

"I'm in touch with an Albanian woman in Stockton. Heartbreaking story. I'm trying to work out how to help her. Well, so far I have no ideas about what I can do. It could be totally separate but I'm guessing it's not."

"Where did you meet her?" Danny was all ears.

"Yeah. We've never met. She can't leave her building. She needs help."

"What the fuck is this, Mol? What is it you're telling me?" Danny was getting agitated already.

Molly was tempted to tell him to fuck off and get his brains blown out. She was getting sight of her own agitation.

Stevie intervened. "Take your time, Mol. Just listen for a minute, Danny, man."

"It's alright, Stevie, we're all good," Molly said.

Danny softened. "Sorry, I didn't mean to be sharp, go on."

Molly continued. "She phones me when she has the chance.

Like I said, we've never met. We've been in touch for a couple of months, maybe eight or nine phone calls."

Molly swallowed, she was aware that she had their full attention and she felt even more nervous. "I've linked up with the English Collective of Prostitutes. It's a campaign group. I like to think of it as a trade union for sex workers, but yeah, it's not really. Anyway, I've left my number for other local workers to get in touch with me. If they want to. Emina first phoned me a couple of months ago. She's held in Stockton. Her English is really good. She's not really a prostitute, Danny… she's a slave."

Danny was listening now, settling down, good as gold.

Molly continued. "Danny, there are tens of thousands of slaves here in the UK. Can you believe it? It's 2022 and there are fifty million slaves in the world. Sorry, I'm losing my thread but it's incredible, it's crazy. Anyway, while I've talked to Emina, I've picked up a few snippets that might be useful for you to know."

Molly was doing okay but she suddenly felt a bit nauseous. She was about to ask for Danny's help which wouldn't be easy. Sometimes Molly needed help for all sorts of reasons. But despite her neediness, help was something that she struggled to ask for and that she struggled even more to accept. One more deep breath. "Please, Danny, I want to get Emina free. I don't know what to do. I need your help."

Danny was flabbergasted. Who the hell was he talking to here? Molly? He'd entered Molly's dingy bedsit to visit the sister who he always argued with, who was a fucked up heroin using prostitute. Now he was talking to a trade union shop steward, working for international rescue (Thunderbirds are go) trying to help an Albanian sex slave in Stockton. Funny old world.

Molly waited for a couple of seconds. She was incurably impatient. "I'm asking politely, please will you help me, Danny?" She believed in him. She knew how powerful Danny could be and she had no one else to ask.

"I can't promise, Molly, but I'll help you if I can."

It was as much as Molly could hope for. She continued. "There's a guy called Erdi… I think that's the name." She watched him respond with recognition. "They're all in Fulham Road in Stockton. Emina and two other women are locked up all day and sex slaves at night. Emina does some office work for Erdi. So you know, she knows a few things, hears what Erdi is saying. I've been over there, stood right outside. I've been a couple of times, just to have a look. I've probably been within fifty feet of Emina. It felt weird, you know, so close and yet…"

Danny was starting to enjoy his new working relationship with Molly. "This is gold dust, Mol. Anything else?"

"Emina thinks that Erdi's married. He lives in Yarm." She watched Danny and Stevie exchange a look across the table.

"Where in Yarm? What's the address?" Stevie was excited. Danny could pop over to Yarm and do whatever one drugs baron does to his rival. Then they could all get back to working comfortably again.

"I don't know." Molly was ahead of them both. "He works on Fulham Road. He lives in Yarm. For fuck's sake, it's not rocket science. Everyday he leaves work, gets into his Mercedes and drives home. There's only one route, Stevie. Park your Corsa around the corner from Fulham Road and follow him home."

Danny closed his eyes, then released a long lung full of air. Game changed. This past couple of weeks he'd been on the back foot, caught napping if truth be told. It had felt bad. He'd chastised himself but with this information he was back in the box seat, back in position. Almost.

"Thanks, Mol. Is there any more?"

"Emina lives on the top floor, above a café. She said it's number 12 on the café door. They have red curtains." That was pretty well everything she'd gained from Emina. "She speaks really good English. She used to be a teacher."

Danny looked at Stevie. "Another day at the movies. I'll come with you."

Molly got the impression that her usefulness had ended. "Oi, never mind the fucking movies." To her amazement, Danny didn't take the bait.

"We'll find out where he lives, Molly. We'll find out who he's married to. That'll shift the balance. I don't know what else yet but I'll help Emina if I can. I owe you, Molly. Big time." Danny had never seemed to value anything that Molly had said before. "I don't suppose you know what model of Mercedes he drives?"

"It's black." Molly's offence evaporated.

The boys got to their feet, preparing to leave, maybe park up around the corner from Fulham Road.

Then Molly had a thought. "You better give me your number, Danny."

It was a day for miracles… he gave her his number.

# OPEN DOOR, OPEN MIC

Maisie had butterflies in her stomach. It was just a couple of songs, a low key open mic event. She wasn't nervous about singing, she just hoped that Sean arrived on time and sober. She checked her phone and she looked towards the door. Nothing. Then suddenly someone sat beside her.

It was Sue Bellamy. "Hello, Maisie, haven't seen you for years. Are you okay?"

"Hi, Sue. Yeah, I'm fine. You?" Maisie replied.

"Yes, I'm good, I'm singing tonight. Are you singing, Maisie?"

"Yeah, just a couple of songs if my guitar player turns up. It's been a while since you and I last shared a stage, Sue. Who'd have thought?"

"I know, amazing! Listen, Maisie, a word in your ear. I hear your John's in league with the Albanians. He loves his notoriety, doesn't he? Seriously though, Maisie, I hope he knows what he's doing. Those guys don't take prisoners. I'm sorry, Maisie, but you know, I thought you might want the heads up."

"No, no. I appreciate it, Sue. And I hope all goes well tonight. Break a leg, babe. I look forward to having a listen."

Maisie was a bit fazed. She watched Sue return to her seat and then saw Sean making his way to the table. He had his guitar but something wasn't right.

Sean sank heavily on to a seat beside Maisie. The right side of his face was swollen and strangely coloured, just a few hours along a journey towards a fully formed black eye.

"Who's done that?" Asked Maisie.

Sean chuckled, then winced. "It was your brother, the one you never told me about. John."

"Why?

"Hmm, interesting question." It was the best Sean could do.

"Hmm, interesting answer, Sean. How badly are you hurt? Are we still playing tonight?"

"Well, I could try, but not really. I was asleep. Your brother opened the car door and thumped me. I've taken paracetamol but I've got a monster headache."

"And you've been drinking. Fuck, I was looking forward to tonight. Come on, I'll walk you home, we'll have coffee. We need to have a chat."

Maisie felt for him. He was in pain, but she was exasperated. She'd had to grow up with John but she had nothing to do with him now. Sean, fucking dickhead. He'd always been the same, drawn to the wrong people. No comfort for Maisie there. But she wanted to know what had brought Sean and her brother to blows.

They resumed their conversation in Sean's living room. Maisie made coffee and had a proper look at Sean's injury. "No broken bones, no cuts. John must be losing his touch. So, I have to ask, Sean… what is your connection with John?"

Sean took a breath. "Your brother's working with an Albanian gang, selling drugs all over Teesside. I assume that I was targeted because I'm a friend of Danny Hutton."

"Christ… John. What is he doing? I bumped into an old school friend tonight. She said the same thing. I know nothing, Sean. I never speak to John. We don't get on but my little sister still lives with him. You need to tell your big mate Danny Hutton to get up to speed. If my fucking brother's got the drop on him…" She paused for a moment. "Well, he's not all he's cracked up to be – John's a drongo." Maisie heard alarm bells. "I'll have to go to the house. I need to check on June. I really want to get her out. She can come and live with me."

As a young child, Maisie had done her best to shield June but with limited success. She'd had her hands full protecting herself. When she and John were growing up, she'd answered her big brother's attempts to bully her, punch for punch. She had been fierce and unyielding, squeezing her small bony hands into fists to stand up to John. She'd scratched and bitten, screamed into his ears, spat in his face. John was two years older and twice his sister's size, but he didn't need any of the trouble Maisie was giving. Out on the streets, getting that kind of attention from your kid sister wasn't the image that John wished to promote.

He learned to ignore Maisie, until he was fifteen and inflated with testosterone, when he'd punched her in the mouth. He'd given no warning but Maisie was always alert, she'd swayed back defensively although not far enough to fully evade her brother's fist. Her top lip had split against her teeth but she'd stayed on her feet and looked up at John, shocked and full of fury. John had seen blood trickling down her chin. He'd laughed for a second, pleased after all those years to have finally crushed Maisie's spirited resistance.

That was always a problem with John… he celebrated victory too soon. While her brother was enjoying the sweet fruit of victory, Maisie focused. She could taste blood, she had a fucking mouthful of it. She wasn't going to scratch and bite, they weren't kids anymore, but she did spit, a good gobful of blood and saliva, delivered without a trace of feminine charm. John just had time to look down at the specks of bloody spittle across the front of his shirt before Maisie's right foot found his testicles. Plum pie.

Maisie had fled the violence of her family when she was sixteen years old, and then she'd worked all hours to build a new life. And now it was Sean, of all people, who was sending her back home. "I've asked her before, poor June, she's frightened of John but she's frightened to move."

Sean was all guilt and repentance. "I'm sorry, Maisie. About tonight. I was going to ask you about John. But I can't tell Danny. I fucked up. I shouldn't have been out this morning, he won't be pleased. But I'll take you over to Stockton if you want to go for June."

# LOOKING FOR ERDI

They were parked up in Stevie's Corsa. Stevie was pleased that he and Danny had talked the previous day, but in truth he was still just as troubled and uncertain as he'd been twenty-four hours earlier. It seemed strange to Stevie that in these circumstances they should feel the need to follow Erdi.

"Why are we doing this, Danny? Seriously, man, I'm here with you again in the car and we're on the watch, taking in a new movie with a car chase. Why exactly are we doing this?"

"I'm going to meet with Erdi. I don't know when. The bastard's keeping me waiting. I'm taking a chance, Stevie. I can't see any other way. I don't want any of us getting hurt. I don't suppose he'll be generous, he clearly wants us gone. So I'll have to talk to him, see what he has to say. I don't have anything to work with, Stevie. He holds the cards. I want to know where he lives."

"That's good, you know, meeting with him. I get it, Danny, if we have to move aside. It's just that I don't really get why I'm here today. Whatever." Danny's answer hadn't helped him. He felt the need to change topic. "Did you know that Seth's got a little boy?"

Danny's head swivelled to face Stevie. He couldn't believe what he'd heard from his friend. "What? You mean like a child?"

Stevie was laughing, suddenly he was happy. "Yeah, man. Seth's a dad. He's called him Daniel. Fuck knows why! I'm his uncle, so are you, and Sean. He told me not to say anything but you know, given the circumstances, I wanted to mention it. Fucking crazy, man… Seth's a family man. Who'd have thought?"

Danny was really struggling to process this information. He didn't have a compartment in his brain for father stuff, he couldn't form an image, he couldn't conceptualise Seth as a man with a conventional family, as part of a couple with a child. "Wow, that's shocked me, I had no idea." Danny really was shocked, almost speechless, as he tried to update his image of Seth. He felt light-headed. What had Seth done? What had he become? Had he somehow stepped into the world where normal people lived? "When did this happen? I mean, how old is Daniel?"

"He's thirteen months. It's brilliant, Danny. I can't wait to meet him. And Jen. We should have a party, get everyone together." Stevie paused and then refocused. They both watched the traffic for a while, having missed the previous ten minutes. "But what I was trying to say was that Seth, he needs a career change, Danny… he's got Daniel and Jen to consider. Seth needs to go and do something else. He'll be fine, Sean'll be the same as ever, Beth's got the shops, Mol, fucking hell, Danny, Molly's moving along. They're all growing up. It's just you and me, Danny… we're the ones with no new life." Stevie didn't seem to be too worried, but he'd made a fair point.

Danny was unable to share Stevie's joyful reception to Seth's new family. He felt uncomfortable. "Have you told Beth about Daniel?"

"No, it's just you and me. I'm supposed to be keeping quiet. You tell her if you want, Danny, yeah, tell Beth to organise a get together, invite us all. I want to be Uncle Stevie. I want to meet my nephew."

Danny was starting to absorb the information and he was happy in a way, pleased that Seth had surprised them and fair enough, best to move on from the hard drugs and violence, for Seth for sure, maybe for them all. "I can't believe he hasn't told us, Stevie. A baby boy. Bloody hell, I didn't see that one coming. And yeah, I'm not sure about today, I just want to make sure we all get out in one piece and it won't do any harm to know where Erdi lives. There's nothing else I can tell you."

Something in Stevie had started to shift. In the absence of viable strategy, he'd moved towards desperation and fantasy. He'd spent the previous evening dreaming about alternative futures. "We could go travelling, Danny. Fuck off to Thailand or Cambodia, have a gap year, see the world while we plan a new future."

Danny smiled, His business might be lost, but not Stevie, his brother. It got dark. They'd have to try again tomorrow, maybe pay more attention to the traffic.

# PARTY PLANS

Stevie was all over the place. He'd spent three hours in the Corsa with Danny. They'd been to the cinema and managed to miss the film. Either Erdi had taken an inexplicable detour on his way home, or they'd missed him while they were talking. The talking and the missing. Both had contributed to Stevie's scrambled brain. A liberal sprinkling of THC may have played a small part.

His conversation with Danny in the car had left him confused. Their business enterprise appeared to be coming to an end and although neither he nor Danny had any ideas about what might come next, they had both begun to accept the possibility. That in itself was surprising. Their little Teesside class A drugs empire had given them their adult lives, their wealth and their identities. Danny Hutton looked set to be pushed aside, overpowered, half ready to accept enforced redundancy.

Maybe their adaptability was a gift from broken homes – coping with change, bad news and disappointment, just another day in the lives of looked after children.

But it wasn't the Danny Hutton that Stevie knew. Seth had said the same thing a few days ago. Was it just a few days since he'd talked with Seth? It felt much longer. When Danny was threatened, he never walked away. That's what Seth had said and that was playing on Stevie's mind. Something wasn't right with Danny, his attitude, his acceptance, his hesitations. Stevie didn't know what to make of it all. He decided to phone Beth.

Stevie and Beth had almost missed each other at Malton Court. She went off to live with her mum two months after his arrival. But they'd built a relationship over the past few years and they got along well together. It was only when there was some sensitive family business that he noticed some hesitation. He felt it now, especially as he needed to talk about Danny but he phoned, he'd find a way.

Beth answered her phone. "Hey, Stevie, have you got my fella with you?"

Not quite the start Stevie had hoped for. "No, isn't he with you?" Obviously not. "He'll be at the gym." Stevie was thrown, already he felt he'd made a bad decision. He didn't know whether Danny talked to Beth about his work. He didn't know whether Danny talked to her about anything. He felt unsure about what he should say. That was always a precarious position for Stevie, when he didn't know what to say, he might say anything. He managed to stay quiet.

Beth noted the silence. "I wanted to see him tonight," she said. "Is something wrong?"

Stevie was back at his flat. He'd had a smoke, he'd got himself comfortable, settled and warm after a couple of hours sitting in a cold car. Nevertheless, Beth's direct question unsettled him. He started to sweat. He was standing in the space between Danny and Beth. He didn't want to be there, he needed to move. "Hey, what about Seth? Amazing." He'd bottled it.

Beth was a bit confused. Stevie was no trouble but he wasn't in the habit of phoning her and she noted his evasion. She appreciated Seth's qualities and characteristics but in Beth's experience 'amazing' didn't fit the profile. "What about Seth?"

Stevie was aware that he was about to betray Seth's confidence for the second time but hey, it felt like good news week. "He's a family man. He's with Jen, they've got a baby boy and guess what... he's called Daniel." He really ought to have left Seth to deliver his own news in his own time but too late now. Stevie would make it up to him, maybe buy him a coffee.

Beth was stunned. "Really? Seth has a baby? How old is he?"

Stevie's discomfort was alleviated. He was back in his new Uncle Stevie buzz. As soon as he thought about Daniel (who he was yet to lay eyes on) he felt happy. Weird. "He's thirteen months, already a decent footy player, I reckon. Listen Beth, it's been a funny old week, there's a few things going on, we need to get together. All of us."

Something was happening to Stevie. The events and conversations during the previous several days had penetrated – he was affected. Erdi, John fucking Stanton, Molly, Seth, Danny, all on the move, everything changing.

He wasn't fumbling anymore. He delivered his next comments with authority. "We'll have a little party for Seth. We'll need a few days to get organised, a week on Sunday, Beth, at your's. Two o'clock in the afternoon. Get a cake, make some jelly for little Daniel. You tell Sean and Molly, and I'll speak to Seth. I'll have to phone him, I have to be somewhere tomorrow. I'll be seeing Danny again, so I'll tell him about the party. I'll see you in a few days. Beth?"

Beth was taken aback. Stevie sounded like he was taking charge. Suddenly she felt more worried about Danny than ever before, and she felt an urgent need to see him. Her instinct was to accept Stevie's instructions without question.

"Alright, I'll be ready. I have the shop open on Sundays but I'll work something out with my interior designer." Beth paused. She was worried about Elizabeth. "I might invite her actually, maybe her husband as well but that's fine, she's lovely. I wanted to introduce her to Danny. Yeah, that'll be lovely, Stevie. I haven't seen Molly for weeks."

Stevie had stepped forward for a minute. He wanted to make sure that they all gathered together. Seth's family introductions were part of the motivation but there was something more than that, although he didn't fully understand his own suggestion. There was a feeling of urgency, a gathering storm, a need to be amongst friends, to be in the heart of his own fragmented family.

He ended the call to Beth and he realised that he'd have to front up with Danny when they made their second attempt to find Erdi on his way home from work. He'd taken charge impressively when he talked Beth. It had been an uncharacteristic and inspired moment of leadership. It lasted for long enough to gain Beth's support, then it was over and it dawned upon Stevie that there were a couple of things he'd need to tell Danny... he'd have to find the right moment.

# FINDING ERDI

It was twenty-four hours later and they were parked in the same space, watching with better attention. It was new territory for Danny and for Stevie. They were half way out of the room but still hadn't really thought about closing the door. They were talking about conceding to a stronger rival... perhaps they would give everything to Erdi. Just as soon as they'd followed him home and taken a look at whoever he was married to.

Danny was a hard man to read. He'd stayed at the gym, ignoring Stevie's prompt to bring Beth up to speed with Seth's family circumstances.

They'd been in position for almost an hour. Stevie was uncomfortable. He still hadn't managed to confess, the right moment yet to reveal itself.

He went ahead regardless. "I thought you were in Saltburn these days."

Danny was grumpy. "I am mostly."

Stevie was still uncomfortable. "But not last night. I phoned Beth."

Danny was more than grumpy. "You didn't tell her about Seth, did you?" Danny wasn't asking, he was simply stating what he assumed to be a fact.

In all the time that Danny and Stevie had been friends and business partners, Danny had never hit him, never even given him a threatening look. But in this moment, Stevie wondered if he might have pushed his luck too far.

"Yeah, I told her. She's arranging the party. A week on Sunday at two." The same unconvincing bluster he always used when he feared that his luck had run out.

They both saw the black Mercedes at exactly the same moment. Stevie thanked the god he'd never believed in. He sparked up the Corsa and they began to follow their man. Erdi was alone and in view, three cars ahead, easy to follow. It was almost dark already.

Stevie decided to push his luck even further. "How are things with you and Beth?"

Danny ignored the question as Stevie had expected. It was Danny's first defence against difficult questions – ignore the question, then watch the asker reconsider. It worked ninety nine times out a hundred. Once in a blue moon, Sean might have a second go.

They kept a safe distance behind Erdi.

Stevie pursued his death wish a step further. "I've never stayed with anyone, Danny. I don't seem to get very close with my girlfriends. I won't let women get close to me, not just women, pretty well everyone. I like the look of it with other people, being together with someone, holding hands, but no, anyway, I just wondered about how you get on with it, you and Beth."

Erdi's appearance was well timed, Danny's irritation was almost appeased, his focus had shifted and he was beginning to relax, Stevie had moved on, he was talking about himself. But then he threw it back to Danny again, who flashed an angry glance across to his driver.

Stevie was concentrating on Erdi's Mercedes but he felt Danny's glance. "Fuck, I thought you were going to hit me there," said Stevie, still keeping half an eye on his passenger.

"So did I," lied Danny. "It's not easy, Stevie. Beth's pretty good, she's better than me. Fucking hell, Stevie. You know who I am." His anger had evaporated and he surprised himself and his driver by answering the question. "I'm trying my best but I don't think I can do it. I don't think I can be with someone. I'm damaged goods, Stevie. I don't want to disappoint Beth. I can't tell her. I can't tell her I'm leaving and I can't tell her I'm staying."

Erdi took a right turn into a housing estate out in the suburban sprawl surrounding what had once been a small North Yorkshire market town. Stevie was watching with full concentration, they needed to stay with their target all the way to his secret world.

Danny hadn't finished.

Stevie still couldn't quite believe that he'd started.

"I think I found my dad a few days back. Me and Sean were parked up, just watching the world. Anyway, I saw him and I shoved his fucking head into a wall. That's pretty fucked up,

Stevie, not really the thing to do when you bump into your dad. I don't think that's what normal people are expected to do. Slam their old fella's head into a brick wall? I don't know, Stevie, I don't know who he was and I don't know who I am either. I have no father and no mother. Believe me, Stevie, I'm a bastard. I must have come from somewhere. I don't know where. A bad place, I guess. I'm fit for nothing, except for dealing shit in a dark street. And it looks as if that's going now. There'll be nothing left."

Erdi took another turn, then he signalled left and pulled onto a drive alongside a detached house. It was only just detached, a metre from identical houses on both sides. There was a garage but he left his Mercedes on the drive, a message to the neighbours, daddy's home.

Stevie drove twenty metres past the house and pulled over. He turned the engine off and released his seat belt.

Stevie's set of unexpected conversations had extended further. For the third time in less than a week, he was hearing a friend starting to tell a story. Just stories, stories that had waited for their telling, unsure of their voice, emerging fearfully yet with courage, with Stevie a confused witness.

"You're Danny Hutton. Just in case you were still wondering." Stevie looked across at Danny. "You're my best mate, Danny. I'm here because of you." Stevie was starting to get the hang of this real conversation shit.

Danny moved on so quickly that it appeared as if Stevie's comments had been missed. Seth had texted him the previous evening and passed on a message from Erdi giving the time and place for a meeting. "I've got a meeting with Erdi arranged in a few days, maybe he'll kill me. I'm not frightened and I don't care if I die, it's nothing to me, this fuck up of a life. But going home to Beth in Saltburn tonight, that scares me, Stevie. I know how to fight and I think I'll know how to die, but I don't know how to be with Beth."

These were familiar thoughts for Danny. For more than five years he'd bounced between the gym and Beth, feeling unable and unworthy. The good times were easily forgotten, the struggles always loomed large. "So there you go, Stevie, that's how things are going with me and Beth. I need you to be back here on Monday morning, before eight. Bring a flask and some food, stay all day, watch every minute, see who comes out and who goes in. Get everything you can, then do it all again on Tuesday, I need to know more than Erdi wants me to know, before I meet him. Get me the goods, Stevie."

Stevie wanted to say something. He felt an enormous wave of sadness. He might have drowned. "Okay." That was all he could manage, his voice small. He started the car and drove Danny back into town.

In their confessions they'd each admitted a problem with the eternal dream, human closeness, and, in their confessions, they'd become closer.

# SPREADING THE NEWS

He'd arrived at 7am and was parked at a discreet distance. The Corsa was much more than a car. It was an object of affection, an indulgence. Stevie had wasted good money on a few pimpy enhancements — a set of alloys, a slight tint to the windows and a new set of seats with deep bottom of the ocean blue upholstery. Nevertheless, even with the Bose speakers and the racing green respray, it was an aging Vauxhall Corsa.

It held a thousand memories, echoes of love and laughter. It had transported Stevie far from youthful innocence. It had made him important and it had made him feel important. The Corsa had always been there for him, offering a thousand possibilities. But in the end, it had driven him to a life in crime.

Stevie was unable to think rationally about the car. It was an emotional connection. He kept it in mint condition, outings once or twice each week just to keep everything lubricated and warm. Mostly these days he kept it garaged at his house in the suburbs. He had a new Porsche 911 Speedster for everyday use around town but for cinema duties he always went back to the Corsa. For Stevie this was a luxury car. It was a privilege to sit cocooned in the deep blue ocean driver's seat. To passers-by it was a no interest, nobody car, invisible when it was thirty yards up the road from your house.

At eight thirty, just as Stevie finished his cold coffee, the front door opened and out they came. Come to daddy. Erdi, a young woman, two small children, both male, dressed in short grey trousers and blue school blazers. Result. Stevie watched Erdi kiss his wife and then each of his children, before getting into the Mercedes. He drove away, leaving the others, the family, out on the drive.

The woman opened the garage and reversed her Toyota Aygo out on to the drive. She got the boys, in their smart school uniforms, into the car. Stevie followed. He watched the kids being dropped off and escorted into school and he followed the Toyota back to the house. Stevie had the goods. The wife, the two children, the house, the school. Power, waiting to be unleashed.

He phoned Seth, he explained his circumstances and he gave instructions that would allow Seth to join him without any unnecessary drama. Seth understood that there was a crisis and agreed without hesitation but with trepidation. Twenty minutes later he was in Stevie's forever impressive Vauxhall Corsa, in a personality free area of Yarm, with two coffees.

Stevie opened the car door and for the first time in many years, he greeted Seth without mentioning coffee. "Seth, great to see you, man. Come on in, how you doing?"

Seth was a bit shocked and slightly disappointed. He'd spent half of the previous week rehearsing a new response. He'd never been this ready. He understood Stevie's extraordinary welcome as a bad sign and his trepidation upgraded to alarm. "Yeah, I'm all over the place, Stevie. I bought some coffee." Still nothing... fuck.

Stevie accepted his latte with good grace. "You're a better man than me, Seth, thanks for coming."

The aroma from the coffee filled the car and they sat quietly for a moment, watching the world through the windscreen.

Stevie gave voice to his thoughts. "Yeah, it's all a bit fucked up as far as I can see, Seth. I'm watching Erdi's house, very interesting as it turns out, major leverage. Seth, I want you to know that Daniel is a consideration as far as I'm concerned. We need to get Danny up to pace, Seth. We need to take stock."

This was Stevie's tactic, convince Seth that consideration for Daniel underpinned everything, win some favour and then tell him he'd spilt the beans all over town.

"We need to get together, all of us... you know, catch up and stuff. And yeah, Seth, you know when we talked about Jen and my main man Daniel, who I'm guessing can't wait to meet his Uncle Stevie...well, I let it slip with Danny."

Stevie pushed the left half of his bottom lip up, so that it covered half of his top lip, and he bit lightly on the right side of his bottom lip with his upper teeth. At the same time he raised his right eyebrow and half closed his left eye. It was his best attempt to blend contrition and confession. Seth was disarmed before he'd loaded.

"You look fucking weird." He hadn't meant to say it out loud, there you go.

That was as good as Stevie could have hoped for. "Yeah, I'm sorry, Seth. But since I'd already spilled the beans, I told Beth as well. Last night."

Seth was listening. "Right."

Stevie continued, in for a penny. "And I phoned Mol and you won't believe it, Seth, but it slipped out again. So basically, mate, everybody knows."

Seth believed him, then he corrected him. "You haven't told Sean."

"No, that's true enough, but Beth's told him."

Seth didn't mind at all. He'd been struggling with the prospect of updating them all about his family. Problem solved.

Stevie noted his friend's indifference and went for the jackpot. "Yeah, she had to tell him because of the party."

"What party?"

"A week on Sunday, at Beth's house in Saltburn. Fucking Saltburn, man, we're going up in the world. She's got a garden and shit. Daniel will love it. So will Jen. We want to welcome her into the family, Seth, and we all want to meet our nephew, little trooper, he's already got aunts and uncles all over the place." Stevie had no idea how Seth would respond.

"I don't know Stevie. I was expecting a different conversation, I thought maybe we were going to war." Seth was fine. He wasn't sure about Jen but why not, all of the introductions done in one afternoon. "But I don't see why not, if Jen's okay, yeah great."

Seth wasn't a fast thinker but he was a thinker. He really had been expecting the call to arms. He'd thought about the rival operators and he knew Danny well enough. He was worried for his friends and for himself. Even still, with a young child to consider, he'd answer the call. He couldn't refuse Danny, he couldn't let him go forward alone. But he was afraid and he was hoping that Danny would walk away.

And of course he'd been thinking about his family. He had two families now. He was part of both but there needed to be some separation. He'd given so much of himself for Danny. But he'd given a big part of himself to Jen. Seth was taking his first steps in a different direction, he was growing away, he was developing. He was a father.

He'd experienced a tension within himself, holding his two families apart, wondering what Jen would make of them all, and what they'd all think about her and Daniel. That's all he'd needed to do. He should've thought of it sooner… just tell Stevie, then tell him to keep it quiet, job done. A few days later, the whole world knows and there's a party.

# ALL THE BETHS

Beth first met Elizabeth soon after the Table Leg opened early in 2021. There were many exciting changes in Beth's life, a new shop and a new house, a whole new life in a quaint Victorian seaside town.

Elizabeth became a frequent visitor to the shop. She and Rob were approaching their wedding and she bought a few pieces to add some life and colour to Rob's grey and masculine home.

She and Beth chatted. Elizabeth noticed that Beth had great taste and everything in the shop was bang on trend. When Elizabeth had free time, she would go to the shop. They spoke the same language and they talked for hours.

Elizabeth and Beth launched Table Leg Interior Design as a joint venture, business partners in an offshoot from the shop. The new business quickly began to thrive. Elizabeth married Rob and moved into her husband's house. She and Beth got along well. They both had worry and doubt about their partners, but nothing was ever said… their dialogue was focused on starting their business. They always had so much work stuff to talk about, the personal domain would have to wait.

But as time passed, with their relationship and their enterprise established, Elizabeth had allowed Beth to see something more of herself, some vulnerability. Nothing specific, just the mention of Rob's name with a troubled face, testing Beth's response. She was careful and offered her clues in a way that left Beth with a choice. She could let the remarks slip by or she could pay attention. Each time that Elizabeth gave a clue, she would take a quick look across at Beth, eager to read her colleague's response.

Beth was a perceptive woman. She'd heard the early warnings and she could feel that something more was coming. She didn't have to wait for long.

For Elizabeth, work was protection, a place of refuge. She'd always been happy to leave her troubles at home. But after a particularly abusive verbal attack from Rob, Elizabeth had been unable to shake it off. She had been visibly upset. Beth had asked if she was okay, Elizabeth had said that her husband could be a bastard.

That was all she'd said. It seemed to help her regain her composure. She'd apologised to Beth and they got back to work. But in the days that followed, Elizabeth started to unload and thankfully her friend was receptive. Beth was listening. Elizabeth told her that she'd got into a hole and that she was working out how to end her marital relationship.

She didn't give too much detail. She felt embarrassed. She didn't like Rob's behaviour, but for much of the time she was blaming herself. She'd made a bad decision to marry him and now she was putting up with his appalling treatment. Elizabeth felt trapped and she feared negative judgement as she revealed to Beth the sad secrets in her home life.

Nevertheless, she had started to open up which brought some relief. She'd been alone with her trouble, now she had a friend. She told Beth that Rob was quite controlling and that he could be unkind when he got into a mood.

Elizabeth had watched Rob getting more irritable and she'd noticed that he was spending less time at the unit where he and Mark operated their business. She'd asked him if there were problems. He'd mumbled something inaudible and left the room.

She had developed expertise as her husband's observer. She needed to pick up early signals to guide her own strategy. She could see that her husband was stressed out, his behaviour was changing, something was wrong and Elizabeth was suffering the consequences.

For the eight months of their marriage, Rob had kept some parameters around his cruelty. He delivered verbal and emotional abuse effectively but, until very recently, he'd never laid hands on her. Then it changed… he crossed a line. First it was a shove, then it progressed further. He'd grab her wrists or her arms, hold her so that she couldn't move.

He really gripped tightly. He'd left a few bruises and patches of angry red skin. Elizabeth had known for months that she disliked her husband but now she was frightened of him. She started to wear long sleeves. It wasn't a good place to be, finding ways to disguise her partner's violence.

Normally Rob was fastidious. Everything would be in its place, no detail overlooked but not so much these days. His concentration was slipping, he seemed distracted. Elizabeth took the opportunity to look at some of his correspondence. She was shocked to discover the size of his overdraft and horrified by his mortgage arrears. They had reached a level which had led the lender to threaten repossession.

Elizabeth had been upset that Rob never mentioned the possibility of re-registering the property in joint names when they were newly married. She didn't mind so much now. It was his house and his mortgage. She hoped the solicitors would agree.

Elizabeth opened a new and intimidating dialogue. She told him that she'd found a bank statement and asked questions about the business. She'd thought about it carefully, maybe she could help him, maybe he'd be glad to share the burden.

He got angry, accused her of invading his privacy. He grabbed her upper arms and shook her while he shouted abuse. He shook so hard that he lost his hold and Elizabeth tried to escape but Rob grabbed again. He held her wrists, squeezed hard and twisted her skin till she was bruised and burned. She felt the pain and she felt her fear. Rob shoved her away. He seemed satisfied.

Twenty minutes later he apologised. That was unusual. Rob had administered his maltreatment routinely, they were long past the apology stage. Then they talked, even more unusual. Elizabeth surprised herself, offering her support and suggesting that they arrange appointments with the bank and the building society. Rob nodded his assent. Let her try. Why not?

She went into the Table Leg the next morning. Beth caught sight of some bruising on her wrists. Elizabeth tried to tug her shirt sleeve back into place, but it was too late.

Beth had waited patiently, giving Elizabeth the space that she needed. But at that point, she voiced her concern without hesitation. "Jesus Christ, Elizabeth, what've you done to your arms?" She was guessing the answer even as she asked the question. "Has Rob done that?"

Elizabeth attempted to defend him. "Rob's under enormous pressure, Beth. Sales have dried up, the business is failing. That can't be easy for him. It's no wonder that he's been bad tempered."

Beth had always found the courage to reach out when someone needed help. She held Elizabeth's hand and she lifted the sleeve back to look properly at the marks. "And he's taking it out on you. What do you want to do?"

Elizabeth straightened her back, re-covered her bruises. "I don't know. I didn't know about any of it, Beth. Rob's in trouble. I can't leave him now." She looked up at her business partner, hoping in vain for affirmation. "I'll have to try and help. We'll go to the bank, see if we can work something out. What else can I do?"

Beth tried once more. "Lots of people have money worries, lots of men have problems at work, my Danny included, but you won't find bruises on my arms, Elizabeth. I can give you help if you need it, you can come and stay at my house if you want to. I mean it. We can shut the shop and go right now to collect your things. I think that's the way to go."

"Thanks, Beth, you're too kind. I'll be fine. Honestly, I'll be alright. I think we've sort of cleared the air." Elizabeth tried to believe her own words. As it turned out, she was fine… until the next time.

# BROKEN PROMISES

Beth hadn't seen Danny for over two weeks. He'd been at the gym since the day after his meeting with the boys, the morning after their unexpected sex.

It didn't surprise Beth. Their intimacy had reached a new level... he'd probably be gone forever. Beth understood and normally she'd have waited until he was ready to face her again, but she also felt concerned. Danny had told her that there was a new threat in town, and she'd had conversations with Molly and Stevie which had disturbed her. Danny was absent, and Beth once again was worried that she'd lose him. A week later she was a week late. Beth's menstrual cycle was reliably regular. Whoops.

Beth had taken her contraceptive pills since she and Danny first started having sex. She'd continued for a couple of months into their period of abstinence, but then she decided to give her body a holiday. There was no sign of Danny's interest returning. She took the pill until she ran out but she didn't get a repeat prescription.

She hadn't expected the resumption. She'd surprised herself.

She did three tests, all positive, all confirming what she already knew. Bloody hell. It seemed incredible... one unprotected night and bingo. It was an accident, an unplanned pregnancy, but Beth's child was wanted, and would be cherished. It would be a child with a good mother and hopefully some sort of part-time father.

That would be a matter for Danny. Beth was surprised. She was a bit anxious about how he would react but she was over the moon. It was a moment of enormous significance, the answer to a deep calling, she was more than ready. The mother that Beth had always been would be exalted.

Beth knew there was risk. She knew that most of the people who maltreat children were themselves badly treated as children. For some people such experiences are a stimulus to promote attentive and thoughtful parenting for the next generation, but it could go either way.

Similar thoughts had entered her mind when she heard about

Seth's little boy. Danny and Seth, big lads, gym buddies, both with their insecurities, neither of them knew their fathers, both with violent tendencies, neither of them at ease, both quite risky prospective fathers.

And of course Danny had been clear from day one. He'd always maintained his message – no children – right through their relationship and she'd promised him more than once, there would be no children. Her promises were broken now and when she looked at her tests, she couldn't stop the thought as it invaded her mind… would Danny be able, would he be safe?

She had to think about it. Beth could never forgive herself if she exposed her own child to an unworthy father. Not after her own experiences. So she allowed her thoughts, her doubts and her fears and she found some solace. She looked back, remembering Danny's rage as a young boy, his struggles, and she examined her own assessment, with her instincts as a mother who must look after her child. Danny was hard work but, for all of his struggles, he'd never shown malice or bad intention with her. She felt he'd be okay and she hoped with all of her heart.

She'd made up her mind to confide in Elizabeth, who had her own relationship problems, but when Elizabeth arrived late for work with fresh bruising around her wrists, Beth reviewed her intentions. "What exactly is he doing to you, Elizabeth?"

Elizabeth held out her arms. "Just this. And shouting. He has strong hands, he squeezes and twists. I thought it had stopped. He's under enormous pressure. But that's it, he hasn't hit me. Once he has a hold of my wrists, he knows that I can't move."

Beth shook her head, jumbled her thoughts. Elizabeth distressed, Danny absent and a baby starting to grow inside her. "Everything I said to you last time still holds, Elizabeth. Come and stay at mine."

"No, no. Thanks, Beth. Rob and I talked last night. Like never before, something is shifting, I'm sure of it. He's never opened up like that before. I married him. I made a commitment, I can't just walk. I'm going to give it another try, So's Rob. He promised."

Rob and Elizabeth weren't the first couple to try again, to tell themselves that the impossible might become possible if they could simply try a little harder. Beth remained unconvinced but she stayed quiet.

'*I can't just walk.*' That's what Elizabeth had said. Danny had said something similar about his work. What was the problem? If you don't want to stay, then leave. Surely it is a simple thing to understand. Why should leaving your mistakes behind be so difficult?

The shop was doing good trade. Beth waited for an hour, allowing Elizabeth to become settled. Elizabeth's homelife was clearly problematic but she continued to pull her weight at work, and she agreed to manage the shop while Beth took some time out.

Then she phoned Danny. She was desperate to tell him the news but he was at the gym every night. It was only a couple of days until the get together for Seth and his newly revealed family and she still hadn't seen Danny. She phoned him in the middle of the morning and asked him to drive her out onto the moors. It was a glorious day, cold and sunny.

Just over an hour later, they were out of the car and walking through glorious moorland, both of them happy to be there, taking in the space and the quiet. They found a rock and sat for a while.

Beth had found the right place and she hoped, the right moment. She hadn't realised how nervous she was feeling until she heard herself start the wrong conversation. "Elizabeth, my interior designer, has problems with her husband. He's hurting her, Danny. Her wrists looked red raw this morning."

Danny wasn't qualified to give relationship advice. "What do you want me to do, Beth?"

"No, nothing, it's just that she had new bruises today. It's on my mind, that's all. They're going to try again. I wanted to talk about something else." She felt like a nervous teenager, unsure of herself, unsure of her impact in the world. "Danny, I'm pregnant. Congratulations, you're going to be a father."

That was pretty well it, she'd told him. She waited. They were both facing south-east. They were up pretty high, it was a clear day, and they could see for miles across the moors and dales. Just Danny and Beth and the sheep and the wildlife. No better place on Earth to receive unexpected news.

Danny was surprised, that was his first emotion. It was quickly superseded by a couple of seconds of mental paralysis, then he spoke. "Wow, Beth, that's big news. Are you okay?"

He looked at her, swallowed and inside himself he panicked but he kept it hidden. He could have a good panic later when he was alone.

Beth smiled. "Yes, I'm fine. I'm glad that I'm pregnant. It's wonderful." Beth wanted to let him know that the big news was also good news and she wanted to be brief, she wanted to hear from Danny. Danny had never indicated any change in his position. She really didn't have a clue how he would react.

But unintentionally, she spoke again. "It was that night after the board meeting. I stopped taking the pill six months ago, Danny. We weren't having any sex and I took the opportunity to have a break. I just thought it'd be a good idea. Anyway, you know what happened, Christ, you made a hell of a noise when you came that night."

"Beth, please, you can't just say things like that." Danny was squirming with intense embarrassment, despite the accuracy of Beth's observation.

Beth suddenly felt a bit more grown up. "Oh for fuck's sake, Danny. Chill out. It was lovely. It was the perfect way to get pregnant." She'd thought about it and she absolutely believed it. It had been a beautiful moment. Danny had been highly aroused, tense and needy, a tight spring desperate for release.

But there was more than that. Danny was a young man who needed to develop an understanding of parental love. And Beth had a sense that this might be a healing gift to her troubled man. She believed in Danny. Together they could care for a child, be a real family.

Danny smiled. He turned towards her now to face her. He was

drifting amongst a range of unknown emotions and as he drifted, he experienced a sense of wonder. Beth was pregnant, they would have a child, he'd participated in a miracle.

Tension and surrender, intensity, hesitation, doubt, irrepressible and desperate lust, uncertainty, shame, obligation, compliance, self-loathing and love, the seeds of Danny Hutton, given to Beth, the mother. There were so many feelings jostling for position, but it was no contest, happiness won through. No denying it, Danny was made up.

He shuffled across their rock seat until he bumped into Beth, then he put his arm around her shoulder, his first gesture as a newly expectant and protective father.

And they sat, Beth and Danny on a rock, satisfied in their creative endeavour. They had endured for near on six years as a couple, their love – sometimes surrounded by doubt, sometimes impossible – was undiminished.

# NERVOUS JOHN

When it first started, John was just as high as a kite. He was helping himself to plenty of coke, but the flow of cash was his favourite hit. That was what made him giggle when he laid alone in his bed. During the first few weeks, he'd laughed and partied.

Initially he'd revelled in his new gangster status… big money and good drugs. He got himself a shiny set of wheels, some new clothes from TK Maxx, decent gear. As far as John was concerned his Primark days were behind him.

But it had all come from nowhere, as a gift. He wasn't ready. He was picking up huge piles of cash without fully understanding where it was all coming from. Every day. He was distributing big quantities of heroin, cocaine and MDMA. John had no idea what to do with the cash. He was afraid to take it to his local TSB branch, his skill set didn't include money laundering. He filled one kitchen drawer after another. He giggled, not too far away from hysteria. John was way, way out of his depth.

John had adopted Finn Duncan as his number two. Finn had his contacts, he took his opportunities. It worked for them both. The White Lion was their meeting place, their pub. It was Finn who pointed out that Erdi seemed to be an unnecessarily generous partner and asked why he'd chosen John for this high earning and senior role, when he clearly had a whole army of Albanian personnel in play?

That had given John pause for thought. He found himself without answers. It didn't make sense. They were two and a half pints into their daily meeting. They had dealt with essential business.

Finn couldn't contain his curiosity. "You've been putting yourself about I hear? Giving Sean Murphy a slap."

"I haven't given anyone a slap, Finn. Who's Sean Murphy?" John was puzzled.

"Nobody much, a failed musician who drinks too much," Finn said.

John raised his glass. "I'll drink to that."

"And who just so happens to be Danny Hutton's best mate. That was a bold move. You must be cocksure. I'll tell you now, John, when Danny Hutton comes calling, leave me out. Alright? I'm sure your Albanian friends will do whatever's necessary." Finn glanced across towards John and winked. "Anyway, you're carrying plenty of heat, big man."

John was still puzzled. "Who's Danny Hutton?"

Finn cheerfully misunderstood. "Absolutely, mate, never heard of him."

John tried again. "I'm asking you, Finn. Who the fuck is Danny Hutton?"

The penny dropped. Finn's smiles and admiration disappeared. He gave John a brief summary of Danny's business interests and reputation.

Three rapidly consumed pints of strong lager after a light lunch was a well-practised routine. But John felt unusually sober. "I've never met the guy, never heard of him."

Finn was staggered. "Well, why did you give Sean Murphy a bump?"

"I haven't heard of Sean Murphy either and I haven't hit anybody, Finn. Someone's got their wires crossed."

Finn was struggling. "Well, I've heard different. The word is that you've battered Murphy. And that you did it to send Danny Hutton a message. You need to have a chat with your man, Erdi. Because Danny Hutton will get that message, whether you sent it or not."

So John was nervous. It had taken him a while but eventually John understood that he was being used by Erdi. These kids were flying about selling his gear and he didn't really have control of any of it. John had no clue where Erdi's drugs came from, he didn't really know who exactly Erdi was. He was nervous. He was in play. What to do?

So John did what any self respecting gangster who's got himself into deep shit would do, he got himself a gun. Finn knew a guy. He paid three grand. No problem, John needed the drawer space. So there it was: John Stanton, armed and shitting bricks, desperately seeking Erdi.

# ERDI AND FRIENDS

Erdi's decision to make use of John Stanton had been thoughtful. Unfriendly and exploitative, but thoughtful nevertheless. If rivals or police felt sufficiently interested to observe the new wave of street selling, they would find a trail that led to John. That suited Erdi very well. He would be invisible. John had been mugged, he'd become so deeply entrenched in his delusions of grandeur that he'd been fool enough to accept a poisoned chalice.

John had swallowed Erdi's story without a question, eager to please like a good-hearted but stupid dog, although Erdi suspected that John's request for an urgent meeting was probably indication that he was catching up. It'd taken him long enough.

And it had worked perfectly well. Danny and his boys had sniffed around, got eyes on John and then he'd got a message through Fatos. Danny wanted to meet. Perfect, they were queueing up at his door to be slaughtered. He took his time. He didn't reply to either John or Danny. Let them sweat and sell drugs. English scum.

He waited because he could. He had way too much firepower for Danny Hutton, and John Stanton was an insignificant distraction who'd already served his purpose. Erdi was sitting comfortably. He was happy to have them both waiting nervously, playing with his power. He'd choose the moment to deliver their bad news. He'd half hoped that Danny might dispose of John but no worries, Erdi would have to clean up his own debris.

Erdi let five days pass before he responded to John's cry for help. He had his people watching The White Lion. He wanted to give John a surprise. John sat with Finn Duncan. Finn had been tempted to pull back when he'd realised that John knew nothing about his rivals. He was more watchful and less active but still spending time with his newly rich friend.

They'd had a few drinks (all bought by John) when Erdi walked in. "You want to talk to me, John?"

John was unprepared for Erdi's unscheduled visit. He had Finn with him and a shiny new gun in his jacket pocket. Unfortunately

John hadn't told Finn how worried he was. John had practised bravado all of his life. He'd indicated to Finn that he and Erdi were buddies so long as Erdi behaved himself.

So this unannounced appearance was awkward. John had some questions and some comments to make, but with Erdi's imposing figure standing in front of him and Finn beside him, he couldn't think. "Hi, Erdi. Have a seat." It was the best he could do.

Erdi accepted John's polite invitation. He sat down and then sat back. Erdi was relaxed. "Maybe your friend would like to buy me a beer?" Erdi looked at John while he spoke and then at Finn as he completed his suggestion.

Finn started to laugh, assuming this was a light-hearted, witty remark, a bit of banter, but then John looked across at him and nodded.

John's face was a picture. He was attempting to create an expression of urgency and fear (for fuck's sake, get up and get him a beer) while at the same time confirming that he was the senior partner and that all was well in the world. It was a tough task.

In amongst John's shifting facial features, Finn saw the fear and understood that John's friendly relationship with Erdi may have been misrepresented. He went to the bar, paid for Erdi's drink and delivered it to the table. Then made his excuses to leave.

"I don't have much time, John. What do you want?" Erdi didn't care what John wanted.

"These people you have selling the gear, they're everywhere, they're too conspicuous. I think we need to cool things down. It could get dangerous." That wasn't too bad. It was pretty well what John needed to say.

"Yes, they are conspicuous. I wanted Danny Hutton to see them." Erdi was past pleasantries, he couldn't be bothered to disguise his intentions anymore. There was no need.

John was rattled now. He could see how little Erdi cared. "I've heard all about Danny Hutton. I'm telling you Erdi, he's bad news."

Erdi looked at John with disdain. "Don't worry, John. Danny Hutton won't want to waste his energy with shit like you. I feel the same way. Our business has concluded." Erdi got to his feet and walked out, his beer unfinished.

John sat alone in The White Lion nursing his lager, his friend and his former business partner both gone. John had his gun in his jacket pocket. It never entered into his thoughts during Erdi's humiliating farewell.

For several weeks he'd collected the street takings and passed on Erdi's products. By the time John recognised that his role added no value whatsoever, he was known all over town as the new man, the guy who had the balls to stick two fingers up to Danny Hutton. He felt like a fool. And everyone would be able to see how easily he'd been used.

John just hoped and prayed that it was all over. He still had a handgun, a drawer full of cash and a good supply of cocaine. He'd survive the embarrassment and he hoped that Danny had a forgiving nature.

Erdi was also glad it was over for John. He'd never have to smell him again. One relationship ended, one was still in need of attention. He'd give Danny the courtesy of an appointment, although Erdi would once again give the time and the location. Only one man in charge.

The location was important. Erdi avoided indoor venues for meetings of this nature. Seats were needed, relative quiet and a range of options for arrivals and departures. So he chose the pond in Albert Park. It was perfect, quiet benches tucked away out of sight, paths, bushes and high hedges. Erdi was particularly keen that he found a place where lots of parking options could be considered, a meeting place offering approaches from all directions. Which meant they were unlikely to park in the same street and that his plans for Danny Hutton would not be witnessed.

He sent his message to Danny: Tuesday 6th December, 2pm.

# THE STANTON KIDS

Maisie stood before Sean's bathroom mirror, looking with admonishment at her reflected image. Silently she criticised herself, echoing her father's voice. Sean's house was a mess, the bathroom needed a good clean. She knew that Sean wasn't lazy or dirty. He just didn't do that stuff, not any of it. He couldn't cook, he was unable to manage money… those kind of skills weren't in him.

He was always busy with music, listening and playing. He loved to read and write, mostly he played his guitar. He played like nobody else. Maisie liked his music but she also liked his application, his attention to detail, his exacting standards. He took it seriously and she felt the same way.

All the same, she was cross with herself for staying over. She'd make clear that it had meant nothing more than the moment, then she'd leave. She went back to his kitchen. "Morning, Sean."

Sean had the same breakfast every morning, a mug of tea and a cigarette. His chair was pushed back from the kitchen table, his guitar in position. "There's tea in the pot, Maisie."

"Thanks. Your bathroom's worse than your garden. I know, it's re-wilding. You need to give it a clean, Sean." Maisie washed a mug and poured her tea.

"Yeah, sorry, I didn't expect you'd be staying. I'll clean it later."

Maisie started her explanation, her extrication. "No, neither did I. But you know, you'd been punched. And it was my brother. I sort of felt guilty. It was a weird day. How's your eye?"

"It's sore but not like last night," said Sean. "Yeah, that was all a bit weird. I've known you for more than five years and you've never told me you have a brother."

"Yes. Alright! Fuck it. You mentioned that last night. John's no one to me, Sean. What happened with you, whatever Sue Bellamy was telling me, that's your world, Sean. I know nothing of it. Yeah, John's my brother. I can't erase the genes." Maisie was angry. With Sean, with her brother, and with herself. "What's going on with John? What's your involvement?"

Danny's instruction had been to make discreet enquiries and to stop the movie nights. It wasn't going well. Now Maisie was angry with him. "That's the first time I've met John. Quite an introduction, but I've told you what I know, Maisie. It's not really my world either."

Maisie was exasperated. "Sometime next week. I'll need to go over to Stockton. I need to get June out of there. You can take me."

"Can't wait. Will we be staying for tea?" said Sean, daring to smile.

Maisie found a space for her half-empty mug on a busy kitchen table. She slammed the door on her way out.

•

Maisie had made the journey back to her family home in Stockton many times. She'd visited June pretty regularly over the years and she'd set her up with a phone.

It hadn't been easy to arrange. She needed June to let her know when John was out of the house at a time when Sean was free to drive and when she had space between her shifts.

Maisie was always glad to see her sister but these were worrying circumstances. Sue Bellamy's warning, then Sean's information. John could fuck up all day and every day, not a problem, but if June was in trouble, Maisie needed to know.

Sean was a fool in love. He'd managed to do exactly what Danny had asked him to avoid, he'd alerted John Stanton's sister. It was too late to claw it back. The cat was out of the bag and trotting across to Stockton.

Maisie was worried about June, and Sean was trying to make amends with Maisie. So he took her in his car and parked up around the corner to wait, one more drive through movie. Maisie would phone him when she was ready to go or if she encountered any difficulties.

They arrived outside of her childhood home at two o'clock on a Wednesday afternoon. June was at home and John was out.

June wasn't too bad, she'd gained a few pounds in weight, she had the house in good order and she was pleased to receive a visit from her sister.

June's survival was testimony to her resilience and her fortitude. She'd lived through more than twenty years of maltreatment from her father and from John. Billy had been the worst, he could be really quite cruel. June had felt pleased when John threw their father out… she'd understood her brother's heartless eviction as an act of generosity.

Of course, John's reasoning had been entirely selfish. Billy had become unproductive and well past his sell by date, a stain on the sofa, dead meat. John had given no proper warning. He gave his father one week to get his stuff packed and get out of the house.

Nevertheless, it brought a big change for June. She was under no illusions about her brother. He was a dickhead, but a better and less cruel class of dickhead than her father. In the weeks and months after Billy's departure, June felt her burden ease. She moved a little more freely, she was less anxious in the shops and she could watch whatever she wanted to on the telly.

It wasn't much but in the context of June's miserable life, it was an improvement. She was curious about the cash that John was stuffing into the kitchen drawers and he'd shown her his hand gun. June cleaned his clothes and his room, she shopped and she cooked his meals and if he got shot in a gunfight, June would either laugh or cry. Maybe both.

June admired her big sister. She got a real lift when Maisie visited and she felt bereft when she left again, anticipating a bleak future, feeling alone and forever unloved.

She and Maisie exchanged greetings. Maisie told June how well their mum was doing. She checked that June had plenty of credit left on her phone.

On her previous two visits Maisie had mentioned the prospect of June coming to live in her flat, sounding her out, but June had been reticent, fearful. Maisie could see that both the house and June were looking relatively well. She reiterated the message, trying to reassure her sister that a move was possible. June had heard Maisie's sales pitch on previous occasions but she'd also heard John's perspective. He needed her in Stockton.

June listened and she nodded. She understood that Maisie was making a genuine proposal. She didn't give an answer one way or the other. It was difficult for June. It would be a leap into the unknown. She got anxious when she tried to imagine change of such enormous proportions. She didn't want to stay but she was frightened to leave.

The relationship between Maisie and June had formed within a repressive home environment, where loud men dominated and ruled. Maisie was both fortunate and resourceful. Given the circumstances, she'd done pretty well.

She was a few years older than June, who was less fortunate. They never spoke much and they didn't spend much time together. The oppression and the age gap combined and conspired to hold them apart and yet strangely they became close. Although they never connected with a verbal dialogue, they understood each other with natural ease, and even without words, their communication was intricate and complex, infused with an older sister's love.

As young children, they'd always used eye contact and facial expression to communicate. It was their own language, nuanced and precise. From their expressions and their recognitions, they exchanged information. The turn of a head, the shift in a shoulder, the sway of a step. An inhalation of sorrowful breath. All day long, conscious and unconscious, in their restricted circumstances, they expressed their sisterly bond. Solid as a rock, sharing everything without a spoken word. It was a language that the other family members couldn't understand but Maisie and June...? They were fluent and habitual speakers.

Nothing had changed as they'd grown older. They never chatted very much but they sat and looked at each other and off they'd go, a thousand thoughts and feelings, a trillion neurons firing in half a second. No words could give such a rich account of themselves and their sister.

Maisie had come to see her sister, a simple and a beautiful

thing. June was touched by her sister's outstretched arm. Maisie, with her gestures and her smiles, gave sustenance, sisterhood and hope.

So they sat for a while allowing their breathing to settle and then to synchronise and they gained a sense of eloquent conversation. Their own language, born from the brutality of their family, delivered everything that each of them needed. Without a word being spoken.

June sat at a small table in a cramped kitchen, appreciating her big sister's support. She'd peeled some potatoes and trimmed the carrots. There was just the white cabbage still to prepare. She built a pile of waste on a page of yesterday's newspaper.

This was June's life, making John's food, cleaning John's clothes.

June broke the spell. She spoke, there were one or two matters that Maisie might want to consider. "John's bringing wads of cash home, Maisie. Loads of gear and Finn Duncan's been coming round."

"So I hear. Has anybody else been round?" Maisie waited.

June shook her head. "No, and John's out most of the time. It's just been two or three months. He seemed to be buzzing at first, but not anymore. He's been in a foul mood." They drank their tea, the TV stayed on, June's constant companion. "And he's got himself a gun."

Maisie's alarm was renewed. How the hell had John got himself into all of this? Why did he feel the need to carry a gun? "Oh my god. June, I'm worried. There'll be trouble coming. Christ, John with a gun, in a bad mood. Fuck." She started again to urge June to come away with her but then the she heard the front door close.

John walked into the kitchen. He was in an angry mood, and seeing Maisie in his house didn't help him. He didn't want Maisie sitting at his kitchen table, he didn't want Maisie in existence. Maisie had no intention of engaging in any kind of exchange with her brother. She stood and put on her coat. She needed to go and she would have left quietly if John had allowed her.

John was increasingly troubled by his new found good fortune.

Erdi had dismissed him, Finn had disappeared. He still had drawers filled with cash but even that was starting to bother him. The giggling days were behind him, he felt more trapped than June. And guess what? His long lost sister, Maisie, showed up… well, well. He'd never felt more pleased to see her. He took off his coat, then reached into his jacket and pulled out his gun. Gangster John, scaring his little sister. He looked across at Maisie, making sure that she'd seen, and placed the gun on the work surface to the left of the kitchen sink.

"What do you want?" John regained his position standing in front of the door.

Maisie kept it simple. "I came to see June, but I'll go now."

"I don't want you coming here anymore, Maisie, you got me? You don't ever set foot in my house again. Understood?" He was shouting, deliberately winding himself up, getting ready. She had no one to protect her, nowhere to run. John would deliver his revenge. "Have you got a kick for my bollocks today, Maisie? Eh? Come on, you're a game lass, come and take a shot. You've done it before. Let's have it." John stood a few feet from her. He'd waited a long time, almost a lifetime, for this moment.

Maisie faltered. She was a game lass and she had given an impressive account of herself in her previous encounters with brother John but today, looking at the intimidating figure standing in front of her, she wasn't confident. She tried again. "I'd better go, June. I'll be in touch."

She started towards the door, John waited in her path. He grabbed her violently, pushing her against the wall, the fingers of his left hand half covering her nose and mouth and the heel of his palm pressed against her throat. She gasped and struggled, but he was unbelievably strong. She couldn't resist, not this time. John Stanton had his sister pinned to the wall, gasping for breath.

Maisie struggled, panicked, but she couldn't move. For her first sixteen years, she'd held this man, this monster, at bay. She'd survived in his presence, she'd swallowed his stench and she'd made her escape. But it was all up now. Maisie was done. John had her by the throat. She was at his mercy. John didn't do mercy.

June wasn't a chef. She wasn't particularly interested in food. John wanted his tea, she cooked. She used an electric oven, fan assisted. She had a ceramic hob with an electric grill, a present from John. And she did all of her prepping at the kitchen table with one paring knife, a four inch blade. She kept it well sharpened. It had a good pointy end.

In all of her life, June had never hurt a fly. She'd never kicked, punched, slapped or scratched another of God's creatures. She'd received plenty, but had never been the provider of violent acts. She had had no practice, she had no technique. She didn't know what to do, but she felt desperately anxious. She stood up from her chair, her paring knife in her hand, and she could see Maisie's eyes wide open with terror. June wished she had some way to help her sister. She was on her feet but she was hesitant and uncertain.

Maisie tried to move, but John had her pressed hard against the kitchen wall. Her eyes darted in all directions and she saw June, standing and frozen. Maisie's right forearm was half free. She opened and closed her fingers, quickly and repeatedly, beckoning, grasping, reaching out, communicating to her sister.

June got the message. She walked three steps towards her sister and placed the black handle of her paring knife into the palm of Maisie's half free right hand. Then she sat back down. Maisie was losing her strength, unable to breathe. It really felt as if John intended to kill her.

She positioned the knife in her hand. She didn't have enough movement to get proper backswing, but she gathered herself and pushed her hand towards John. It was nothing much but she felt the blade sinking into him. She pushed again. It was enough to get the full four inch blade inserted into the back of John's right thigh, about half way between the knee and the buttock. John winced, groaned and faltered, all at the same time. Then he screamed in pain as Maisie withdrew her sister's paring knife.

She wasn't even aware that she'd withdrawn the blade. Nevertheless, she'd managed to twist the knife. Only a few degrees and without either malice or intent but a bit of a twist makes all the difference. A quick, clean in and out – no problem, hardly felt it, it'd mend later. But fifteen careless degrees of rotation, ooh mama, what a difference, big motherfucking pain.

John felt the pain but he didn't know what had happened. He couldn't understand how the situation had changed. Somehow Maisie had done him again. The pain in his leg was severe and the blood was flowing. John's hand lost strength.

Maisie breathed. Everything seemed to be happening in slow motion. She stepped away, released and looked at John staggering backwards and screaming in pain. Then she saw a rapidly expanding bloodstain on his jeans. She dropped the knife and looked across at June, half a second of eye contact and she understood everything. Maisie looked down at the knife on the floor, also stained with blood.

John still didn't know what had happened. The pain in his leg was intense and he could feel the blood soaking into his jeans. He was dizzy, but he was still on his feet.

This wasn't John's best day. He was fighting Maisie again. His gun sat waiting on the kitchen worktop, cold engineering, a killing device, a three thousand pound investment ready to pay the dividend. Maisie was starting to recover, getting some air into her lungs. She looked across towards the sink and she saw it, her brother's gun and her family's violence. It was in them all, even June.

John followed her eyes, silent and unmoving. He was still fighting. The race began. Maisie flew. John had a gammy leg. She claimed her trophy, the gun for which her brother had paid three thousand pounds. To protect him, to save his life. Meanwhile John, her big bully brother, the new man in Teesside, stumbled, his knifed leg bleeding and hurting.

John arrived at the finish line two seconds too late. He dropped to his knees, defeated by Maisie – his fucking mummy's special girl, the shit-arse teacher's pet – and he looked up to watch her holding his gun.

Maisie felt sick in her stomach, appalled by this culmination to their sibling rivalry. Nevertheless, adrenaline was pulsing through her veins and she was still fighting for her life. She slammed the gleaming hard metal into the side of John's worthless head. All of the family business was done. Go, Johnny, go, go.

John was almost unconscious, badly dazed. He dropped to the floor. Maisie and June exchanged a look, a thousand words at least. June ran upstairs. She packed a few items of clothing and a few other personal belongings into a rucksack and ran back to her kitchen. Her brother John, a heap lying on the floor, her sister Maisie, asking the question again with one slightly raised eyebrow.

*This is it, June.*

*This is it. Are you ready?*

*June?*

June answered with a shy smile, it seemed to be a good moment to relocate.

Maisie messaged Sean: come round to the back door, might need a hand. June opened a kitchen drawer. She grabbed hands full, a drawer full of twenty pound notes, stuffing them into the rucksack, emptying the drawer, then on to the next one, every last note, not one left behind.

Sean knocked. Maisie invited him inside. The kitchen was a bit of a mess, there was blood on the floor. Then he saw a man who looked half dead. Sean worked out pretty quickly where the spilled blood had come from. He was alarmed. "Who the hell's that?"

"Very funny, Sean. June's coming back with us. We'll get some bags into the car and go." Maisie had blood on one hand and a gun in the other.

Sean took the gun from her. "What's happened here?"

"This is my family. You were lucky, you never had one. We'll talk later. Right now we need to go." Maisie passed one of the bags to Sean. She watched him as he got sight of the cash. "Later, Sean."

June Stanton was moving house. She was frightened. She was celebrating whatever it was that she had with her sister and she had a bag full of cash. June took a look around the room. She'd lived every day of her life in this house. She looked at her brother, who seemed to have lost consciousness. She left him the paring knife. The vegetables were all prepped… he'd have to make his own tea.

Maisie watched in amazement as her sister greedily crammed the last remaining money into her bag. *A bit of a dark horse, our June.* She led them to the front door but June ran back up to the bathroom. She'd forgotten her toothbrush. They walked out into the street, stumbled into Sean's Beamer and he drove them home, to a new home in the sun.

Inevitably, Seth heard the whisper. John Stanton had given Sean a good hiding. It was an unanticipated development but, in Seth's estimation, a quite serious one. No one had seen or heard from Sean for several days. Danny also seemed to be lying low. Seth was confused, at the moment when Stanton had officially started the hostilities, Danny had fucked off home. He called Stevie. They met at the south entrance to Albert Park and made their way to the pond.

Seth had suggested the meeting. He was concerned about Danny's failure to respond, starting to wonder if he'd have to fill the space that Danny appeared to have left vacant. He was hoping that Stevie might shed some light. "When did you last see Danny?"

"I haven't seen him for a couple of days but we talked on the phone this morning. He was out buying ice cream for Daniel. He seemed fine." Stevie sat on a bench, then immediately stood again. He was unsettled.

Several days had passed since Seth had heard the rumour about Stanton and Sean. "What did he say about Sean?"

"He didn't talk about Sean." Stevie was puzzled. "Why would he?"

This time Seth tried sitting. "Stanton beat Sean up last week. It's started, Stevie. That was a declaration of war." He jumped back to his feet, the seat of his trousers cold and wet. "And what's Danny's response? Sit around for a few days, then pop out to buy ice cream. The Albanians must be bricking it."

Stevie had spent more time tailing Erdi. He'd taken a look at Fulham Road. But Stanton had dropped off the radar, Danny had lost interest. "I didn't know about Sean. I'm pretty sure that Danny doesn't know either. How is he? Sean, I mean. Where is he?" Stevie's cogs were turning fast now but he couldn't make sense of it.

They stood for a moment, both men occupied by confusion. Seth spoke first. "Well, I actually haven't seen Sean. I assume he'll be at his house. But, no, I don't know how he is. He won't be well. Stanton knows how to use his fists."

Stevie forgot about the wet seat and sat down again.

"This fucking bench is wet," he said as he stood back up again. "Seriously, Seth, why does Erdi want to meet Danny here? It's a shithole, it's winter. Why here?"

"Good question. Who knows? We should be here, Stevie. Danny's not at the fucking races, man. He's acting all wrong. The Danny Hutton that I've known all these years would have heard about Sean and he'd have wasted Stanton. I mean, forget about Erdi and the turf war. Stanton's beaten up his best mate. Danny would kill him, he wouldn't hesitate for a second. End of story." Seth was convinced now that Danny was compromised.

"So what do we do, Seth? He's told me he wants out. I think he means it. He's walking. He'll come here next week and give Erdi the green light." But still he felt puzzled. "But why Albert Park, why here? Unless…"

"Unless what?" Seth asked.

"Unless he's decided to take Danny out. It's early December, Seth. Take a look around. There's no one else here. It's not duck feeding season. It's cold, miserable and it's deserted… it's perfect. Erdi could crack Danny's head open, shove him into the pond and walk off without a care. I can see the headline… 'pond death for pond life'." He chuckled, amused by his own black humour. Even in this moment of murderous possibilities, Stevie couldn't help himself.

"I hope you're wrong, Stevie. But you might be right. Listen, I've been in the middle of them, with the messages for the meeting. Erdi's probably had eyes on me. But somehow one of us needs to be here on Tuesday, just in case. If Danny wants to walk, fine, we'll sit quiet and watch him walk. But if Erdi's planning his execution, then we need to be ready. I'll be right outside, Stevie, just a phone call away, but you're our man in the park, mate." Seth was already doubting himself.

Stevie was in no doubt whatsoever. "You must be fucking

joking. We need to tell Danny not to come, surely that's a better way forward."

"He'll go to the meeting. We'll see him at the party on Sunday. You see if you can dissuade him. Best of luck to you. We can all have a chat. But Danny will still go." Seth looked directly at Stevie. "And we'll be in place." He wasn't asking, he was telling Stevie.

# SNOW STORM

While Stevie and Seth walked through Albert Park, Danny walked in Saltburn. He felt like he'd been chasing around forever, first looking for John Stanton, then following Erdi. Running hard but progressing slowly. It had all happened in a period of five or six weeks. Elizabeth Bennett had appeared like a ghost. Now Beth was pregnant. It was way too much and it had all happened too fast for Danny. It had fazed him.

He'd been out of sorts. And off his game. Prevaricating. Then he finally got word about his meeting with Erdi in Albert Park. He could slow down, collect his thoughts. After Beth had given him her news, he stayed with her in Saltburn, holidaying at home.

He was pleased to spend time with Beth, together with their secret. Saltburn was a small and sleepy town. Danny felt no emotional connection but at least he felt free from danger, as if these leafy streets were off limits, a demilitarised zone.

The world seemed to slow down. Instead of hunting down his rivals, Danny was out buying sausage rolls and ice cream. While Beth was at work, Danny went walking. He walked in the woodland, he walked on the beach, he walked in the town. He saw the people, families, workers, friends and lovers. He wondered if he could be part of this foreign place where Beth, mother to their bundle of cells, had moved her life. Maybe the walks would help.

Saltburn felt weird, not his natural environment. It was a truth he'd never felt comfortable with but it was undeniable. Out on the streets, on the wrong side of the tracks, in darkness, with the damage and the desperation, he'd always felt at home. But he knew that Beth loved her new home town, he'd have to do a lot more walking… maybe one day.

Danny had some things to think about and some decisions to make. He was conflicted. He had no doubt anymore, his days as a drugs dealer were numbered. Recent events had developed a half held notion into a clear recognition. He'd had more than enough. Given that realisation, Erdi's arrival might have been welcomed. His timing was perfect.

Unfortunately, Erdi's manners had been less than perfect. He'd challenged Danny Hutton, Erdi had made an aggressive move and he'd hidden behind John Stanton. That was the conflicting factor. Timing and logic played no part. Each of Danny's walks took him to the same dilemma: he wanted out but he couldn't persuade himself to walk meekly away.

He kept thinking about it, bending it one way, then another. He looked to the heavens, to the ocean, anywhere to give him a solution. An icy December wind brought a sudden and wild flurry of snow. Danny found shelter in a bar and to his astonishment, the landlord was able to offer a choice of two single malt whiskys. That was a new experience. He smiled, inviting fate into his life. It seemed like a miracle. It was unusual for Danny to visit a bar. Mostly his whisky drinking took place at home.

He greeted the landlord. "Good afternoon. I like your bar. You have an unusually good choice of whiskys."

The landlord's face lit up. "I love my whiskys. I've got a better selection at home. What can I get you?"

Danny was suddenly enjoying himself, smiling even. "What do you recommend? It's freezing cold outside and I need to figure something out. What fits the bill?"

The landlord initiated the handshake. "I'm Clive. Definitely the Talisker, a bit of spice, it'll warm you and sharpen your thinking. The Oban's too smokey, best leave that one alone."

"Good to meet you, Clive. I'm Danny. I'd better have the Talisker then."

Clive poured the whisky. He waited.

Danny wrapped his hand around the glass, took a sniff. Then a small sip. He closed his eyes for a second, sensing a hint of cinnamon. "Smooth and warm, very nice."

Clive was satisfied. "What are you trying to figure out?"

"No need to beat about the bush, Clive. A competitor is trying to take over my business. I'll be meeting him in a few days but I can't decide how to play it."

"I have my bar, Danny, but I'm not much of a businessman really. But I happen to know a few things about competition. You see, I'm a backgammon player." Clive reached for the bottle of Talisker, then walked out from behind the bar to sit alongside his customer.

Danny Hutton was never a child of the universe, he didn't believe in God and he didn't believe in fate. But he'd stumbled into an empty bar, taking shelter from the storm and found Clive, a malt whisky enthusiast who played backgammon. And who claimed expertise on competition.

"I play backgammon, Clive, or I used to when I was a kid."

"Really?" Clive was as pleasantly spooked by their common interests as Danny. "You've come to right bar, Danny, a well timed entrance." Clive smiled as he spoke. "There are three key principles." He paused. "For backgammon, for competition and for living life. And timing, my friend, is the first principle."

Clive was enjoying himself. He grabbed a glass and poured himself a whisky, then he added a top up into Danny's glass. "I can run you through them if you're interested?"

Danny nodded, encouraging his host to continue. Clive needed no encouragement. He was a barman from another age. He wanted his bar to be a part of the community, filled with local drinkers whose burdens would lighten as he generously offered his support and wisdom. Twenty years earlier he'd had his wish, his bar had been filled with regulars. But now it had all changed, tourists, craft beers and Japanese gin. He'd lost interest. He'd been trying to retire for three years but the tourists kept coming. He was delighted to meet a man who appreciated good whisky and who played backgammon. He smiled as he received Danny's quiet encouragement.

He began the exposition of his wisdom. "Timing's a big one. You need patience and nerves of steel. You have to be prepared to wait, sit in, wait for the moment. You know the game, Danny, your opponent can boss it right through the game but then it can turn right around at the end. The last chance saloon isn't the worst place in the world to enjoy a glass of whisky. Only brave men drink there, with patience and hope. You have to play with hope, Danny. The dice seem to know."

Danny was loving it. He sipped from his generously refilled glass, happy to indulge his new friend. "Okay, timing, patience, nerves of steel and hope. That's four."

Clive corrected him. "No, that's just the first principle. Timing is the principle but if you lose your nerve or your patience or your hope, then you lose your timing. Alright. Second principle." Clive took a drink. "Be ahead of your opponent. I don't mean on the board, that'll always fluctuate, but be ahead in your thinking. You don't want to be catching up, you don't want to be level. Get in front, stay in front. Out-think your opponent."

Danny had no questions. He accepted the wisdom. "Next principle?"

"Strategic risk." Clive beamed with pride. "Mostly you play the percentages, Danny, stay in the game. But there'll be moments of opportunity, and the timing has to be right, when you can make a rogue move, take a risk, win the reward. The high risk option is what your opponent least wants and most fears. That's the place to go, towards danger, that's where trophies are won." Clive lifted his glass and gulped the remainder of his whisky.

Danny was a little light-headed. There was something about Clive. He was good natured, reassuring. Danny had only intended to spend ten minutes while the snow and the wind settled down so that he could make his way back to Beth's house. But he remained in his seat. He felt comforted and at the same time slightly unsettled. It was a unique experience for him, accepting Clive's paternal bar-room wisdom.

Clive watched his long-awaited customer and caught a glimpse of something. "Are you alright, son?"

Danny swallowed and cleared his throat. "Yeah, I'm good, a better backgammon player than I was twenty minutes ago." He looked out through a window. "I think the snow's blown over, I'd better go. Thanks for the whisky, Clive." He stood up and made ready to leave.

Clive ignored his customer's intentions. "No problem, Danny, good to meet you. Yeah, there's something else, just one more thing. Things never go as planned in this crazy world, the dice will always have their say." He smiled. "Be ready for a surprise, life's full of them."

Danny buttoned up his jacket. "Sound advice."

Clive seemed to be satisfied, almost ready to release his customer. "Well, the Talisker has seen you through the bad weather. Don't forget, Danny… get the timing right. Get thinking, get ahead. Think like a winner, throw the dice with hope. You'll work it out, don't you worry."

"I'll do my best but it's not a backgammon board out there, Clive, it's real life." Danny headed to the door.

Clive offered a parting shot. "Backgammon's just like real life, Danny. You make plans and you throw the dice. May the best man win. Enjoy your weekend."

Danny walked slowly back home. Something had changed. He didn't feel quite recovered, but his mood had lightened. He chuckled to himself as he thought about Clive solving life's problems on a backgammon board. For weeks he'd stumbled, feeling lost, now he'd found a little hope and he hoped that he was walking back to himself.

# THE PARTY

Stevie and Molly travelled to Saltburn on the train. They'd set out early so that they could take a walk on the beach and look around the town. Saltburn had become home to Beth but it was still a day out at the seaside for Mol. They enjoyed a liquid lunch and wandered into the town square across the road from Table Leg, half hidden by the queue at the bus stop. A woman and a man emerged from the Table Leg door.

"Shit." Molly turned her back to the shop as she spoke, suddenly mortified.

Stevie noted her discomfort with amusement. Stevie did his best to find amusement in everything. He scanned across the road to see what had disturbed Molly and immediately recognised Rob leaving the shop.

"Whoa, interesting," said Stevie who also turned his back. "This guy gets around, he's everywhere."

Molly half turned to look again as Rob and his companion walked away. "He's one of my clients."

"Yeah I know, he dropped you off when me and Sean were waiting for you the other night. Rob Thomas, he's a client of mine as well. He's a knob but his money's fine. He takes way too much coke, his nasal passages must be lined with steel. Mind you, he's overdue, maybe he's been buying from Stanton. He comes into Middlesbrough. I'd no idea he was a Saltburn man."

"No, me neither."

Stevie had been selling gear to Rob for more than a year but he had never got to know him well. "What's he like, Molly?"

"He gives me the creeps. He just about stays onside but he makes sure that I feel like dirt, the way he looks at me, he's rough and the way he talks to me…" Molly paused, momentarily experiencing the feeling that Rob Thomas's visits had always provoked in her. She could almost taste him and she wanted to spit on the pavement. She restrained herself.

Then she re-engaged with Stevie. "He talks to me like I'm a filthy whore."

Stevie empathised deeply with Molly's disgust. For at least a second, then the laughter burst out of him. "I wonder why that might be, Mol!"

Molly couldn't help herself. She exploded her way into the raucous laughter party with her appallingly insensitive friend. Half a dozen rubber necks in the bus queue turned to check them out.

•

Seth was very nervous, much more so than he'd anticipated. He'd breathed a sigh of relief when Stevie blabbed. He thought that revealing the knowledge was the job done. But when Sunday arrived Seth became very nervous.

When he'd first got out of bed, he thought he had Covid and he told Jen they'd have to cancel. Jen was also nervous. She knew that she'd be judged today but she wasn't about to let this opportunity slip away.

She'd always accepted Seth's vague references to his work. When she first met him, she was quite excited by his reputation and she'd heard plenty of whispers… her man was a close associate of the infamous Danny Hutton. Well, now she was going to meet the man himself. She informed Seth that he didn't have Covid (as she had done dozens of times before), no need to cancel.

Jen had a bright head on her shoulders, she was switched on, and generally quite confident within her home and work environments. Maybe it was because of Seth being nervous, anyway, she felt tense. A whole group of Seth's closest people, his other family, in a house she'd never been to before. So they were a bit tetchy with each other.

Daniel picked up the mood and got crabby. All three of them were out of sorts. They got a bag full of baby gear into the car and drove to Saltburn. Daniel fell asleep in the car. Jen stayed quiet but her mood picked up as they approached the house.

"Very nice. Serious money."

It was the first time that Seth had been to the house. "Yeah, it looks nice." He looked at the sleeping child, then he looked at Jen. "You'll like Beth." He parked on the drive where there was plenty of room. It was an impressive house. They unloaded with care and walked with their bags and their baby to ring the doorbell.

•

It had been a busy day for Beth. She opened the shop on Sundays and the Christmas trade was peaking. She could hardly believe the sales figures. Energy prices were through the roof, inflation soaring. Beth had increased her standing order to the local food bank. She knew there were plenty of people struggling to stay warm and to feed their families. But she was still selling Christmas tree decorations at £7 a shot, all day, every day.

And just to complicate matters, Elizabeth appeared to be moving towards a crisis in her marriage. Beth had offered comfort as best she could. Elizabeth had bruised wrists and arms from a recent row. Last week she was desperate to escape, this week she was trying to build bridges.

Beth had invited her to the house to meet Danny and the others. She hadn't intended to include Rob but at the last minute, mindful of Elizabeth's foolish wish to patch things up, she told her to bring Rob.

She bought a cake, that was all she had time for. She had a few snacks, they'd be fine. She was busy. Beth was worried about Elizabeth but she was happy. She was pregnant and she'd told Danny. It was too early to spread the news. Danny had been a bit spooked but no complaints. And he'd stayed in Saltburn for two whole nights, the dutiful father. This really this was a moment of great excitement for Beth… she would have a child.

Danny was hard work, frequently absent without leave and apparently unable to commit. Nevertheless, their relationship had endured and now they were waiting for their baby. She buzzed around the house, moving things from one place to another, just nervous energy. The house looked fabulous, of course.

Danny looked at ease. He was moving at a slow pace, he was speaking softly. These were usually reliable indicators of a relaxed mood. And he was relaxed, although not fully at ease. He knew at the back of his mind that just a few days before Beth had told him she was pregnant, he'd arranged a dangerous, potentially fatal meeting. It was on his mind. He knew it would be risky but he felt he had to meet with Erdi. It wasn't just about practicalities, it was a personal statement. Perhaps it would be Danny's last stand, sitting down on a park bench.

But then he'd met Clive, who had appeared like a fairy godmother, talking cheerfully about backgammon. When Danny had wandered into Clive's bar two days earlier, he'd been full of uncertainty. Clive's guiding principles had not been forgotten. Danny's approach had clarified.

He'd spent the past couple of days talking with some of his close business associates, preparing the ground for his withdrawal. He was more than ready to move on, he just needed to be ready for Erdi, who had chosen to demonstrate his power, to intimidate.

Danny had told Stevie just a few days earlier that he didn't mind the prospect of death and he'd spoken truthfully but as a prospective father, his position had shifted.

What a shift it was. For as long as he could remember, Danny had always got on with his life. He got out of bed every morning and he got through the days. And he got through the nights, all the nights he'd lain in the quiet and the darkness, alone with his demons. He'd kept going.

He had never seriously contemplated suicide. He'd surprised more than one psychiatrist with that claim. Nevertheless, he didn't like living and he'd never worried about the prospect of death, the moment when the demons would die with him.

And now, one careless fuck later, it was different, something had shifted. He'd carry on being a miserable sod but he wanted to live. Danny didn't walk away from anything, and he wouldn't walk away from his child, from his role as a father.

Danny was unconvinced about his suitability. He'd been a drug dealer for all of his working life, he had a long history of violence and he had committed murder. He had no healthy experience of being cared for by a father. He was a victim of abuses, a looked after child. He was all over the place, all of the time. The prospect gave him both fear and excitement. But even with his dubious qualifications, he'd give it his best shot, so long as Erdi didn't give him his.

Danny definitely wasn't a party animal. Nor was he a fan of social gatherings. This whole getting the family together vibe did nothing for Danny. He liked his brothers and sisters one at a time. And even then, not too often. If Beth hadn't been pregnant, he'd have made an early exit and headed back to the gym. But for now, he was staying in Saltburn.

He was in the kitchen, looking at his phone. Beth was busy, in and out, when the bell rang.

"I'll go," Danny said and went to greet the first guest.

It was Sean. He was early and needed to talk to Danny. Sean had been nervous for several days as he'd anticipated this little catch up. He could only imagine that Danny would be annoyed. He'd kept watching after Danny had called them off, he'd been punched by an unidentified attacker, and he'd finished up at Stanton's house where there was a gun, a knife, a drawer full of twenties and a stabbing.

"Hi, Danny. I need to have a quiet word."

Danny took him through to the conservatory at the back of the house. Danny was trying to make the move to Saltburn but it still felt like a foreign land. He felt like an unwelcome visitor in his own front room. It was posh. There were soft furnishings and clean floors. It felt very different to the gym. At least he felt comfortable in the conservatory. They sat in wicker chairs, looking out on what was left of this December day.

Beth shouted hello from the kitchen. Sean didn't reply. He spoke to Danny. "I need to update you on a couple of developments."

Danny noticed the residual bruising under Sean's left eye. "Who's hit you?

"I thought it was John Stanton," Sean replied.

Danny spoke again. He'd got well past caring about Stanton. Things had moved on. "Where?"

Sean cleared his throat. "It was where we'd parked when you jumped out and wasted that guy. I was worried, I decided to go back and see what was what. You never said a word, Danny. Anyway, I fell asleep. This guy, whoever he was, opened the car door and punched me. He said he was John Stanton and then he buggered off."

"Why?"

"I don't know. I thought you might know something about it. I saw his car, a grey Lexus."

Danny hadn't expected this. He was puzzled. "When was this, Sean?"

"It was a few days after we'd been up there. Maisie was pissed off. We had to miss the open mic." Sean knew that Danny would be annoyed, and tried to offer something more helpful. "It wasn't Stanton, Danny, I'm fine. It was probably just some dickhead acting on impulse, you know, saw me sleeping and couldn't resist. It's all done and dusted."

"Definitely not. Not in a Lexus. Not saying he was John Stanton. But I don't understand. It must have been one of Erdi's guys." Danny's thoughts were racing, maybe it had been opportunism. "And he definitely claimed to be Stanton?"

"Yes."

"And you believed him but now you don't?" Danny was getting impatient. He knew his brother well... there was more to come. "Whatever it is, Sean, just fucking tell me."

"About a week later I gave Maisie a lift. She'd heard rumours about John, she was worried and she wanted to go and check on her little sister. So you know, I thought I'd better go with her. I met John Stanton... it wasn't the guy who'd hit me." Sean paused for a moment. "Stanton had a gun, Danny."

They'd never progressed to guns. Middlesbrough wasn't much of a gun town. Danny didn't want a gun. He didn't like the idea of shooting someone. "Tell me what happened, Sean."

"I never actually saw him. I was waiting outside in the car. June,

Maisie's sister, was at the house by herself when we arrived but then John turned up. They had a row, well, a fight, Maisie stabbed him in his left leg and she gave him a pistol whipping."

"Fucking hell." Danny was more than surprised. "According to Seth, Stanton's a big lad. And he was armed with a gun. And his kid sister walks in and stabs his leg, sorry, his left leg. And then gives him a slap with his own gun. You've got interesting taste in women, Sean."

"Yeah, Maisie's a feisty bugger. Believe me. She sent me a message, she needed help. I went into the house, that's when I got to see John. He was in a bad way, groaning on the kitchen floor. He wasn't the same guy who'd hit me. Maisie's sister, June, took a drawer full of cash. I took John's gun. I'm guessing that he won't be pleased." Sean waited. He hadn't spent any time with Danny since the incident at the post office.

Danny was quiet. He knew that things had moved on and he quite liked the idea that John Stanton had got his comeuppance. But fucking Sean... he was clueless. He'd taken his own path, he'd said too much to Maisie, then he'd assisted her in her rescue mission and he didn't tell Danny about any of it. "You should have told me sooner, Sean."

"I'm sorry, man, you just disappeared after you'd wasted that guy by the post office and you left me out after that. I thought you didn't want to see me. What was that about? Who the hell was he?"

Sean was right. Danny had left him out and he hadn't wanted to see him. He had preferred to avoid the question that Sean had now asked. "I don't know who he was. He'd hurt me when I was very young. It's a scary thing, Sean, but that's everything I know. That's a fucking scary thing." Danny was visibly affected.

Sean seemed to have moved the conversation on successfully, which was nice but he recognised the seriousness of the new topic. "So how are you doing now?"

"I'm all over the place. It knocked me over. All these years, he's been two miles down the road, free as a bird. And I'll never know. Who he is, what he did, maybe it was because of him that

I finished up at Malton Court. I'll never fucking know, I'll never know who he was and I feel like I'll never properly know who I am."

Sean saw Beth as she appeared in the conservatory doorway, trying to say hello. He held up a hand to send her back out. Beth stopped and returned to the kitchen. She must have felt the mood. Sean was curious, something was coming out of Danny Hutton, something he'd never seen before.

"There are things you'll never know, Danny. The same with me. We have to live with that. We're looked after children, that's our song. It's probably best that way. He hurt you. He hurt you badly, so badly that you had to batter him. How much detail do you want? I'm telling you, you forget that stuff for good reason. I've spent most of my life looking for things I can't ever find. It's no use. No use looking back. It can't be changed. I'm with you always, but I won't have that. You know exactly who you are. You know what you dream about, you know what you struggle with, you know what it's like in your head. That's you, Danny, don't tell me you're not real. Who've I been hanging with all these years? You're a complex fucker, no question, but you're as real as every other human being I've met. You're Danny Hutton from Malton Court. So now you know. I don't care who you came from, I'm only interested in the miserable fucker sitting in front of me. That's you, Danny."

Danny listened. Only Sean, no one else, could command his attention like this. He didn't just listen, he heard every healing word. Sean, with his profanity and wisdom, whose careless incompetence might have put his life at risk, who had the courage to reach out to him in the darkest night. The brother who loved him. Fucking brothers.

They sat in their wicker chairs, these looked after children, friends and brothers, in Beth's posh house and they watched the afternoon light, changing.

•

The doorbell rang again. Danny and Sean sat quietly, neither of them made a move to answer the door. Beth glared at them through a wall and went to greet the next arrivals. Molly and Stevie. She immediately repaired her mood and embraced Molly, warm and happy.

Beth led them into the house and on in to the kitchen. "Sean and Danny are in the conservatory." Stevie was sent on his way. Happy to take the cue, he wandered through, leaving Beth alone with Molly. He appeared to be in good form.

Stephen Hunter, retiring cocaine dealer, entrepreneur, man about town and more recently, psychotherapist, was enjoying the day. He was enjoying the miracle of Molly Lopez, walking with her on the beach at Saltburn, top stuff. They were having a laugh, brother and sister in a good phase.

Stevie had felt highly uncomfortable during the previous day when he and Seth had done a recce in Albert Park, but today, rather strangely, he was untroubled by the crossroads at which he was waiting. He'd had a smoke before setting out and he'd had a couple of beers with Molly. The combination seemed to be helping him to accept his fate, he'd had a good run. Erdi... whoever... let them have it.

Stevie was taking his time, he was thinking, taking stock. Stevie would find something. He was more worried about Danny, who had been uncharacteristically uncertain, not quite at the top of his game and surprisingly accepting of Erdi's aggressive takeover. Stevie was unconvinced about Danny's judgement, accepting Erdi's invitation to meet in Albert Park. He was equally unconvinced by Seth's proposed defensive manoeuvre, particularly his own role as Johnny Superhero.

Stevie felt a new connection with Seth and with Molly. He had reached a view that the conversations he'd had with each of them during the past couple of weeks were a significant part of the change he was experiencing. Just at the moment when the business looked set to fold, he'd bumped into these personal encounters. They had provided some compensation and Stevie connected it all together. Even today's little gathering felt like a sign, another reminder that his Malton Court family mattered. He liked the way they could come together. They would all feel the value of their family bonds today.

He'd worked well with Danny throughout it all. The circumstances in which each of them had lived through the first fifteen years of their lives could hardly have contrasted more sharply – they were unlikely friends, brought together by a turn of fate. They had maintained their rhythm and their rhyme through ten years of honest trading. Now they'd arrived at the end, together and contented. Stevie didn't want any mistakes in this final stage, he needed to convince Danny to think again about the meeting with Erdi. He had a bad feeling about it. Albert Park? It felt wrong to Stevie. Particularly so since Seth had asked him to hide by the pond.

The conservatory was quiet, a sympathetic witness to Danny and Sean's conversation, serene and contemplative, the perfect setting for profound reflection. Then the moment was disturbed, shattered by Stevie's invasion.

"Hey guys, me and Mol have just got here. Anybody fancy a line?"

Sean often found Stevie's lightness of heart irritating. His conversation with Danny had been serious and the moment of quiet contemplation had felt peaceful. He decided on irony, Stevie would never know. "Room reading at its brilliant best, Stevie. I'll pass, thanks."

Sean had judged accurately. Stevie missed the irony but he did detect something of Sean's disapproving tone. "Suit yourself, you miserable fucker. Danny?"

Danny gestured an invitation, or instruction, allowing Stevie to sit. "Sean's just been updating me on John Stanton."

Stevie looked at Sean, noting the remains of his black eye. "Yeah, Seth told me that Stanton had taken a pop. What happened?"

Sean repeated the tale, including the latest instalment in the sibling rivalry between Maisie and John.

Stevie was surprised. He and Seth had made their secret plans based on the assumption that Stanton had attacked Sean. "Jesus, so John Stanton is unlikely to come chasing after you. And you don't know who it was that whacked you?"

Danny answered. "Who the hell do you think it was, driving a Lexus?"

Stevie was catching up. "Well, at least John Stanton's slowed down. It's a bit odd though, targeting Sean. One punch, I don't get that."

Danny agreed. "Me neither."

Stevie turned to Sean. "What did you do with the gun?" And then to Danny. "You could take it to your meeting with Erdi, Danny. I don't trust that meeting. I'm serious. I've been thinking about it… why Albert Park? It's fucking December, man. Wouldn't it make more sense to meet indoors, among people?"

Danny understood the danger but he knew that at some point he'd have to sit down and talk with Erdi. It was the only way to conclude their business without one of them dead. Since his chat with Clive, he felt less inclined to allow Erdi to dictate terms. He appreciated Stevie's reservations but sooner or later, the two men would have to face each other.

•

Molly had enjoyed her day out with Stevie. This was a rare luxury for Molly… a day off, a day out, a day with her family.

"Let's go on the train," she'd said. Stevie, owner of a Porsche, agreed. "Let's walk on the beach," she'd said. Stevie, in Timberland trainers, agreed again. "Let's have an ice cream," she'd said. Stevie, half a stone overweight, agreed. "Let's go to the party," she'd said.

Stevie, the coolest dude in town, offered his arm.

Molly was a grown and growing woman… she was finding a new perspective on her career in sex work, a new understanding of a hundred other things.

Molly had got politicised. She'd read the stories on the English Collective of Prostitutes website and she'd understood something about the injustices, the abuses, the oppression and the inequalities between innocent babies, neither earned nor deserved. This new understanding was helping Molly through the changes she was going through. She'd never had this much self respect in her life... who could say what Molly Lopez might do next?

She'd had a blast spending time with Stevie but she was pleased that Beth sent him away. She felt the need to ensure that Beth was fully informed about Emina's slave master. Like Stevie, she had doubts about Danny's judgement.

Although Beth had decided not to tell anyone else about her pregnancy, she was already tempted to tell Molly. "It's great to see you, Molly. You look fantastic."

Stevie had had the same experience a few days earlier, seeing Molly and being pleasantly surprised to notice how well she looked.

Of course, Molly rejected the compliment. "Fuck off, Beth."

Beth was still fetching and carrying, to no great effect. She gave Molly's hand a squeeze as she moved past her. "You look lovely, Molly, and don't tell me to fuck off." Beth knew how to handle Molly, hide the compliment behind a telling off and she'd get away with it.

Molly smiled. She enjoyed Beth's mothering manner. There would be more guests coming, she needed to take this moment of opportunity. "How's Danny?"

The problem was that they were each thinking about different things. For a moment Beth thought Molly was talking about his reaction to her being pregnant. Then she remembered that Molly didn't know.

"He's okay. Well, he's all over the place, the same as ever, Molly. Never mind Danny, how are you?"

"I'm pretty good. Me and Stevie came over this morning. We've been for a walk on the beach. We've had a laugh. He's trying to be a good brother. He's absolutely fucking clueless but it's nice that he's trying. It's lovely here... the house, Saltburn, for fuck's sake. You've come up in the world. And this place... Jesus, it's a bloody mansion. I saw the shop, we didn't go in but I want to see it." Molly was strolling around the spacious kitchen, taking in the extent of her sister's success. There was a big armchair and two white sofas in front of the fireplace. It was more than twice the size of Molly's whole flat.

Beth spoke regularly to Molly on the phone but it'd been a while since they'd been in the same room. Beth was uplifted. "Yeah, you have to come and see Table Leg. My friend's coming later. She's an interior designer. We're doing some work together. It's all moving along. Hey, what about Seth?"

Molly shared her friend's sense of amazement. "Unbelievable. Seth! He never said a word to any of us." Molly was genuinely excited about Seth but her concern for Danny needed expression. "Listen, Beth, sorry to change the subject but while we've got a minute, I'm worried about this meeting Danny's going to on Tuesday. The guy he's meeting… he's a nasty piece of work."

Molly's concern sailed smoothly over Beth's head. "Yeah, well, Danny's no angel, Mol. He can look after himself. Honestly, don't worry." The doorbell rang again. "I bet that's Seth." She was already hurrying on her way to the front door.

●

Having waited almost two seconds after ringing the bell, Seth was again convinced that he was going down with Covid. He was about to describe his key symptoms to Jen when Beth opened the door. She was about to begin loud and cheerful greetings but Seth put a finger to his lips. "He fell asleep in the car. He'll need another hour or two."

Beth reduced her ambitions and settled for a big smile. She moved aside while Seth lifted Daniel's carry cot into the house and she moved towards Jen. "Hello, Jen. I'm Beth. Come on in."

Seth waited. "Where shall I put him?"

Beth showed them into the parlour, a grand Victorian sitting room. Seth still moved as if he was overweight. Make no mistake, Seth was still able to enjoy a pie but getting rip fit with Danny had made a big difference. He'd remained steadfast in his determination to keep in shape. But even after all of these years, he still had an awkward sway to his shoulders, an apology in his movement – I'm sorry for being a fat kid. It became exaggerated when he knew he was being watched, evaluated. He lumbered into the room and lowered Daniel to the floor. Jen placed her bag full of baby gear next to the cot and they all crept back out.

Beth turned to Jen again, this time to initiate her into the women's wing of the family.

"I've known Seth since he was twelve, we all have, and we found out about you and Daniel last week." She made a facial expression that said 'need I say more'.

Jen responded with her eyebrows and a shake of her head... *I understand perfectly*.

Beth continued anyway, just to be sure. "Men."

She turned back to Seth. "The boys are in the conservatory, Seth... just through the back. Go and say hello. Danny will get you a drink."

Seth followed the instructions and found the others. "Hey guys, how you doing? Nice place, Danny."

Danny went first. "I'm all over the shop, man."

Sean and Stevie followed, enjoying the bonding ritual.

Seth looked across at Sean. "I hear you met John Stanton."

It was Seth's turn to find out what had been happening in Sean's life. "It's been a bad couple of weeks for Stanton. Apparently his working relationship with the Albanians is over. It's just Erdi now, Danny. What do you think about Albert Park?"

All eyes moved to Danny. He took a moment to consider. "The first time that we met was outside as well, near the library. I don't know why he's gone for Albert Park, it might be raining, or snow. It snowed here yesterday. But I need to talk with him. I'll have my wits about me on Tuesday, Seth. Don't worry about that."

Seth was unusually outspoken. "I am worried about it. I could still try and get another message through, ask for a change of venue."

Danny shook his head. "It's the day after tomorrow. I'll deal with it, trust me. Have you brought Daniel and Jen?"

Seth gained a little encouragement. Danny sounded much

more himself. He accepted the diversion. "He fell asleep in the car. He'll need another hour."

Stevie was beside himself with frustration. "Poor little bugger's missing the party, Seth. Give him a shout, man. Tell him his Uncle Stevie's here."

The four of them together, the board of directors, friends and brothers, settled into the late afternoon. They'd had the work update, then they were able to move on. There was plenty of banter. And over the course of about an hour they had some fun, horse play, laughter. It was a rare and beautiful moment. The four of them together, daft kids, joshing.

•

While the boys were in the conservatory, Beth, Molly and Jen had a good chat. They were enjoying their own exclusive event. Beth took a moment, watching herself, acting and reflecting simultaneously. She felt good, her home and her family, her future. She hadn't expected such a fine gathering. Beth was happy to spend time with Molly and she noted with interest that Jen seemed to be doing well in retail.

They talked about the house and about men. They had a great hour together.

They were all comfortable, they could have sat for hours in their two groupings. Until suddenly it all changed. The doorbell rang and Daniel woke up. Jen went to get Daniel who was demonstrating the power of his lungs and the pain of his solitude. The four men ambled from the conservatory into the kitchen. At the same time Elizabeth and Rob followed Beth into the opposite end of the same expansive room. And instantly, no one was comfortable.

It had been a difficult year for Rob. Elizabeth had clearly struggled with the adjustment to married life. Rob remained mystified by her struggle, just a few new routines and duties and yet she'd found either objection or incompetence for every requirement. Modern women seemed so confused. And then of course there were the financial issues. One minute he was doing well… the height of the pandemic had been Rob's finest business hour but during these last several months sales had declined to almost nothing. Unlike the overheads and his huge mortgage repayments, not to mention the cost of cocaine and sex workers.

Rob was in serious trouble, so serious that he'd accepted Elizabeth's suggestion to give their marriage one last try. The alternative was to be left on his own, facing repossession and bankruptcy. So here he was, entering the home of his 'let's try again' wife's business partner for an afternoon party, celebrating the existence of someone else's child. Not a prospect that Rob anticipated with relish, but as Rob was discovering, you do some crazy shit when you're trying again.

He stumbled into the room assuming that he'd know no one. But as he made his way into the spacious kitchen, he half recognised a woman with dark hair and olive skin. He couldn't place her. He stepped forward with Elizabeth, half listening to the introductions.

There were too many people to remember all at once but Beth went ahead anyway.

"Everyone, this is Elizabeth. She works with me at Table Leg, and this is Rob."

Rob noted that his own introduction had been restricted to three letters. He decided to let it pass and listened as Beth continued.

"Hello, Rob. I'm Beth. This is Danny, Sean, Molly…"

Rob was already feeling out of place. Yes, yes, you're Beth. Danny, Sean, Molly.

Molly?

Molly! Rob looked at the olive skinned woman who he'd paid to have sex with on countless occasions. Why was she in the room? What kind of a party was this? What on earth was he to do? He had no idea so he did nothing. Then things got worse. Danny, whose name Rob had remembered, a man who carried an intimidating physical presence, approached Elizabeth.

"Hello, Elizabeth. Good to see you." Danny walked across

to her, gave a warm and reassuring smile and steered her away towards the conservatory. "I think you'll like the conservatory, it's my favourite part of the house. Come on, I'll show you."

Rob was deeply entrenched in excruciating discomfort. He tried to turn away from Molly, still unable to find a response. He'd have to do his best to ignore her and hope that she'd be discreet. He sensed that he wasn't the only person in the room to be experiencing some hesitation. His wife's disappearance seemed to have had an unsettling effect.

Rob needed someone to give him support, discretion. Something, anything. He hardly dared lift his head. He could feel Molly's stare, waiting for acknowledgement. Then he heard a familiar voice. Praise the Lord. And he did raise his head. Stevie Hunter, his cocaine dealer. Not great but at least Elizabeth knew about his drug habit. No, not great, but not terminal.

He clocked Molly's happy smile and turned to Stevie. Rob replied, grateful for some direction, at the same moment when Stevie turned his attention to his noisy nephew.

"Hi, Stevie," said Rob, his gratitude evaporating as he realised he was talking to Stevie's back. He re-evaluated, and shifted his attention to Sean, with whom he shared neither history nor secrets. He approached Sean hopefully, desperately.

Sean had his own perspective and was more than ready to chat with Rob. "Hello, Rob. I saw you the other night, when you dropped Molly off. Nice car. Does Elizabeth know about you and Molly?" It wasn't an unreasonable question and Sean was genuinely curious.

Rob was caught off guard. As far as Rob was concerned, their paths had never crossed. He wanted to simply turn on his heels and walk back out of the house and that was clearly his best option... he could only go backwards if he stayed. He stayed. Rob saw trouble everywhere he looked. He'd assumed that Sean would be ready to engage in polite conversation, maybe talk about the weather.

Rob was now not only excruciatingly uncomfortable, he was stumbling without direction. Sean's indiscretion forced him once again to reconsider his options. He shot a cold glare towards Sean and turned again. He decided to talk to Molly. After all, they were intimately acquainted.

Molly had an insistent grin. It was there, all over her face and it wasn't going away. And with Elizabeth gone to the conservatory and Stevie captivated by his nephew, she decided to break the ice. "Yo, Rob, I can't wait to meet your wife." Even as she spoke, her grin was unmoved. The fact that she'd just lost a customer made no difference.

Rob hated her and he started to feel angry with Elizabeth, the stupid bitch who'd thrown him to the lions, then disappeared with Charles Atlas. Where the hell was she? What was she doing?

•

Danny had responded characteristically to this awkward moment. He'd trusted his instincts, taken control, decisive and immediate action. The prospect of having his historic connection to Elizabeth exposed and explained in front of the others was unsettling, too much discomfort. He'd taken the only action he could… this catch up required privacy.

They'd made their escape and Danny was calm now.

"Please sit down, Elizabeth. You've been on my mind, after that morning when you walked up out of the woods. How are you?"

Elizabeth wasn't calm, but she was grateful that he'd ushered her into a private space.

"Oh, a bit up and down at the moment. I didn't think you'd recognised me, Danny. I only half recognised you, you've grown. It wasn't until a couple of hours had passed that I knew it was you."

"I'm pretty good with faces. It's funny. Beth has talked about you lots of times. I never made the connection, not even after I'd seen you. It never occurred to me." Danny had actually dreaded the prospect of having to sit and talk with Elizabeth. Now that it was happening, it felt fine. He was in control.

Elizabeth had been more than surprised to meet Danny in these circumstances, invited to his house. She'd also been nervous about the prospect of meeting him again. She'd more or less persuaded herself that their coincidence by the woods was unlikely to reoccur. She smiled now. "I've been the same. I've heard Beth mention you lots of times."

The discomfort was all gone and they sat quietly for a few moments. Then Rob, a bit red in the face, appeared.

He walked briskly across the conservatory. "We have to go, Elizabeth. Something's come up."

Danny watched with interest. Rob was clearly feeling a sense of urgency.

As he spoke, Rob reached down and took hold of Elizabeth's arm, urging her quite forcefully to get up from her seat.

"Ooh."

Rob had found a tender area of bruising and he'd disturbed her carefully worn shirt sleeve, revealing some of the marks on her wrist.

Elizabeth replaced her sleeve with care.

Danny continued his watch, missing nothing.

Rob was about to reiterate his message but he hesitated as he watched Danny ease purposefully to his feet, his large frame already warning Rob.

He took a step back. "Sorry to interrupt but something urgent has come up. Me and Elizabeth have to leave."

Danny had seen enough. He put his right hand on Rob's shoulder and moved him with imposing strength back out of the room. As they reached the doorway, he spoke quietly and with a touch of menace. "Fuck off out of my house. Don't ever come back." Danny had seen a vulnerable person. He'd made his assessment and with carefully chosen words, he'd decided to intervene. He'd remove Elizabeth from her family home and find a place of safety for her.

Rob did what he should have done five minutes earlier. He walked out of the house without saying a word to anyone.

Danny went back to his seat. "I hope that was alright. Beth

mentioned to me that you and Rob were having some problems. I told him to leave. You don't want to be anywhere near a man who treats you like that."

Elizabeth was tearful but already recovering. "Yes, that's perfectly alright. I'm embarrassed. I've been foolish enough to hope that he might change his ways. I should have known better."

At that moment Beth appeared in the doorway with Daniel in her arms. She'd watched Rob make his exit. Danny mouthed a silent message of reassurance. He looked at Beth, awestruck to see her holding Daniel. The image left him so choked that he couldn't speak. His tears were flowing faster than Elizabeth's.

It was rescue city in the conservatory. Elizabeth's turn. She stood, she let her palm rest for a second on Danny's shoulder as she walked towards Beth.

She said a cheery hello to Daniel, who was enjoying his popularity, and then turned to look at Beth. "I knew Danny when he was a young child. It was a surprise to find him here today. We just need a minute, Beth. I'm so sorry about Rob. Has he gone?"

Beth nodded. "Yes, he's gone." She went back into the kitchen.

Elizabeth walked back to Danny. "Perhaps we should go back through. Beth must be puzzled." She gestured encouragement.

Danny accepted his cue, following behind her. "I might need to ask you some questions, Elizabeth. Not right now, some other time."

She glanced back to him. "Yes, of course."

•

Beth had looked forward to this gathering. It was her first chance to show the house to her friends and to Elizabeth, to host a small party, provide warmth and welcome. It was great to meet Daniel and Jen, but clearly something was wrong. Danny and Elizabeth had wandered into the conservatory and Rob had made a swift and silent exit.

The whole thing reminded her of the Godfather films: the family fun out front and the private meetings with Marlon

Brando in the back room. Danny had been in there the whole afternoon, one meeting after another. Now it was Elizabeth, her new business partner and guess what? She knew Danny, who'd been giving it Godfather in the conservatory all bloody day.

She knew that Elizabeth and Rob had problems but Danny's involvement was unexplained. Daniel wriggled in her arms. She granted his release, lowering him down onto unsteady feet.

Daniel trotted across the room to his dad.

Several hearts melted. Seth scooped him up, his big hands wrapping gently around Daniel's delicate frame, and he let his son sit on his forearm, his large hand holding him secure… a father full of love, protecting.

Stevie followed. "Hello, Daniel, my man. I'm Stevie." Stevie moved his eyes to look at Seth. "Seth, he looks like you, I mean, whoa, he's just like you, make the payments, buddy, that's your son."

It was true, Daniel was a chip off the old block. Seth had replicated his genes. Job done, function fulfilled. He beamed. "Hey Daniel, this is in fact your Uncle Stevie."

Daniel appeared unimpressed, allowing a little regurgitated milk to run down his dimpled chin.

Beth tried to take it all in. There were still a few gaps to fill.

Molly offered her assistance and gave Beth a quick update on Rob, then asked, "What's the score with Danny and Elizabeth?"

"I don't know yet, Molly. They've met before, a long time ago. That's all I know. I've only just found that out." Even as she spoke, Danny and Elizabeth walked back into the kitchen.

Danny went to say hello to Jen and to meet Daniel. Elizabeth came to join Molly and Beth.

Elizabeth proceeded as Danny had suggested – that they should simply tell Beth the truth, no secrets, no shame. Easy as that.

"I used to be a social worker, Beth, twenty years ago. That's when I met Danny. I was involved when he first went to Malton Court. How incredible to find him here with you, I can't quite believe it. He seems lovely."

"Wow, that is incredible." It was an odd moment for Beth. She appreciated Elizabeth's explanation and she felt better just knowing how they'd met. On the other hand, she felt jealousy arising in her. Danny belonged to her. She didn't like the idea of Elizabeth having her own deeply personal connection to Danny.

Beth felt nervous. Danny had a tendency to be spooked by echoes from his past. She wondered what this reunion would mean. She looked across at Danny. He seemed at ease but she remembered what Molly had said earlier. Suddenly Beth was reminded of how little she knew about Danny's early life. She'd caught glimpses of his working world but Molly's words of warning had surprised her. Beth knew Danny at home. That was pretty well it. There were big pieces of his life, past and present, that were hidden from her. She experienced a moment of insecurity, and sadness.

The next couple of hours passed more easily. Daniel stole the show and Seth gave his proud dad routine to great effect. Beth was happy that Danny had invited Elizabeth to stay at Stevie's house. They couldn't send her back to Rob. And she heard her Brando-esque partner ask Stevie's permission, about ten minutes after Elizabeth had gladly accepted his generous offer. Molly found a minute to ask Danny to be careful in his dealings with Erdi. Danny was listening. The warnings were coming thick and fast. They were no different to the ones he'd given himself... he had his own perspective on the scheduled meeting.

It was six o'clock on a dark December evening. The kitchen sofas were filled with conversation and smiles, a room filled with warm human interaction. Then Sean decided to leave, and Molly and Stevie asked him for a ride back into town. They took Elizabeth. Seth and Jen took the opportunity to make their own departure. It all happened in five minutes, and just Danny and Beth were left.

Beth felt tired. What a day, that kind of tired. She wanted her own meeting with the Godfather, she'd had to wait all afternoon. She took his arm and led him once again into the conservatory.

He was tense after almost five hours of continuous social

240

contact, including another meeting with Elizabeth and the warnings from Stevie and Molly.

Beth sat him down, then she went out to fetch the whisky, Glencairn glasses, well filled with a rich and peaty Bowmore. She turned out the lights and took her position behind his chair. "You look tense, Danny," she said as she started her massage.

His neck and shoulders were tight, unyielding to begin with, but she was patient and she worked her hands well.

Danny appreciated the sentiment and the massage. He needed both. He started to move his shoulders, one way, then another. He felt untied. He settled again and Beth continued her massage. She knew how badly he would want to retreat to the sanctuary of the gym and how big a deal it was that he'd remained.

She wanted him to have a quiet space here, in her presence. She could feel his shoulders relaxing and then the neck muscles. Beth continued her massage for a few minutes more. Then she caressed his neck and she kissed his cheek. She found her whisky and then took her seat. She didn't look at Danny. She'd give him as long as he needed.

She stared out from a dimmed conservatory to a dark December night and she let the Bowmore deliver its sympathy and its splendour. And Danny accepted all of her gifts, the massage, the whisky, the understanding, the patience and the silence. Beth knew the value of not speaking… she'd done it before.

After all of the fun and the frolic there he sat, Danny Hutton, in Beth's posh house in Saltburn, glad to be home.

·

It was a cold evening to be standing out on the street, hidden beneath the dark and naked trees. The last of the guests seemed to have departed. The young Kosovar had seen enough… the party was over. He headed off to Stockton to meet his old friend.

# PART FOUR

# A WALK IN THE PARK

Danny had been steadfast in his role as party host, alongside Beth from beginning to end, but he went back to the gym to prepare for his rendezvous with Erdi. It was only a couple of days since the family gathering but the warmth and the laughter were long gone, only the warnings and the wisdom had travelled with him. He'd felt the need for solitude and he wanted to get his head into a different space. He'd gone back to the gym to find some hope, to find himself, to become ready.

Beth's shops, the house in Saltburn… they were alien worlds, pretensions of respectability. He still needed his bolthole: a cooker, a fridge, a bed, a bathroom and all of the gym equipment. In all the years he'd had the place, he'd never bothered to do much with it. He'd converted the old shower block into a modern bathroom. There was a television and a couple of easy chairs. It was a dump but it still felt more like home than anywhere else.

He had lain awake most of the night. Remembering. A stream of uninvited images had passed through his mind. After all of those early years, head-fucked by his parents, sent here, there and everywhere in the care system. Throwing his child body into walls in fits of rage. There had been a thousand restless and lonely nights throughout this young man's troubled life. One or two more still to come.

He needed to collect his thoughts. He'd had some time now to understand that his life was changing. He knew that he needed to move on, but nevertheless, he anticipated a challenging day. He was unsure about the future, he was unsure about this day. He'd faced every challenge that his young life had thrown at him, he'd never been defeated and he'd always fought. Always. He needed to get through the next hour, and then… well, who could tell? It was a day for possibilities.

His perspective had extended with the news that he was to be a father. The timing was pretty good. Danny still worried about his struggle to stay with Beth. He was worried also that he'd fail as a father. He'd do his best with both Beth and their child, and he was excited about the baby. That had surprised him. Stay alive today, Danny Hutton.

Maybe he'd talk with Elizabeth, ask a few questions. There would be some kind of future but first he had to find a way to deal with Erdi. The man who wanted to steal his turf, the man who he held responsible for Sean's black eye. He glanced at his phone. The minutes were taking hours. He just wanted it done.

He was up well ahead of the winter sun, wondering if he was a man condemned, waiting to be hanged. Maybe. Maybe not. He lifted weights through most of the morning, just passing time. He was impatient and apprehensive, desperate to get moving. Still, he chastised himself. He should've made his move much earlier. Perhaps it had been laziness, maybe complacency. Either way, his response to Erdi had been sleepy. He'd allowed his rival to gain ground, ascendency.

Today Danny had some catching up to do. Just a few days earlier, he'd still felt paralysed by indecision. His serendipitous encounter with Clive had offered good guidance. It was time, he would take a strategic risk.

It got to 1.30. He went down to his car and drove to Albert Park. He was more than fifteen minutes early and he drove around the park perimeter, detoured around some of the surrounding streets.

He had no intention of attending the meeting. Clive's bar-room wisdom had convinced him. He just wanted to take a look, make sure that the timing was right. He'd found some hope and he'd waited patiently. The steel of his nerve had never been a concern. He saw Erdi's Mercedes first, no passengers. Erdi had arrived exactly on time for their previous meeting and had walked without urgency to meet his rival. Not so this time. Erdi was early.

Danny drove around a corner and saw Stevie's Corsa. The image appeared to Danny as a curve ball. Stevie, close to the battlefield? An unexpected throw of the dice. Then came another… his phone rang.

•

Emina had enjoyed her breakfast. The food was the same every day but this was a Tuesday, so Debora was in a good mood. She had talked again with Molly. They were talking quite freely, exchanging information. Someone out there in the free world knew about her. Molly was an unlikely saviour but her presence and her support meant something to Emina. Molly and her friend Danny were her only sources of hope.

Then she was taken to the office. It was just another day. Erdi wasn't very communicative. He seemed preoccupied. Emina entered the offices expecting the Tuesday routines with which she had become familiar but she quickly noticed unusual activity. Luan was in the office, then a younger man arrived… a stranger. The same man had visited the brothel late on the previous night. He'd chosen Debora, who had remained unusually quiet after he'd gone.

There was something in the air. Emina was keenly alert and highly curious.

Emina kept her head down and her ears open. She thought that she knew everything that was going on in Erdi's world but this morning something was happening and Emina knew nothing. She could feel a different atmosphere, an unusual mood. She watched and she listened, her senses heightened and focussed by anxiety.

During the middle of the day, Erdi unlocked his safe, an ancient cast iron container. The three men gathered into a tight group. Emina couldn't be certain but it appeared that each man took possession of a gun from the safe. There were more uncharacteristic behaviours and a feeling of nervous tension across the offices. This wasn't a regular Tuesday morning, the discussions were guarded, half hidden, softly spoken.

Emina kept herself busy, quietly attending to the conversations. And as the morning progressed, she picked up more information. The pieces came in fragments: Albert Park, the pond, meeting at a bench, two o'clock. From these fragments and her understanding of the morning's activity, she gained an increasingly clear and chilling picture. Erdi and his companions were planning an execution.

She'd strained to listen but in the end the stranger made things easy.

Alex Toka first met Erdi in Bedford. Although Alex was ten years younger than Erdi, they were both Kosovars whose fathers had died fighting for the Kosovo Liberation Army. That had connected them. His father had been brave but he'd left seven-year-old Alex alone with his mother. She became one of twenty thousand victims of sexual assault during the conflict. His heart had seemed to freeze when young Alex first witnessed his mother's rape and then her murder. He wandered out from the family home and into the streets, his blood running cold, and watched the mosque in which his family had always prayed, burn to the ground. From that moment, Alex had to find his own way, without guidance from his parents or from God.

He kept wandering for the next two years. He stole food and he survived. He was easily groomed into a criminal gang and his unique talent became apparent... Alex could kill. Even at twelve years old, he could point a gun with a steady hand, he could pull the trigger without hesitation and he felt no remorse when the deed was done. He was smuggled into the UK in 2015 as a specialist worker. He was the best in the business and he responded affirmatively when Erdi requested his help up in Teesside.

He sat casually on the corner of Emina's desk. He was well dressed. Tall, dark and handsome, but even with his confident smile and his calm demeanour, his presence chilled her.

"Hi, you're pretty. Maybe I'll come to see you tonight."

Emina's work in the brothel had never before been mentioned in the offices. Alex wasn't a man who respected boundaries. He seemed to understand that he was unsettling Emina. His smile grew large. He placed a cold and manicured hand against her cheek.

It was a violation. Emina tried to remain impassive. But she shuddered inside.

"First, I have a job to do. Later we can celebrate together." He allowed his hand to slide slowly from Emina's cheek, watching her discomfort.

She recovered impressively. "What job are you going to do?"

"I'm going to kill a man. An Englishman, a drug dealer. When I see you tonight, the world will be a better place than it is now because Danny Hutton, English scum, will be gone." Alex laughed.

Emina winced and she remained silent. With a few words, an uninvited intimacy, and a cruel smile, this man had frightened her. She was trembling. "I wish you luck," she said, unable to meet his gaze.

Alex laughed again. He stood up, towering over Emina and much too close to her. Then he was gone.

Emina had confirmation… Danny Hutton – Molly's friend, the man who might help her get free – was to be murdered.

Emina witnessed the presence of three furtive men together in the offices for the whole morning and then all of a sudden they were gone. Their movements had been guarded, then the mood changed and they marched out of the building, swift and purposeful, leaving Emina alone except for Zamir in the next office. It was 1.15. Frenk had been in earlier and attached half a dozen phones to the charger. Only six, there were usually more than that. Emina was discouraged. She needed to make a call, she had to warn Molly, her lifeline… and now Danny's lifeline.

Her body temperature and her heartrate had increased. She was sweating. Zamir seemed unusually attentive to her, perhaps he too was affected by the morning's events. Emina needed to make the call. Fifteen minutes passed, Zamir had clearly been briefed to watch her, and he was relentless. Then Frenk came back in. He didn't even look at the phones, he went straight through to Zamir, and they were locked in conversation. Emina assumed that they were probably talking about Danny Hutton's execution.

She took her opportunity, she had to, it wasn't perfect but she wasn't staying in the second chance hotel. Frenk would take the phones from the charger on his way back out. She stole a phone from Frenk's charging point while the two men were engrossed in their private conversation. She was getting better at this James Bond shit. She had her phone, she just needed a minute to make the call. The clock was ticking like a time bomb. Emina needed to make the call.

Suddenly the vibe shifted in the next office, Zamir and Frenk stopped speaking and turned to look through the glass partition at Emina. She was doing her best, just quietly attending to her spreadsheet, her heart pounding, her fear overpowering. Their observation went on for another ten minutes. She could feel their staring eyes. She didn't look up. Emina's hands were shaking.

Then Frenk was on the move. He came through and unhooked the phones from the charger, all five of them. He threw them into his bag, still staring at Emina and left the building. Zamir resumed his watch. Emina had her phone.

Zamir was good. He kept his attention focused on Emina for another ten minutes until his own phone rang. Emina watched him look at the ringing phone. He answered the call, and for a moment at least his attention would be diverted.

This was as good as it was going to get. She turned her back and punched in the numbers, her heart racing, praying to God that her friend would answer.

God was listening. Emina heard Molly greet the call. "Molly, thank God, it's me, Emina. Molly, please listen to me. Danny is in danger. Erdi is going to Albert Park with two other men to meet Danny at two o'clock. I've listened to them all morning. They have guns, they are going to shoot Danny. On a bench, near a pond. You must tell him not to go, you have to stop him. Phone him now. Don't let Danny go to meet Erdi, he will be shot."

She ended the call.

Emina's perspective was limited. She could see nothing of the world outside. She'd never met Danny. She'd gained information and judged her response. She was surprised by her own sense of urgency but, as ever, she delivered her message efficiently. She was in deep now, she'd stolen a phone and she'd made her call. She slid the phone back towards the charger, leaving it half hidden by loose paper documents. Then another surprise, Zamir took her back to her living quarters. She waited with Valmira and

Debora. She could do nothing more. She'd have to wait and hope as the consequences from her actions unfolded.

•

Molly sat alone in her flat, thinking quickly. Her phone had displayed 'unknown caller' but she'd decided to accept her uninvited stranger, the habit of a lifetime. Now she could hardly breathe. She was almost paralysed by the burden of responsibility. Danny's life was in her hands. If she failed to give him Emina's message, he would be shot in Albert Park.

Molly appreciated Emina's courage and she wondered what danger her friend may now face. It was a day of phone calls, one received and one to make. Five minutes and a few words, life and death.

She had to shake herself. *Move, Molly.* She made the call. *Come on, Danny, pick up your fucking phone.*

Danny hesitated but he took Molly's call. "Molly, I'm busy. Can I call you back?"

"No," Molly shouted. "Emina has just phoned. She watched Erdi and two others leave with guns. They're planning to shoot you, Danny. At the pond. You mustn't go to Albert Park. That's all she said."

"Okay, thanks. I'm not going to the meeting." In truth, Danny hadn't known what to expect from Erdi. He was disappointed with his rival but not surprised. He didn't feel malice. Erdi had carefully planned his execution but Danny was cool enough with that. He fully understood what was necessary to overthrow a drugs baron. Been there and done it.

His intention had been to go to Erdi's house. Two young children and a loving wife might shift the balance in a negotiation. Erdi's family was his ace card and his only card. But now he changed his plan. This was an unexpected set of dice, he needed to adapt. Clive would be proud.

Molly grew restless. "What are you going to do?"

"I'll go and get your friend at Fulham Road. Can you phone her?"

"Christ, Danny, I hope you know what you're doing. But no, I can't phone. Why?"

Danny needed to get busy. "Never mind. If she phones again, tell her and her friends to pack a bag. I'm on my way." He killed the call and phoned Stevie.

"Danny," whispered Stevie.

"Your car's parked close to Albert Park. Where are you?" Danny asked.

Stevie's whispering continued. "I'm in the park, wedged between a wall and a prickly bush, freezing my bollocks off. I've been here for nearly two hours. It was Seth's idea."

"There's three guys in the park waiting to shoot me, Stevie. Can you see anyone?

"No. I've seen a couple of dog walkers. That's it." Seth had found a hiding place with a view across the pond but Stevie had opted for a more considered position, two hundred metres further away and with no sight of water.

Danny was exasperated and slightly amused. "What the hell are you doing?" He didn't wait to hear Stevie's reply. "Listen, I have to go. Get the fuck out of Albert Park. Try not to get shot. Erdi's Mercedes is parked around the corner from the Corsa. Give him a puncture. I'll call you later."

# BETH

Beth had a lot going on. Table Leg was thriving, the Christmas trade was gaining pace, and she was pregnant. Twenty years had passed since she'd first arrived at Malton Court. It was only ten miles from Middlesbrough to Saltburn but it had been a long journey. She'd made a life for herself. She was hungry for the future.

Beth had never wasted her energy complaining. Even through challenging times, she had always tried to be positive. And the challenges had been many.

And yet she'd arrived at a moment in her life that offered fulfilment. Everything was falling into place. Even Danny seemed to be changing, making ready for this new adventure. He'd not only accepted her pregnancy, he seemed to be pleased about it.

Sometimes Beth felt something close to guilt. Her life in Saltburn, with her home and her shop, was held at arm's length from Danny's dangerous world. She was safely cocooned. She had never developed the street wisdom that seemed to come as second nature to Molly and the others. They stood alongside Danny wherever he went, while Beth stayed safe at home.

She'd reacted dismissively at the party when Molly had cautioned her about Danny's meeting. But she hadn't forgotten. Molly's warning had caught in the back of her mind, and now that it was Tuesday, Molly's words replayed. Beth's interest felt stronger now and she wondered what would take place in Albert Park.

She felt a bit uneasy, nothing more than that. She'd be glad when this day was done. There was nothing she could do. She wouldn't beat herself up for staying safe today, not with a baby growing inside her. She kept herself busy at the shop through the morning, but her sense of unease wouldn't settle. Elizabeth was taking a couple of days off following her separation from Rob. But Beth had employed Josie… primarily for the Christmas season although Beth had already decided to keep her on. Josie was excellent and Beth would need more help in the shop as her pregnancy progressed. She felt the need to be home. She could decorate the Christmas tree. So she handed Josie the keys and by 2pm she was back at the house.

Danny had left a jacket hanging on the back of a kitchen chair. It brought a smile to her face – gradually more of his clothes had moved from the gym. Even still though, hanging on a visitor's hook. And she could just about feel him in the house now. Just a small presence, gradually her man was making his way home. It was slow progress, he still needed time alone at the gym but the balance was shifting. He'd stayed with her the night after the party but he'd been back at the gym the next morning. She wanted him back in Saltburn tonight.

They were together now.

She occupied her house with hope in her heart. It was a cold December day. It was just a short walk home from Table Leg, ten minutes at most, but long enough for her to have felt the chill of winter. She and Danny had danced around the central heating thermostat for two years. Danny, uncomfortably warm, would turn the temperature down while Beth's back was turned, and she'd turn it back up at the first opportunity. She smiled to herself as she turned up the heating and settled into a sofa. She decided that she'd cook tonight.

Her need to see Danny tonight felt too strong to hold. She sent him a text asking him to phone.

# DANNY HUTTON – FREEDOM FIGHTER

He was a marked man. There was a bullet waiting for him. Really, he should have headed for home, found some cover and taken some time to think, or talked to Stevie and Beth. Instead, he was busy making his way to a twist in the tale. He was driving across to the centre of Stockton to pick up three sex slaves who were imprisoned in the headquarters of the violent criminal who was busy trying to kill him. Danny couldn't be sure how this diversion might help him. He was following his instinct, making a rogue move and he owed Molly... the person, of all the people in the world, who'd given him vital information, who'd called this afternoon, trying to save his life. And she'd been assisted by one of his rescue targets. He'd chosen and adapted his strategy. Now he'd throw his own dice.

Danny turned into Fulham Road and looked for the café, number twelve. He looked up to the top floor windows and sure enough, there were red curtains, just as Molly had specified. Danny still didn't know how this day would end. During the short drive, he'd wrestled with some doubt. He hadn't had time to think this through and he couldn't be sure who or what might greet his entrance into Erdi's world.

Too late now, he'd arrived and parked his Range Rover. In his thinking, Danny could experience doubt and hesitation. Not so for his actions. When Danny asserted himself in action, he moved with absolute certainty.

He activated the car locks and entered the building. He was in a café. In the far corner, a set of stairs offered him direction. He walked through the café, not bothering to look at the customers. He was moving swiftly. He ascended two flights of stairs, three steps at a time until he reached the top floor, land of the red curtains.

He stood before a locked door. The first kick split the frame, the second took the door off its hinges. The mixture of terror and hope on the women's faces was a sight to see. Danny felt alive... Danny Hutton, still living. The hesitation that had crept into him, got into his head, was all gone.

All three women stood before him, their possessions in plastic carrier bags on the floor. "Emina?"

She replied. "Danny? I phoned Molly, she said you would come."

"We have to go quickly, Emina."

It was all a bit crazy. "We are ready." Emina and Valmira were indeed desperately ready.

But not Debora. "I'll stay here," she said.

In the rush and the urgency, this announcement met a brief silence. Debora had surprised herself. Her bag was packed but her heart wasn't in it… her heart was with Genti. She hadn't rehearsed for this moment, she had no time to think and yet she heard her own words and learned her decision, she would stay.

Valmira tried to persuade her friend. "Please, Debora, we came here together, we've suffered together." It was true, they were bonded through shared experience and trauma. They had picked each other up from the floor, bathed one another's wounds. "We should leave together. You have to come."

They'd still been girls really, when fate had brought them together in Stockton, sweetened with naivety and inexperience. Now they were women… weary, soured with disillusionment. The door that had held them lay broken on the floor. The escape that had seemed impossible, beckoning.

Emina also tried. "Debora, we are leaving. Danny has come for us. We have a chance to leave. Please, Debora, we have to move quickly." Emina hadn't planned for this either, although as she looked across at her friend, she understood that it was Genti who held Debora now. "Maybe you can still find him, Debora. When he knows that you're gone, maybe he will follow. He isn't a prisoner."

"If I leave now, I'll never see him again." She would stay, she couldn't walk away from Genti. She loved him. "I'm staying." She looked at her two dear friends, tears streaming down her cheeks. "Go quickly. God bless you on your next journey."

Danny accepted her refusal. He didn't wait around. "Okay, let's go." He turned and started back down the stairs with Valmira and Emina following behind, each of them carrying a bag of worthless possessions, trying to believe in Danny.

As they descended the stairs, Valmira asked, "Where is Fatos?"

Danny stopped. "What are you saying? Who's Fatos?"

Emina answered, her English skills needed. "He is Erdi's man, a strong man, violent. He will stop us if he's in the café."

"Does he have a gun?" Danny didn't want to facilitate his own execution. He'd already toyed with that idea earlier in the afternoon.

"I don't know." That was all Emina could offer.

Danny took off again down the stairs, moving quickly.

By the time they got back down to the café, Fatos was waiting for them, standing with his arms folded across his chest, already looking forward to his fun. An unexpected bonus in the middle of a Tuesday afternoon.

The confidence in Fatos's smile faltered, just for half a second when he saw the size of Danny but he stood his ground and re-crafted his sadistic grin.

Danny noted his hesitation, that tiny moment of doubt. He looked across straight into Fatos's eyes and he saw it again, twitching facial muscles and a slight scent of fear. Two almost imperceptible twitches, that was enough for Danny. He had gained position. For Danny, there wasn't any hesitation, no doubt, he was filled with confidence. Fatos had neither a gun nor the self-belief to worry him. Already, Danny knew he was in control.

Danny stepped forward as Valmira and Emina edged down the final few stairs and into the back of the café. There were eight customers in the café, all Albanian men, plus Fatos and Joel who ran the café.

Fatos glared at the women. "Back upstairs."

Danny smiled at the distraction. He'd allowed Fatos's first lapse to go unpunished. This time he reacted. Danny kicked the back of a seated customer, sending both the chair and its occupant across the floor. An innocent man half way through a late lunch tumbled into Fatos's legs. Fatos stumbled, almost lost balance.

Danny was swift and unerringly certain. One kick and one

right hand punch. Both blows delivered with accuracy and power, before Fatos could reorientate his attention from the man at his feet to the one who had just destroyed him. He'd just met Danny Hutton, with adrenaline.

While Fatos was spitting out a couple of teeth, Danny calmly led the women out into the street. Danny still hadn't really stopped to think what came next. He got them into the back of the car and drove away.

He checked the mirror… no one in pursuit.

# ERDI, ALONE ON A PARK BENCH

Erdi hadn't forgotten his first meeting with Danny. This time he parked in an unlikely street and timed his arrival with both care and attention to detail. His men were in place. Luan, his lion, discreetly patrolling the surrounding area, watching for surprises. He was grumpy. It was a damp afternoon, grey and cold. Erdi felt the same way.

He felt nervous, sitting on a bench in Albert Park. Today he had to get his own hands dirty. He didn't know what to expect from Danny, but his plan was solid and simple. Alex would fire the gun, an Obsidian 45 with supressor. Erdi had chosen the bench but Alex had selected his weapon. Alex would fire from about four metres into the back of Danny's head. Erdi and Luan were also armed in case events took an unexpected turn. That was unlikely. Murders are straightforward if they're well planned. Alex never missed.

Erdi was in place thirty minutes before Danny's arrival time. He spent a few minutes alone with his murderous thoughts. He didn't like this part of his work and he wasn't without a moral conscience. Mostly he tried not to think about his criminal activities. When avoidance failed, he found explanations for himself that just about worked. That was the reason for the absolute separation between work and home. The man in Yarm, husband and father, the family man, that was who he was. Work was what he did. Emina was his secretary. He never went to the brothel.

At five to two, Erdi started to suspect he'd be stood up. There was still time but he just had a feeling that something wasn't quite right. He waited. 2pm came and went. He waited still but he knew now that Danny wasn't coming. Erdi got more grumpy, angry with himself. He'd planned for every entrance and exit. He had a ready response to every move that Danny might make. But he hadn't planned for Danny's absence.

The minutes ticked by. Still Erdi waited, although he knew that the meeting time had passed. Danny Hutton was elsewhere.

All three men returned from their posts back to the cars.

The front passenger tyre on Erdi's Mercedes was completely flat. This was a new experience for Erdi. No one stood him up and no one messed with his wheels. Erdi wasn't grumpy anymore, he was ticking. What kind of an attack was that? A flat tyre!

He addressed Luan. "He's been here. We'll change the wheel and get back to Fulham Road." It wasn't a plan, it was instinct. Get back to the castle, alongside the troops, with full access to all weapons. Erdi's work phone vibrated. He took the call. It was Joel from the café who gave him a brief summary of Danny's impact on the late lunchtime trading and the potential for a quiet night in the brothel. He couldn't talk for long… he needed to get Fatos to A&E.

Erdi had the firepower, he had the numbers. But Danny had surprised him. It was a declaration of war, no doubt about that, and Erdi was starting to falter. He turned again to Luan. "He's been to Fulham Road. He's taken two of the women. Fatos is hurt. And we're three fucking moves behind him." He felt desperately impatient while the car was fixed. At least the delay gave him a moment to think.

Ten wasted minutes later, Erdi and Luan drove back to Stockton, looking for answers.

# HOUSE CALL

When Danny had driven out of Fulham Road, he'd headed towards Yarm, gaining a bit of distance before he turned into an Aldi carpark.

Danny parked up, released his seat belt and turned to see Emina and Valmira locked in an embrace. What else could they do but hold each other. He watched them. They held each other tightly and with such tenderness, Danny was moved. He was choking up, the magnitude and the impact of his actions suddenly apparent to him.

He'd never seen two recently freed sex slaves before. It was a powerful image. Their silent embrace continued. Danny could see the right side of Valmira's face, her eyes closed and wet with tears, her trembling head pushed into Emina's shoulder.

He waited, still deeply moved, his heartrate slowing. It went on, almost forever. Eventually the women moved apart, slowly relaxing their arms, leaning away so that they could look at each other.

Danny felt himself an intruder and yet he was transfixed, compelled to witness the image before him. Two women quietly sobbing, utterly overcome. Valmira raised her right hand, an open generous palm to reach Emina's left cheek and gently wipe away a few tears. Emina kissed her friend's tender hand. Then she reached out to return the intimacy, offering her own hand. He marvelled at the affection between them, then he managed to disengage.

He jumped out of the car, giving them a moment of privacy and himself a chance to breathe in some cold air. It'd had become an eventful day. He too was affected. He took a minute, breathing with long deliberate breaths, pushing his cheeks out like a trumpeter each time he exhaled. He cleared his nostrils and his head.

A woman wheeled her shopping trolley past him. "You alright, pet?"

"Yeah, I'm good." He looked at her. "Thanks." He got back

inside the car. A couple more big breaths and maybe he could look at them and hold it together. Maybe.

Danny grabbed his water bottle. He swallowed some big mouthfuls and passed the bottle to Emina. "I don't know what you want to do but for now, I'll try to keep you safe."

"Thank you, Danny." Valmira smiled. She hadn't understood what Danny had said. Nevertheless, he seemed to be a nice guy. She was grateful, a bit fazed and quite shaken, but almost smiling. She was at least able to speak although she didn't know what to say and she knew little English. Emina was still shaking and silent, almost in shock.

Danny still had a few things to think about. It was damp and cold and already the daylight seemed to be struggling. "Emina, I need you to listen to me."

"Yes, I hear you."

"I want to make us all safe. Emina, I should be able to take you to meet Molly later. I'll phone her in a minute to let her know I've got you out. You know that Erdi wants to kill me. I have to deal with that. I'm not going to die today. I won't let him kill me."

Emina concentrated, she had to be strong. "He has many people and weapons. There were three men this morning, all with guns. You will have to be very careful, Danny. What can you do?"

Before he could decide exactly what his next move would be, he needed a moment of consideration. Life had become complicated and the long term prospects were uncertain.

Emina had asked a good question. What could he do? The adrenaline was settling, the intensity of the emotional impact was easing, Danny could think again. There was no doubt in Danny's mind that he'd started well. He'd walked in and out of Erdi's Empire State Building on Fulham Road, he'd destroyed Fatos, freed the two women who were sitting quietly in the back of his car and he was less than fifteen minutes drive from Erdi's wife and children. Today he held all the cards, he just had to decide how best to play them. Bearing in mind that tomorrow would surely come.

Danny gave Emina his answer. "I can introduce you to his wife and children." Danny was still thinking on his feet. "At his house in Yarm." He looked at his watch and he hoped that Stevie's intel was accurate and reliable. "The children will be home from school now."

He didn't want to delay. He couldn't be sure how long it would take Erdi to catch up with events. Danny needed to clarify his own intentions and to work out what might be the way forward for his two passengers.

"Yes, Yarm, that's right. He told me he lives in Yarm. I didn't know about his children." Emina was surprised.

"I think we should go there. Erdi won't be home just yet, not after today. Waiting for me, hearing about you guys. I'm guessing that he'll work late. He'll talk to Debora. Why didn't she come?"

"Debora has a boyfriend… she couldn't go without him. What do you want to do at Erdi's house?" Emina detested Erdi. She ought to wish him dead, but she didn't. And she didn't know how she felt about going to his house, meeting his wife. *And* his children.

"Well, first I have to show him that I know where he lives and that I know about his wife and children. He won't like it. I don't really like it myself, but it's all I have to work with. After that I don't really have to do anything more, that'll make us safe. For today at least." Danny had known from the start that he was outnumbered and outgunned. "If I was doing my job properly, I'd take the opportunity to kill him. But I won't do that, there'd be someone else in his place tomorrow. I'm guessing that today's events will reorder Erdi's priorities for a few weeks… we'll see. What about you, Emina? What do you want to say to him?"

Crime and punishment, judgement and justice. Who knows? Lives were being tossed high into a wild wind, dice were being thrown. Danny had no moral objection to a violent turf grab. He understood the dark world in which he and Erdi resided. He also understood that Emina might have her own perspective on crime and punishment. He waited with interest to hear her reply.

Emina's initial reaction was hesitation but she found her voice. "I have some things to say to him. Yes, I have. It feels scary, after what has passed between us. I don't know how to explain, I have been his property, his slave, he stole my life, Valmira's life. It will feel very strange to face him. But I want to do it. I want him to look at me, to see me as a human being making my own choices. I wish I had a way to make him see what he's done." She hesitated again. "I don't want to kill him either."

Danny checked the time… 2.45. "We'll grab some coffee. We need to make a plan. When we get to his house, we need to know exactly what we're going to do. We can have a chat with his wife when we get there. Then we'll bring Erdi back home."

Danny started the car and set off further down the road. He found a drive-through burger bar and bought them coffee and burgers. The coffee was welcome but none of them were hungry. They took less than twenty minutes to formulate their plan before they set off to Erdi's house.

# AGNESA

Agnesa liked to follow regular routines. She'd collected the children and she began to prepare food for the family meal while her boys disappeared into virtual worlds. Despite their immigrant parents, six-year-old Harry and his four year old brother George were Yorkshire boys… and they loved their Xboxes. Agnesa enjoyed a comfortable life. She managed to look away from the dark and murky world in which her husband worked. He'd promised her an impenetrable separation between his work and their domestic family existence. And she couldn't fault him, and for the eight years they'd been together, he'd delivered on his promise. Then late in the afternoon, the skies began to darken.

The doorbell rang.

It was just a regular Tuesday afternoon. Agnesa was entirely free from anxiety when she opened the front door. Her mood changed quickly as Danny pushed himself inside. She understood immediately that she was in danger, although it wasn't until Valmira and Emina also entered her house that she realised the danger was connected to Erdi. She recognised her first intruder as a young and rather frightening Englishman, and she guessed that the women were Albanians. Her boys were just a few metres away, getting two uninterrupted hours of Xbox time before their dad came home. They knew nothing of their father's promise to their mother, broken into a thousand pieces.

Agnesa froze, her routine interrupted, her life changing.

Emina spoke to Agnesa in English. "We've come to see your husband, Erdi. You won't be harmed, nor will the children."

Agnesa heard Emina's words but she was unconvinced. She was breathing fast, her heart pounding, but she met Emina's gaze and she gave her reply. "He's not here. He is working." Agnesa's eyes darted rapidly from one intruder to the next and across to the door of her living room. Then she looked at Emina. "Who are you? Why have you come to the house?"

"My name is Emina. I'll explain to you in a moment. What is your name?"

Agnesa was terrified. She wasn't really able to think but her instincts were sound. She was compliant. "Agnesa Djoni."

Emina continued. "Where are the children?"

Agnesa's level of alarm compounded. "They play Xbox games until their father comes home. He doesn't like them to play on the Xboxes. They are in the living room." Agnesa pointed across the small and crowded hallway to a door on the left of the staircase, fearful for her young sons. She felt that she was collapsing, as if her insides might run out of her. She appealed desperately, "Please, they are innocent children."

Emina proceeded. "We won't harm your children. I give you my word. Do they speak Albanian?"

"Yes, of course. They prefer English, but they are fluent Albanian speakers." Agnesa was starting to breathe again. Despite this intrusion, she recognised that Emina was not hostile… threatening and frightening but at this moment in time, without hostility.

Emina pushed on. "Valmira has young brothers. She likes to be with children. You must explain to them that she is their auntie, visiting from Albania. I want you to tell them to be good boys, maybe watch television with Auntie Valmira."

The three women went to meet Harry and George. It felt surreal to Agnesa, really quite bizarre. The boys accepted their aunt, quickly content to watch Shrek on a movie channel.

Agnesa led Emina back into the hall and on to the kitchen, Danny's presence in the room reigniting her terror. "Would you like some coffee?" Agnesa's emotions were overloaded and she was unsure why she'd offered such a civil welcome. She didn't dare to imagine what might be about to happen. Her guests accepted her hospitality and they sat in conference at her kitchen table.

"I'm sorry, Agnesa," said Emina, "that we have pushed into your house. I'm sorry that Danny and I have frightened you. Please believe me, we won't hurt your children."

Agnesa wanted information. She needed to know what was happening. "Who is Danny? What is he going to do?" She wasn't exactly at ease with Emina but given the circumstances she was just about managing to believe her when she gave assurances that no harm would come to her kids. But Danny hadn't said a word and she didn't like the look of him. Agnesa knew where her husband's use of physical violence had taken him, and she was seriously intimidated by Danny.

Finally, Danny spoke. "I'm going to tell you some things about your husband. I don't know how much you already know or whether you'll believe anything that I say. These women, Emina and Valmira, were kidnapped in Europe and shipped over here in the back of a lorry. They've been held by Erdi in Stockton and used as sex workers. There's three of them, the other one is still there, at Fulham Road. I need to talk to Erdi and, believe me, Agnesa, Erdi needs to talk to me. We need him to come home. I'm going to take a photograph. Where's your phone?"

Agnesa was pretty stunned and still very frightened by Danny but she was glad that he'd spoken. She found him both chilling and childlike. It was a lot to take in, these strangers in her kitchen, bringing strange news. She reached into her bag which was hanging on a kitchen chair and passed her phone to Danny.

Danny addressed both women. "I need you two to sit together for a photograph."

Emina and Agnesa sat side by side while he pointed the camera. "Smile."

They complied like children for a school photograph, both women finding a false grin, each for their own reasons. Danny took the picture and handed the phone back to Agnesa. "I want you to text the photo to Erdi. Tell him to phone you immediately."

Agnesa sent the text, under watchful supervision. Then Danny took her phone, ready to take Erdi's call.

# ERDI

Erdi and Luan arrived back at Fulham Road just before 3pm, about forty minutes after Danny's flying visit. He was trying to catch up, he was puzzled. The remaining witnesses gave clear information. They described Danny Hutton, his actions and his exit. It appeared that Danny's only purpose had been to take the two women. Fatos just happened to get in his way. No one knew why Debora had been left behind. Erdi sent for her.

Debora was duly delivered to his offices. She was frightened. She hadn't seen Erdi for several months. He hadn't changed much. He was perhaps a bit more agitated today.

Erdi was more than agitated, he was desperate and he was confused. It was never going to be his favourite day of the year. He'd started out with a murder to commit. He'd anticipated hearing Danny's acquiescence, watching his sudden death, then settling back into his work.

Now he was back at Fulham Road, his murder uncommitted, Fatos in hospital, and two of the women gone. Emina was gone. Danny Hutton had chosen to fight and he was a step or two ahead of Erdi. These things had happened, but why? Why had he taken the women? How could that help him? It didn't make sense. He wanted an explanation from Debora.

"Where is Emina?" Erdi asked.

Deborah's gazed at the floor. "I don't know where they have gone."

He asked more questions but nothing helpful came from Debora. Erdi was stressed. He needed a clue, he needed to catch up with Danny Hutton and as yet, he was getting nowhere. He wanted to hit Debora. He just felt very angry and frustrated and he felt tempted. He might feel better if he hurt someone. He was exasperated, he shouted and threatened but the miserable whore gave no further information.

His phone pinged, his home phone… only Agnesa had the number. He looked and there they were, sitting side by side, smiling like sisters. His chin dropped down to his chest.

He closed his eyes. He could feel his blood pressure rising. He felt ready to burst. When Erdi was fleeing from his home in Kosovo, travelling through the night, his family gone, he'd felt the same way, stumbling and praying, lost, all control gone.

The separation that he'd managed with such care had ended. Erdi wondered what else was about to reach an end. He'd had his life savagely destroyed, then built himself a new one. What had he now? Erdi looked at Luan. "I have to make a call. Give me a minute, Luan."

Erdi made the call which was answered promptly.

"Hi, Erdi. How you doing?"

Danny's question was more than unsettling, it felt sinister.

Erdi's heart would have dropped into his boots, if it hadn't been there already. He managed to snatch an intake of breath and found his voice. "I'm worried about my children and my wife. What do you want?" Debora was still sitting in front of him. He'd asked Luan to leave but Debora had stayed.

"You should be worried. You've placed them in great danger. I want you to send two of your people outside onto the street. I have a car waiting to pick them up. Debora and Genti. He works in a carwash, he'll be home by now, and Debora, she's probably with you now. Tell them both to pack a bag, then send them out into the street. Tell them to walk over to a white BMW. It's parked back along the road from the café. Tell them to get inside the car. Do exactly what I've told you, Erdi. You've got ten minutes. When I get confirmation that they've left safely, I'll send you another text. Then you can come home, we need to have a chat. Oh and Erdi, don't bring Luan, don't bring anyone. We don't want any unpleasantness, not in front of the children." Danny killed the call.

Erdi looked at Debora, then shouted to Luan. The three of them were reassembled in his office but circumstances had changed, just a touch. He looked at them both. "Who is Genti?"

Debora examined the threadbare carpet.

Luan spoke. "I know him. He works at a carwash. He's a good worker, illegal."

Debora sat quietly.

Erdi turned to her. "You're leaving. You have to pack a bag, very quickly. Then come down to the café, five minutes, no more. Understand?"

She nodded.

Then he turned to Luan. "Take her back. Find Genti. Tell him to pack his things and get him down to the café. Quickly, Luan."

They made their exit and Erdi was left alone at his desk. He was trying not to think. He was trying to push away the images that were invading his imagination. He felt hesitant, he was fearful for his family. He'd lost Emina.

Erdi realised that Danny Hutton would probably have learned from Emina about his plan to shoot him. Not the ideal prerequisite for an amiable negotiation. And suddenly the implications of the day's events started to flood his mind. He was drowning. He lifted his weary body up from his chair, he stepped out into the cold dark afternoon air and breathed some deep breaths.

Luan returned, breathless. Talking as they stood outside on the pavement, they looked back along the road and saw Sean's Beamer, then they strolled to the café.

Debora and Genti arrived in the café at the same moment. They were both equally confused. They were on the move and they didn't know why or where. They'd only ever seen one another on Tuesdays, both of them had been looking forward to their weekly meeting., albeit in different circumstances. They stood, helpless and nervous, hardly daring to look at each other. Something unexpected was happening.

There were no farewell speeches. Erdi gave them their instructions and he watched them scuttle across to the car. Then they were gone.

Less than five minutes later, he received a text from Agnesa. It was time to go home. Erdi ran out to his black Mercedes but once he was ready to drive, he paused. He was desperate to be there and at the same time he didn't want to go. It was difficult for Erdi to imagine that good news was waiting. So he drove slowly home. He pulled on to his drive and he walked to the door of his house. Details of his future were inside.

# KEEPING DANNY SAFE

Sean Murphy in a BMW, allowed two weary souls to climb into the back of the car. Debora and Genti, their lives in carrier bags, with only Erdi's instructions to guide them, nervously met their saviour and their fate.

Sean had received his instructions from Danny thirty minutes earlier. He'd updated Molly and then set out to wait for his passengers. He drove away. Danny had asked him to take his passengers back to Stevie's house in Middlesbrough, a bit of company for Elizabeth.

However, while he'd been waiting on Fulham Road, he'd spotted a grey Lexus. Then there were two men talking as they stood on the pavement. They turned their heads to look back up the road to his car. He recognised one of the men, a familiar figure, the guy who'd claimed to be John Stanton, the bastard who'd whacked him.

Sean drove around the block, making a less than comprehensible explanation to the nervous couple in the back seat, and he texted a thumbs up to Danny. He reparked, further back this time, lights out. And he resumed his watch.

The two men were back out on the pavement. They talked for a minute before one of them climbed into a black Mercedes and drove away from view. Sean now understood that Erdi was likely to be the driver. He decided to wait. Less than ten minutes later, the man who wasn't John Stanton jumped into the Lexus and set off. Sean followed, still no lights.

Luan drove to Erdi's house. Before Erdi had left Fulham Road, he'd given Luan precise instructions. He was to park at a discreet distance and then follow Danny Hutton wherever he took the two women. Erdi had calculated that Debora and Genti would be taken to the same destination. Luan should then return to Fulham Road and report their whereabouts to Erdi, who would plan to recapture the four illegal workers and complete their original objective... Danny's Hutton's murder

However, Luan was an ambitious man. He'd watched his senior colleague screwing up all day. Luan expected that Erdi's position in Teesside was about to become vacant and he was keen to demonstrate his credentials as a likely successor. So he decided to ignore Erdi's instruction to keep weapons out of sight in Yarm and he parked right across the street from the house. Erdi Djoni was yesterday's man, this was Luan's moment. He wouldn't delay Hutton's murder to allow Erdi the chance to claim the glory. Luan intended to kill Danny Hutton at the first opportunity.

Sean drove into an adjacent street. He offered further incomprehensible explanation to his bemused passengers, urging them to sit tight, then crept back towards Erdi's house. He found a space between two parked cars where he was well hidden from Luan's view but with a line of sight to watch his target. The driver's window was down. He saw gleaming metal reflecting street lights. Danny's Range Rover was parked fifty metres further down the road, Erdi's Mercedes was on the drive.

Sean pieced it together. He assumed that Erdi and Danny would be in the house and that the gleaming metal was a gun barrel. He hadn't expected a gunfight but, thanks to his previous failure to follow Danny's instructions, he was appropriately equipped. Given his earlier confrontation with the Lexus driver and considering the gun pointing out from the car window, Sean feared for his friend.

He'd found a place to hide out of view, but the area around the Lexus was open road. There was no cover. He smiled to himself, enjoying the prospect of poetic justice. He looked across at his target, sitting in the driver's seat and wished he'd fall asleep. Somehow, Sean needed to approach this violent man. He'd find a way, Sean could walk easily into scary darkness, he sensed his moment.

He reached into his jacket pocket and allowed Stanton's unused gun to lay in the palm of his hand. There was no option, he'd have to hide in plain sight. He emerged from the path onto the road, whistling out of tune, unsteady in his stride. He caught his left foot against his right heel, an old footballer's trick, almost tripping over, but he chuckled loudly as he stumbled to regain his balance.

Luan looked up and drew his gun back out of sight, waiting for a drunken fool to stagger past. Sean's hand came from his pocket. Sean had fast hands. He wasn't really a fighter but he could throw stones and he could throw a punch. He slammed Stanton's gun into Luan's face, full power. That was that, all done. The man who wasn't John Stanton fell across the passenger seat. Sean looked at him. He was sleeping now. Sean reached inside the car, claiming a second firearm and then the car keys. He took both new possessions and a satisfaction born from revenge back to the Beamer. He edged awkwardly back into the car, taking care to keep his new possession hidden from the view of his nervous passengers. Now that Luan was sound asleep, Sean decided to park up behind Danny's Range Rover. He couldn't drive away until he'd seen his brother emerge into safe territory.

# ELIZABETH

Elizabeth had been at Stevie's house for two nights. He'd let her use his car to go to work in Saltburn. Not the Corsa – there were limits to his generosity – but she could have the Porsche for a while, no problem. She'd gone over to Rob's house the previous day, pulled up in the 911 all by herself, all of her fear gone. Rob watched her pack, she spoke to him… they were done, they both knew.

She hadn't realised what an exciting life Beth led and what interesting friends she had. It was the middle of a Tuesday afternoon. She'd been sorting out a few loose ends, taking it easy, taking it in. She was free from Rob, learning to relax at home again. Then Molly, Seth and Stevie arrived in a bit of a state, excited and worried, talking fast. And it just kept coming. Sean came and went. Molly took a call and she was clearly excited. Some more people were on their way with Sean, an Albanian couple. Apparently, Danny would be bringing some others later.

Amidst all of the chaos, Elizabeth felt light of heart. The burden that she'd carried for the past several months had been lifted from her, let it be. She made tea and she listened. She was enjoying her new freedom, she was beginning again. She was comforted by the warmth and the worry in this chaotic family… her foster family. Short term.

# THE SHORT DRIVE HOME

The conversation had dried up. They were waiting now for Erdi's return. It had been an interesting ten or fifteen minutes for Agnesa. Emina had spoken to her, filled in a few blank spaces.

Emina wasn't a vindictive woman. She took no pleasure from the suffering of another human being. She'd never engaged deeply in philosophical discussions about crime and punishment but during the past couple of hours she'd examined her thoughts about Erdi. She'd asked herself what she wanted for him, how might she make use of her last moments with him.

She had no desire to inflict punishment but she knew that this visit to his house, the involvement of Erdi's wife and children in securing her own and Danny's safety, would have consequences. She'd talked it through with Danny at the burger bar. They had recognised that Emina and the other escapees would have to submit to authority, go to the police and tell their tale… it was their best chance for repatriation. They would be questioned and in order to pursue their own return home, they would have to represent themselves honestly, give credible information.

She'd shared these thoughts with Agnesa.

Emina really didn't want suffering for Erdi and his family but her own rapidly developing sense of justice had found a conclusion: that Erdi's wife got to know who she had married. That was all. The rest she could do nothing about.

So she told her about the brothel. About slavery. About rape. That was a lot. Too much for Agnesa and as she listened, she knew that her marriage had ended.

Danny had been watching the street outside. He opened the front door and ushered Erdi into his own home – it didn't feel like home anymore.

Danny gestured towards the kitchen. Erdi moved inside and found his wife and Emina both seated at the kitchen table.

"Where are the children?" He directed his question to Agnesa.

She answered him. "They are fine, watching a film, playing Xbox." But Erdi's wife didn't look at him. She didn't want to give personal recognition, she wanted him to know that he'd lost her.

Erdi turned to Danny. "So, what now?"

"That's up to you, Erdi. I'm all done." It'd been a long day. Danny was tired. He'd planned to say a few things, announce his early retirement but now that his moment had arrived, he felt inclined to stay quiet. There was too much in the room already. The rivals had had their showdown. For different reasons, they were both surprisingly disinterested in selling drugs and in each other. Other fish to fry. Today they would part without a shot being fired, both vacating the territory they'd fought over.

Emina filled the silence. She addressed Erdi. "We'll go to the police tomorrow." She understood that Erdi was in trouble. Her loathing was undiminished and yet this, her only comment, was a generous parting gift. She'd given Erdi one night to do what he could.

Then a moment of silence filled the room. Emina had nothing more to say. She looked directly at his eyes. Emina was staring into his soul, waiting for acknowledgement. She could see that he didn't want to meet her gaze but she wouldn't be refused. She held her gaze until his head lifted and their eyes met. She looked at him and into him, and for a second she held him to account.

Erdi felt the power of her stare, her courage. He experienced a moment of shame, then he closed his eyes, to Emina and to the world.

Agnesa watched their brief and silent exchange. With great interest.

Emina turned to Danny. "I'll get Valmira."

They left quietly, no goodbyes, no hugs and kisses. Erdi could hear his children playing in the next room, free now from their auntie's gaze. It was Agnesa who went to them. He was left with his thoughts and his choices.

And he had a lot to consider. He was upset by Agnesa's cold shoulder. He watched her go to the children and he was fearful. He wondered if he was losing another family. But Agnesa would have to wait, Emina's call was more pressing. Erdi would have some cleaning up to do at Fulham Road and then he'd need to disappear for a while. It had been a tough day.

But it wasn't all bad news, Luan would be in position… there were still a couple of surprises waiting for Danny Hutton.

•

Danny and Emina had pulled it off. They'd got their heads together and they'd made their plan. And now they'd pulled it off. Emina and Valmira had both escaped Erdi Djoni. Danny had lived to fight another day. The three of them started to walk towards Danny's car.

Danny scanned the street nervously. He was suddenly alarmed. He saw the grey Lexus and immediately he expected to be shot. Danny had the feeling of seeing his fate clearly but too late to do a damn thing about it. He thought about Clive, wishing for a double six. Somehow their walk progressed. His continuing existence felt so unexpected and extraordinary that Danny half wondered if he was already dead. He was amazed as the three of them had almost completed the fifty metre walk, approaching the Range Rover in silence and without interruption.

Then he saw Sean and began to understand his safe passage more clearly.

"What's happening, Sean?"

Sean explained, expecting to be chastised for once again abandoning Danny's instructions.

Danny understood more fully now, Sean had risked his own life to keep him safe. He looked at Sean, felt the meeting of eyes, and he nodded. "Thanks, Sean."

Debora was waving frantically, trying to catch Emina's attention. She had no idea what might happen next but, in this moment of reunion, she felt fine.

Sean smiled. There was the finest of love and loyalty between these two men, but no such words would ever be spoken. Nods and smiles were acknowledgment enough. "I think we should get out of here, Danny. I'll see you back at Stevie's." Then Sean jumped back into the Beamer and away he went.

Neither Valmira nor Emina had responded to Debora. They hadn't had a chance to process the day's events. They were overwhelmed and silent.

Danny took the opportunity to video phone Beth.

Beth had fallen asleep. She awoke to see his smiling face appear on her phone. She accepted the call and his face came alive, although he wasn't smiling. "Danny, you took your time. Are you okay?" She could hear him speaking, she could see him. Already, she felt relieved.

Danny released a long sigh. "It's been a long day. But yes, it's all done and I'm fine."

"Well, get yourself home when you can. I'm cooking tonight and I've decorated the tree," said Beth. She was properly awake now. "I've got to go. I can feel a draught. I must have left a window open."

"Okay, I'll be back in a couple of hours." Danny ended the call.

Emina and Valmira reclaimed their seats in the back of the car and they pulled away.

The two young women stared out through the car windows, feeling like aliens. These busy Middlesbrough streets, the darkness, the streetlights. It all looked scary, like a movie scene passing by, quite unreal. The noises from the traffic, the car wheels on tarmac. It all felt really odd. They were suddenly exposed to the rush and tumble of a world that had been hidden from them. It felt disorientating. Emina was shaking. She'd held it together at Erdi's house, calm and efficient, as always in his presence. She was collapsing now.

Emina and Valmira wanted to return home. They knew that the trauma they had suffered would always be with them, their lives could never be the same, but they had to go back home to live with their pain.

It really had been a long day. Danny had survived. He'd exposed himself to great danger. He'd faced up to and out-manoeuvred his rival, and he'd survived. He experienced the beginning of relief and he whispered to reassure himself, "It's over." He still had some loose ends to tidy up, but his career in illegal drugs was ending. He would work even harder to stay with Beth, watch her belly swell, and prepare to be a father.

They could be together now.

He'd made himself safe, with a little help from his friend, but it would take a while before his heartrate and adrenaline levels could settle. His eyes searched through the car windows, still watching, not yet quite ready to believe. There was a nagging sliver of doubt. He couldn't shake it off and yet he couldn't get a hold of it either. He was just five minutes from Stevie's house now and his thoughts drifted.

He drove on, and he thought ahead, trying to imagine the first face to face meeting between Molly and Emina. Then he thought about Sean and the courage he'd found to protect him. His thoughts couldn't settle anywhere.

He pulled into Stevie's drive and took the women inside to meet Molly. There was quite a gathering in Stevie's front room… a kaleidoscope of emotions, smiling faces, tearful embraces.

And then the illusive sliver of doubt revealed itself. The thought hit him and immediately he was filled with dread… Beth wouldn't allow winter into the house, she'd never leave a window open.

Danny rushed out from the room and into his car. His stomach seemed to be clenching, his jaws were tense. He was afraid. He looked for comfort, reminding himself that he'd just spoken to her a short time ago. But he needed to phone. He needed to know that she was still safe.

Elizabeth saw the expression of terror on Danny's face, and his rapid withdrawal. She immediately followed him outside.

Danny phoned Beth, desperate.

*Come on, Beth. Please, pick up your phone.*

Beth's phone kept on ringing. Danny felt a second wave of panic rise in him.

*Please, Beth.*

Then the ringing stopped and an image of a Christmas tree

filled his phone screen. Danny felt a surge of relief. He released a breath, not daring to speak of the fear he'd felt. He swallowed, composing himself. "Wow, it looks amazing."

"Yes, it is very pretty," said Alex. "You did well to stay alive today, Danny Hutton." Alex scanned the camera across the room, halting his movement to capture an image of Beth lying lifeless on the bloodstained carpet. "Beth, not so well."

Alex ended the call. He'd spoken honestly to Danny, the man who had penetrated Fulham Road to free the women, the first target ever to escape him. He was less impressed by Erdi, after the shambles at Albert Park and switching targets late in the day. Sometimes the winner loses and the loser wins. It's an unfair world. Whatever, his work was done. He walked across the room to view his victim. She was almost as beautiful as his mother had been. It seemed a shame that her dark hair had been spoiled by a trickle of blood, a thin red line from the hole in her skull running to form a gathering stain on the deep pile carpet. That was enough.

Alex was gone.

Danny sat for a moment staring at the screen of his phone. He noticed his own heart beating a steady rhythm through his temples. His face created contortions of disbelief and agony.

Elizabeth stood on the drive, six feet from Danny who was already in the driver's seat of his car. She looked from the darkness, through the windscreen into the brightly lit interior of Danny's Range Rover. She saw the child again, afraid of his own suffering, alone with his pain. The sadness in his eyes seemed to stare out into eternity. She walked around to the side of the car. She opened the door to speak to him. "Danny, what is it?"

"It's Beth. She's been killed." He turned his head far enough to look at her, just briefly. Then he turned away again.

Elizabeth was hit by an enormous intensity of emotions. It didn't seem possible. Her fine friend, generous and caring, her business partner. "No, surely not." She quietened herself, Danny's voice seemed to have come from far away. She knew that their eyes had just met, but already he looked lost to her. She felt sure that this would be unbearable for Danny and she felt afraid for her own safety. She took a step back, still watching him closely. She'd seen this before… Danny, beyond her reach, overcome with an unmanageable burden. She braced herself, anticipating an explosion of rage.

Sean had noted Danny's exit and Elizabeth's concern. He came out onto the drive. "What's happening?"

Elizabeth went to him. "Danny said that Beth has been killed." And she waited expectantly for Sean to contradict her ridiculous assertion. But he didn't.

Sean closed his eyes. He and Beth had been close. He allowed himself a second or two, trying to take it in, and then he put it to one side. He knew that his task now was to be with Danny. He spoke to Elizabeth. "Go inside and tell the others. I'll stay with Danny."

But she approached Danny again. She reached out her right hand and brought her fingers to rest on Danny's forearm. He looked lost but he responded with slight movement. Elizabeth saw his head turn part way towards her. Then she saw his lips open and close again, although she heard nothing. She was surprised to see this acknowledgement, expecting that he'd be gone beyond her reach.

She spoke again. "I'm going inside, Danny. I'll be back in a minute. Sean's here." Then she went back inside the house.

For Sean, fearlessness and instinct had always heavily outscored tact and diplomacy. Sometimes he got it right, sometimes not. He stepped alongside the car. The door remained open. Sean stood in close. They had been close friends for twenty years but there had never been a physical connection. Sean could say anything, but never a touch. Not with anybody really, but definitely not with Danny. Nevertheless, he felt compelled, and with a stuttering awkwardness, he managed to put his right arm across Danny's shoulders. "Hey, Danny."

He felt Danny relax, some kind of acceptance for his clumsy embrace. Sean looked right at him, trying to read Danny's mood.

He needed to hear it from Danny. "Is it true that Beth's been killed?"

Danny closed his eyes, gathered some focus, then turned to address Sean. He nodded, his eyes open again. "Yes. She's dead. Erdi must have given the order after we left his house. Whoever killed her answered my video call. He showed me Beth lying on the living room floor."

"Who was it?" Sean asked.

"I don't know. I don't care. It's Erdi that has to pay." Just saying those words made the pain focus. He wanted to lash out, exact his revenge, make Erdi and every man with him burn, but Danny shook his head slowly. That wasn't him anymore. Beth had changed him and he didn't want to let her down. His blood cooled, the anger subsiding to a dull ache. "I don't want to be here without her. I don't know if I can deal with it, Sean."

"You're doing fine. God knows how but we'll deal with it, Danny. We don't get a choice. Same as ever. We'll play backgammon, drink whisky, throw a few stones. I don't know where this will take us but I'll stay with you. For as long as it takes."

Neither of them were positioned comfortably in their ungainly and incomplete embrace. Danny turned in his seat, towards Sean. Their eyes met for a second. Danny swung his legs out of the car and stood. He closed his eyes and allowed his forehead to fall and rest on Sean's shoulder, allowing Sean to hold him, shutting out the ten thousand demons he'd one day have to face, to accept the love and care of his oldest friend. That was as far as Danny could think or move. He was in his brother's hands now.

Printed in Great Britain
by Amazon